THE HAUNTED SEASON

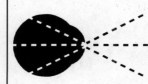

This Large Print Book carries the
Seal of Approval of N.A.V.H.

A MAX TUDOR NOVEL

THE HAUNTED SEASON

G. M. MALLIET

THORNDIKE PRESS
A part of Gale, Cengage Learning

GALE
CENGAGE Learning·

Farmington Hills, Mich • San Francisco • New York • Waterville, Maine
Meriden, Conn • Mason, Ohio • Chicago

GALE
CENGAGE Learning·

LIBRARY OF CONGRESS CATALOGING-IN-PUBLICATION DATA

Malliet, G. M., 1951-
  The haunted season : a Max Tudor novel / by G. M. Malliet. — Large print edition.
    pages cm. — (Thorndike Press large print mystery)
    ISBN 978-1-4104-8549-6 (hardcover) — ISBN 1-4104-8549-8 (hardcover)
  1. Large type books. I. Title.
PS3613.A4535H38 2016
813'.6—dc23   2015031728

Published in 2016 by arrangement with St. Martin's Press, LLC

Printed in Mexico
1 2 3 4 5 6 7 20 19 18 17 16

Again, for my mother

CONTENTS

ACKNOWLEDGMENTS

My thanks to *The Epistle Magazine* of St. Paul's Episcopal Church, Alexandria, Virginia (Lent/Easter edition), for this inspiration: "Remember that the Lord has spoken often through dreams. Who knows what God is saying to the person who appears to be sleeping."

My thanks also to Boris Andjelic, Alexander Bogdanov, and Stephen Redburn for allowing me to lean on their expertise. Any mistakes, as always, are my own.

CAST OF CHARACTERS

The Reverend Destiny Chatsworth: curate newly assigned to assist the Reverend Maxen Tudor of St. Edwold's Church in Nether Monkslip.

Maxen "Max" Tudor: a former MI5 agent turned Anglican priest, Max thought he'd found a measure of peace in the idyllic village of Nether Monkslip — until murder began to invade his Garden of Eden.

Awena Owen: the owner of Goddessspell, the village's New Age shop, Awena also has come to own Max Tudor's heart. The arrival of their child completes the couple's joy.

Mrs. Hooser: vicarage housekeeper and the mother of Tildy Ann and Tom.

Ms. Eugenia Smith-Ganderfort: a church volunteer devoted to Max Tudor. But is she a little *too* devoted?

Elka Garth: owner of the Cavalier Tea Room and Garden.

11

Lord and Lady Bayer Baaden-Boomethistle of Totleigh Hall: currently in residence with the lord's son, Peregrine; his daughter, Rosamund; and the dowager viscountess.

Bill Travis: estate manager and horse trainer at Totleigh Hall, he is rumored to have caught the eye of the lady of the house.

Charles Hargreaves: butler/valet at Totleigh Hall.

Suzanna Winship: the beautiful, outspoken, and ambitious sister of the local doctor.

Chanel Dirkson: a successful author of self-help books whose own life is barely under control.

Dr. Bruce Winship: an expert in general ailments, Suzanna's brother revels in theories of how the criminal mind operates.

Frank Cuthbert: local historian, famous author (*Wherefore Nether Monkslip*), and husband of Mme. Lucie.

Miss Agnes Pitchford: a retired schoolmistress and a walking cross-indexed repository of all village gossip.

Noah Caraway: wealthy owner of Noah's Ark Antiques and of Abbot's Lodge.

Detective Chief Inspector Cotton: the kinetic DCI is again dispatched from Monkslip-super-Mare to investigate a most suspicious death in the placid village of Nether Monkslip.

Dr. Sprottle: an expert in the art of death.

Sergeant Essex: DCI Cotton's no-nonsense assistant.

Candice Thor St. Gabriel and Elspeth Muir: former nannies at Totleigh Hall.

The Right Reverend Nigel St. Stephen: the bishop wants to know why Max Tudor is again involved in murder most sordid.

Lily Iverson: owner of a local knitting and textiles business.

Tara Raine: A lithe, attractive yoga instructor, she rents studio space at Goddessspell.

Major Batton-Smythe: a widower with a passion for history, and for Lily Iverson.

Adam Birch: owner of the Onlie Begetter bookshop.

Mr. Stackpole: the sexton of St. Edwold's Church.

Constable Musteile: an officious man with ambitions to solve a crime, any crime.

Granted that miracles *can* occur, it is, of course, for experience to say whether one has done so on any given occasion.

— C. S. Lewis, *Miracles*

These are the days of miracle and won-der . . .

— Paul Simon and Forere Mothoeloa, "The Boy in the Bubble"

PROLOGUE:
DESTINY

It was springtime, with lingering cold and damp shrouding the somber London streets. The best time of year to be in a steam room.

And as the Reverend Destiny Chatsworth was to discover, a steam room was the ideal place to be for a spot of casual eavesdropping.

Not that *she* would ever eavesdrop. God forbid. That fell somewhere into the same category as gossiping. But if being wrapped up in steam somehow gave people the illusion they were alone and unwitnessed while having a private conversation, she didn't see how it was her fault if she overheard a few things.

Some of them rather shocking.

Destiny being a newly minted priest in the Anglican Communion, the fees for the use of the spa facilities in the exclusive Ladies' University Club, a women-only establishment in St. James's in central

London, would normally be out of the reach of a not-yet-employed curate. But her doting and very wealthy aunt was a member, and as a combination graduation/ordination present she had given Destiny a guest-pass stay at the LUC. Destiny's progressive aunt was tremendously supportive of her niece's new calling: Aunt Jane still considered it an outrage that women had had to wait until 1994 to be ordained as priests in the Anglican Church.

With a few weeks open between her ordination and her first day as curate of St. Edwold's in Nether Monkslip, Destiny was using the time to relax, to catch up on her reading, to shop, to get a decent haircut for once, and to reflect on the glorious new future that awaited her. The question of what to wear was a vexing one: Wearing the religious collar was, for women, a bit trickier than for the men, unless one happened to like gray flannel suits and black shirts, which Destiny did not.

And so she approached her stay at the late-nineteenth-century club as a special treat, and with a sense of saying good-bye to luxury — not just to such stately accommodations and fine food but also to having time free to pamper and indulge herself. Leaving university always meant putting away childish things, but perhaps this was even truer in her case. Destiny was nothing if not earnest in her desire to shine a pure light on an ever-darkening world. And to look appropriately dressed while doing it.

The LUC (its members called themselves the LUCkey ones), which dated to 1885, was modeled on every men's club in London: all leather armchairs, crackling fireplaces in winter, and rustling newspapers. There may have been a bit more floral print in the reading room upholstery and window tiebacks, and crocheted doilies protecting the tabletops, but those were the main differences. In recent years, a modern spa had been installed at great expense, and thus not without rancor and lingering ill feeling among the members of the club's General Committee, many of whom felt that the availability of chess and backgammon boards, having provided sufficient licit diversion for decades, should continue to suffice. Discussions over the spa had reached the same fever pitch as discussions over the movement to modernize the name of the LUC, with Miss Haverdam threatening to chain herself to the fence if this scandalous proposal succeeded.

While men were now permitted to stay as guests in the en suite second-floor rooms, few took advantage of this offer, deterred no doubt by the undeniably, not to say stridently, feminine air of the place. Men, in any event, were strictly forbidden the use of the spa amenities, a concession needed to get the plans for the new spa past the eagle eye of the General Committee.

The new spa was in essence a glamification of what had once consisted of little more than a large wading pool, a sluggish Jacuzzi ("in reality, a large petri dish for mold," as more than one member had described it), and rows of rickety metal lockers. The result, something like a cross between a small school gymnasium and a recently excavated Roman bath, still was more functional than luxurious. But to Destiny Chatsworth, it was like the antechamber to heaven itself. Undressing before an empty locker in the spa's dressing room, she reflected with no little wonder at the good luck that had befallen her. To soon be working for Max Tudor! The Reverend *Max Tudor*! She had known Max from when they were students at St. Barnabas House, Oxford, where he — close to completing his degree as she was just beginning her studies — was already legendary, viewed as a rising star in the Anglican firmament. That he had chosen to become vicar of a small village like Nether Monkslip, when he could have had his pick of parishes, surprised no one who knew him. So to be specially invited to apply for the position as his curate . . . well. It was a feather in her cap, a sign of how hard she'd worked and how far she'd come, and she had to stifle the very human impulse to brag openly. Although she did take every opportunity to insinuate the topic gently into every conversation, she hoped she'd be forgiven for it.

As she disrobed the body she thought of as attractively, even Rubenesquely, plump, she could not help but notice the lithe young woman to her right, who was applying extravagant amounts of perfumed body lotion. Destiny pegged her as a yoga practitioner, and possibly a habitué of the beaches on the Continent. She had skin tanned to a uniform shade of milky tea, which suggested either a stay at a nude resort or frequent recourse to a solarium. Even the aureoles of her nipples blended into the surrounding skin, giving her the plasticized appearance of a Selfridges store dummy awaiting its next costume change.

This superb physical specimen, having draped itself in designer clothing and heels, left behind an old copy of *Bild* magazine on one of the locker room benches. Destiny, who seldom had time for light reading, began leafing idly through the pages, reflecting as she did so that Duchess Kate was starting to show the same uncanny knack for attracting bad press into her life as had Duchess Fergie — for wearing not *quite* enough clothing just as a camera lens was pointed straight at her backside. Despite the perks of the job, Destiny wouldn't trade places with her. Not for longer than an hour. Just long enough to see the parts of Buckingham Palace that were closed to visitors. (Destiny was, among other things, a history buff.)

She put the magazine aside, leaving it for the next person. Somehow, this sort of tabloid "news" had in recent years lost much of its appeal for her.

Once vainer than *Little Women*'s Amy March (and still given to perusing fashion magazines as if they alone held the secrets of the universe), Destiny had, at the age of thirty-five, undergone what most would call a conversion but she thought of as a wake-up call. The first thing that had had to go was her job. She had spent many years in the world's most superficial pursuit (copywriting) in the most superficial of industries (advertising). When the press had begun to reveal more and more that the products she polished and shellacked to a glossy sheen were often produced by slave labor, or were created by destroying the environment, it provided one of the catalysts that propelled her out of her old life and into her new.

Now clutching about her a too-small towel, Destiny warily approached the steam room with all the reluctant wonder of a missionary being asked to witness a pagan ritual for the first time. She had, in fact, never set foot in a steam room before, and she was sure there must be a certain etiquette involved. Did one knock on the door, or just burst in unannounced? Not to mention, surely some sort of safety measures were called for, and she didn't know what they were. If she were to collapse in there alone, would someone come to her aid before she lost two dress sizes? The whole thing was so, well, so Finnish — so very foreign to a girl conventionally raised in a two-up, two-down terraced house in a Plymouth suburb.

In the end, she entered the room slowly, without flourish or announcement, and carefully shut the glazed door behind her. She could just make out two other bodies inside, sitting with legs dangling over an upper wooden ledge. Deep in conversation, they paid her no mind as she entered. They both were wearing white towels wrapped turban-style about their heads and sarong-style around their bodies, so their only identifying markers were their red and pink pedicures. A wall of steam obscured their faces. Destiny tucked herself onto a seat nearest the door, settling into place on a lower bench. She wished she'd thought to wrap her own hair in a towel, as the steam would turn it into the sort of Bride of Frankenstein coils it reverted to when left to its own devices.

All was silence for a long while. Destiny, wondering if she was supposed to chant Viking songs or something, found the novel experience of damp silence so restful, she soon fell asleep, head back and mouth open. She awakened on hearing, in some subconscious way, the two words that had been on her mind for months, and she fully awoke to a shushing sound from one of the women.

"Nether Monkslip," she had heard one of them say. She was sure she hadn't been dreaming.

Then: "It's all right," the other woman said. "She's sound asleep."

Destiny assumed she'd been snoring, a habit brought to her attention by more than one peevish roommate or ex-boyfriend. But some instinct — the tone in the second woman's voice — prevented her from announcing her newly alert state. Instead, she resumed making a snuffling noise interspersed with a snort she hoped approximated the sound one boyfriend had described as the noise a train loaded with panicking donkeys might make as it pulled too fast into the station.

Instinct — plus the fact that she also had heard, very clearly, just as she had awakened, the word *murder.*

When God hands you a coincidence like that, she thought, it is probably good to pay attention. Required, even. There would, or so she reasoned, be ample opportunity to make her presence known to the women once she knew exactly what it was they were saying about her soon-to-be new home. To say anything now, she'd be butting into a conversation that didn't include her. It would be quite rude, really.

She couldn't tell much about the women from their voices as they resumed their conversation. In a locker room, there was ample opportunity to observe the vast variety and shapes of the human body: the yoga practitioners versus the foodies, as it were. Here in this pea soup–like fog, given that the women were dressed in identical towels, there were no visual clues. With their hair covered, and arms and legs mostly obscured in clouds of moist air, they were hard to identify or classify. She would have hazarded that they were both Caucasian, and that was about as far as she was prepared to go.

From their voices, they were young. One quite young, the other possibly older. Well spoken. Posh. Their upper-class accents sounded alike to her ears, except that one had a deeper voice.

Now one woman said, "I can't tell you how ready I am to leave him. But the *stu*pid prenup . . ."

"The solicitor did warn you."

"Yes, I know, thanks. I really never thought it would be an issue. I thought I could cope. I didn't think it would get to be this bad. He's changed so."

"They all do, once the courtship is over."

"Not yet. I don't believe that."

"That, my dear, is because you are a romantic. And look where it's got you."

"Duh. I feel some days as if I'm living out a life sentence. A nice, cushy life sentence. The only thing that livens up that village is the occasional sighting of that heavenly vicar, and he's taken now."

In good conscience, Destiny asked herself later, what could I have done? Snapped my towel at them to get their attention? Loudly cleared my throat and announced that I knew exactly whom and what they were talking about?

But she kept quiet, in fact, because this seemed too good an opportunity to learn more about her soon-to-be village and its people. Nether Monkslip — the village she thought of as battle stations.

Max Tudor's galvanizing effect on the female half of a population she had already witnessed for herself, many times.

But above all, of course, there was that word: *murder*. Had one of the women said "I could murder him"? Or was it "I'm *going* to murder him"? That there had been in the past, or would be in the future, a murder? Destiny wasn't sure exactly what she had heard or what she had dreamed. Only that one word jumped out of the air, as if illuminated in flashing neon lights.

The one word seemed to hang there still, like a word in a cartoon balloon.

Murder.

She again wrestled, but fleetingly, with the thought of chiming in, of announcing herself, but she quickly dropped back into her role of eavesdropper. Well, it was not really eavesdropping, was it? So she assured herself. She sat in plain view — couldn't get much plainer, now could she, nearly naked as she was in this scanty towel? — and the women themselves made little attempt to hide their discussion or even to lower their plummy voices. They assumed discretion, rather like the wealthy and privileged might when speaking in front of their servants. Or perhaps it was anonymity they assumed, like strangers passing time in a train. Destiny had overheard the most amazing arguments and confessions whilst sitting on trains. People assumed they were among people they'd never see again, and somehow it lowered their inhibitions.

Funny she should think of that — that film *Strangers on a Train,* because now one of the women said something about its being a service to humanity if someone would please rid the world of Harold. Or did she say Harry?

The other woman grunted something unintelligible. Then she went on, her voice lower now, saying something like "Too bad: We could have done a swap, helped each other out. Like in that old film."

An unintelligible reply, then: "But God knows where he went to, and good riddance. I'd have been glad of a helping hand."

She laughed, however, so clearly it was

meant as a joke.

Wasn't it?

"It's a wonder he's still alive, the bloody old trout." Destiny wasn't sure who was talking now or whom she was talking about. The slight hiss of steam being expelled through the pipes obscured the sound, distorting it. "Something something," whispered one of the women — it sounded complete gibberish. Then: "Most of these bad-tempered men get a spike or two of high blood pressure and they're gone."

"You remember Bethany? I always suspected —"

"He used to hit her, you know . . . justified. No woman should put up with —"

"When he drinks . . ."

"There are poisons that . . . with alcohol —"

"Shhh."

It was turning into a truly disturbing conversation. A thoroughly detached and unpleasant discussion of the wished-for demise of another human being. But it didn't rise to the level of something Destiny felt she had to put a stop to or intervene in somehow. No one's life was being threatened, after all. Not really. It was just that Harold's and some other man's passing were being considered as events to be anticipated and not regretted.

Bonuses, as it were.

"Nothing to be done about it now."

Another silence, longer this time.

"Isn't there?" the other woman prompted, but softly.

"Sometimes I think . . . You do remember Bethany? No one believed it was an accident."

Destiny, electrified by that one, final word at the end of the sentence — *accident* — forgot to snore. One of the women — the second woman? — gasped softly, and then the room grew very still, the only sound the slight hiss of steam. Both women seemed again to become aware of her, for the shushing sound was heard again, and the second woman said, in a voice that showed the strain, "You're joking of course."

"Yes, yes, that's it. Of course I'm joking."

"Good."

But it was clear from the tone that the other woman did not believe her. And neither did Destiny, who resumed her snoring, more quietly now.

After a very long pause: "I have a friend . . ."

"Good for you."

"No, I mean the kind of friend who can, you know . . . Get things done. Take care of things that need to be taken care of. Obit someone. The kind of person with connections —"

"I should go soon," replied the other woman, hastily cutting her off. She sounded horrified by the drift the conversation had taken.

Destiny, below them, scowled in frustration.

"That mouthbreather of a stepdaughter is coming to collect me in the car. I told her to wait in the library."

"I thought the son was the mouthbreather."

"Him, too. He also chews with his mouth open, for God's sake. How long can male adolescence last, one wonders."

"I could give you a lift."

"Thanks, but I promised I'd take her shopping. The poor thing really is clueless. I'm embarrassed to be seen with her. Oh, did I tell you I saw that guy from the village — what is his name? I thought he never came to London."

As their conversation drifted more into the trivial, it seemed to Destiny it was time either to make her presence known or get the heck out of there. Or stay until she'd lost thirty pounds. The women seemed disinclined also to clamber down and make

31

themselves known, so for a while they all sat in stony silence. Finally, when she could take no more, Destiny created a smoke screen by pouring water on the rocks in the center of the room, and made her escape. It was hard to run with dignity in a towel, but she just managed it.

The two women turned to each other.

"How much do you think she heard?"

"No matter, we won't see her again. Not that she'd recognize us or know who we are. And she couldn't know who or what we were talking about anyway. No one's ever heard of Nether Monkslip, that is certain."

"I'm sure you're right, but that was foolish of me. He just gets me so angry, so . . . so *frus*trated. Just boiling, you know? I forget myself."

Meanwhile, Destiny quickly showered and dressed. Curious as she was about the two women, she was anxious to avoid a meeting that would be embarrassing for all concerned. Surely they were just blowing off steam — and the perfect place for that was a steam room, come to think of it.

By now there were quite a few people in the dressing area. She supposed afternoons before dinner were popular. She heard someone call out, "Eugenia! What on earth are you doing here!" and thought what a nice, old-fashioned name it was. She couldn't help noticing there was a stunned reaction from some of the women in the locker room as she put on her clerical collar. They had all been rather freely discussing their sex lives, along with their rather riotous plans for the evening.

She was getting used to that reaction.

A few days later, she had mostly forgotten the overheard conversation, caught up as she was in enjoying her last few days of freedom. And strange as the steam room conversation had been, she never made a connection between it and the car that narrowly missed her the next day, speeding by and forcing her to jump back on the curb.

She hadn't been watching where she was going, and London was notoriously dangerous.

Thank God she'd soon be in Nether Monkslip, where it was safe.

CHAPTER 1
MAX TUDOR

It was fall, and the patchwork fields around Nether Monkslip were changing color from gold and jade to bronze and topaz in that strange alchemy of the turning seasons.

Father Maxen Tudor sat at his desk in the mellow old vicarage of St. Edwold's, watching his own patch of garden change with the breeze and the moving sunlight. The room was quiet, the only sound the occasional whimper of his dog, Thea, as she chased rabbits in her dreams by the fireplace. A blank word-processing document was open before him and the cursor of his bulky computer blinked, the page waiting empty and undisturbed for his thoughts. It was, he told himself, too nice a day to work.

Autumn was his favorite time of year, and morning his favorite time of day, when his daily parish obligations had been met and he could sit with a cup of coffee, reading and ruminating and planning his next sermon. Time slowed, as if there were nothing to do but wait for the Japanese maple in the garden to cast its shifting red light into the room. While spring was about life and beginnings, fall was, to him, a reminder of the endless cycle-through of seasons: Spring flowers would always return, no matter how bleak their prospects at the moment.

But fall brought special challenges to a man running a small parish almost single-handedly — the Blessing of the Animals, for one. It finally had been decided that having children bring their stuffed animals to church was a better strategy than having everyone pile into St. Edwold's, dragging behind them their live menageries or clasping their favorite pets to their hearts. Max's early Saint Francis Day blessing services had dissolved into an unmitigated chaos and ended in tears when several otherwise-domesticated animals had seized the day, making their various breaks for freedom — hoofing, flying, slithering, and hopping their way down the ancient stone aisles and out the door, which stood open to admit the generally unseasonable warmth of early October in Nether Monkslip. The change to stuffed animals had its opponents among the traditionalists on the Parish Council, however, who now were fighting a rearguard action to move next year's proceedings out-doors.

This year had presented an added challenge in that the duck race, traditionally a springtime event, had been rescheduled to the fall, since the council had deemed the spring weather too chancy. Global warming or no, something in the world had changed, and a duck race held in the rain dampened everyone's spirits.

So in its way, springtime will be easier going, thought Max, despite the fact there was a movement afoot to initiate an ecumenical Lambing Festival, during which children would bring newborn lambs to the church to be blessed. Plenty there, thought Max, to go wrong. But spring was a time of miracles, if you believed in miracles, which Max did, so perhaps all would be well. St. Edwold's cross would be swathed in purple, awaiting the biggest reveal of all.

In the fall began anew the liturgical buildup to the birth of the Christ Child — again a happy focus on new life. And this Christmas season he at last would have help with the avalanche of responsibilities.

Upon the retirement of one of his colleagues, Max had been asked to take on the parishes of Steeple Monkslip and Monkslip Bassett, an impossibility without some sort of assistance, as his bishop readily had agreed. The solution was to allow Max a curate — a recent university graduate, newly ordained. Her name was Destiny Chatsworth.

Max, knowing she was perfect for the job, put her (unusual) name forward to the bishop. She also came highly recommended by her Oxford tutors, which helped his case, although she was not in any sense an academician or great theologian. He wanted her instead for her rare gift of approachability: People quickly trusted her with their feelings and their worries. They forgot themselves around her. He and Awena had her over for dinner, and Awena had pronounced her an ideal fit for the village.

When she was officially assigned to St. Edwold's, Max was so grateful for the help, as he told Awena, he could only hope now that Nether Monkslip was as much her destiny as it was his.

"If I had not come to Nether Monkslip, I might never have met you," he had said to his wife. An unthinkable idea: too frightening to contemplate.

He looked now across the room at the little crèche scene on his office shelf, a memento from his time investigating a murder at Monkbury Abbey. The sight of the primitive clay figures of the Holy Family, and of the cows and lambs that had come to adore this special child, often brought him inspiration. It always settled his mind and brought him peace.

He had a title for his sermon in this season of grace, if little else; the only word that percolated from his brain, beyond context or punctuation or deliberate thought, was *joy*. Joy in his working life as vicar of St. Edwold's, joy in his private life with Awena, joy above all in the safe delivery of their child, Owen. He knew he'd been witness to a miracle at the birth. An everyday miracle, but a miracle just the same. His days with Awena and Owen now were braided together in a happy bond of duty and love. They hoped for another child in the following year.

He turned to his computer, and found his fingers had typed the word *joy* onto the page without his really being aware of it. Reluctantly, he deleted the word from the document, for the topic of his sermon was "Do the Ends Ever Justify the Means?" and it was difficult to see how joy fit in there.

Finally he decided that there was joy in surrender, in living according to Buddhist precepts, in not trying to game the system and force events to turn in a particular direction. That way, thought Max, lies madness. In the long run, mankind did its worst work, and told the most lies, when trying to justify its actions, to impose a certain outcome.

Thy will be done.

The sermon nearly wrote itself, and Max was happily refilling his pen from the inkwell to edit the printed-out pages when his housekeeper, Mrs. Hooser, knocked on his study door. As she was never one to stand on ceremony, the knock was followed immediately by the door's flying open to the shouted announcement, "It's her about the flowers."

Max turned from his task and pasted on a welcoming smile when he saw who "her" was.

Every parish has its "Martha." Or in the case of Nether Monkslip, its Eugenia Smith-Ganderfort. This person is nearly always a female, and nearly always single; a woman who is the Martha of the place — the doer. In the Bible tale, while others get to sit idly at Jesus' feet, listening to him talk, Martha is the one who gets stuck preparing a large meal for the group.

Today's Martha is the one who makes sure the hymnals are stored neatly and that the mice are not destroying them for nesting material. The one who ensures the flowers on the altar have fresh water, that the flower rota gets updated, that the needlepoint kneelers stay in good repair, that the altar is swept and the nave hoovered and the pews cleared of the gloves and scarves and, sometimes, purses and wallets that get left behind by worshipers. She is the person who volunteers for every task, particularly the lowly, behind-the-scene tasks no one else wants to take on or is even aware need doing, like cleaning out the coffee urn or even clearing the graveyard of fallen debris after a storm. The unrewarded, unnoticed chores that keep the wheels of a parish church spinning smoothly. The modern-day Martha's motives for doing all this vary. Sometimes, she is simply a lonely soul with time on her hands. Sometimes, she is just the sort of good-hearted person who needs to feel of use. Sometimes, she is both.

And sometimes, in the case of a charismatic and attractive vicar like Max Tudor, she finds volunteering for the various chores around the church to be the surest way of having some face time with him. To bask for a moment in the sunshine of an extended word of encouragement and thanks from the Reverend Max Tudor.

Along with many other women of the

parish, Eugenia had a sort of schoolgirl crush on Max, and during his bachelor days had plied him with cakes and tuna fish casseroles and, on one occasion, an entire basketful of potatoes. He still was uncertain what he'd been meant to do with that bounty; he couldn't have eaten all of it even if he'd been in training for a marathon. Eugenia still was likely to turn up with a plateful of homemade biscuits, carefully secured with ribbon on a plate decorated with a paper doily. They were "made from love," she had informed him, to his discomfiture, but he told himself she of course meant the Christian sort of love for all mankind.

Today was not one of her baking or cooking days, apparently; in any event, as Max knew well, Saturday was the traditional baking day in the village. Max, putting down his pen, looked at her politely, hoping this would not take long, whatever it was, and wondering what on earth she'd done to her hair.

Eugenia's hair at the best of times resembled a yet-undiscovered form of plant life on the ocean floor, but today there seemed to be rather more of it. She generally styled it tightly permed and knotted into precise quadrants, so that her head resembled a farmer's field awaiting harvest. It was of a

42

neither-here-nor-there shade of blond-gray that reflected no ray of sunshine and emitted no spark of life. Indeed, today it looked as if touched, it might turn to dust, or go up in flames if she ventured too near a heat source.

She was neither fat nor thin, short nor tall, but her waist was thickening with the approach of middle age, a fact cruelly emphasized by the too-tight belt of her shirtwaist dress. The dress was a shiny yellow-green print and, it was to be supposed, a symbol of sprightly youth, but the color of new buds did not necessarily flatter all complexions, and it did not flatter Eugenia's. Besides, the Sprightly Youth ship had sailed for Eugenia many years before. Her legs, sturdy and thin and shielded from the elements by beige spandex, emerged from the dress in a straight line from knee to foot, without apparent benefit of ankle to hold them together — they were what Max's father had called "piano legs." She stood anchored to the ground in flesh-colored pumps, a change from the trainers and heavy white socks she generally wore halfway to her knees. Clutched about her person were various bags and parcels; she had evidently interrupted her shopping for an impromptu visit to the vicarage.

Max noticed her spruced-up appearance only in passing. In his mind, she was a good soul and a much-appreciated, generous volunteer of her time and skills. It was his genial appreciation, of course, that inevitably would lead to trouble, for if Max had a fault, it was that he had been born open and trusting, expecting and generally receiving the best from people. Along with his handsomeness, it was the equivalent of a one-two knockout punch as far as women were concerned. He was largely unaware of his physical attractiveness, a fact that, of course, permanently secured his major heartthrob status among the women of the village.

So it had taken him a while to wonder at the fact that whenever he was in the church, by some odd coincidence, Eugenia also was in the church. If the altar flowers were to be arranged on a Friday at one and Max was otherwise engaged, the rota somehow got shifted in Eugenia's favor for a time when he was sure to be around. Thus the flower-rota skirmishes, often deadly — for it was fondly hoped that such an activity might afford more opportunities to engage the vicar in prolonged conversation — took on curious new layers of subterfuge and ill feeling.

There may have been a Mr. Smith or a

Mr. Ganderfort or a hyphenated personage in her life at some time, and it was rumored there had been such a person, if briefly, decades before. But Eugenia seemed to have mislaid him along the way and now lived alone in one of the little almshouses along the river. Someone — he thought Elka Garth of the Cavalier — had told him she thought Eugenia had a son and grandchild somewhere but that she seldom saw either of them. "I think the son is trying to 'weaponize' the grandchild" was how she put it. "Withhold access as a sort of punishment — for what, I don't know. Such a shame when that happens."

Eugenia was known officially as Ms. Eugenia Smith-Ganderfort, and casually to her friends — although she was not a casual sort of person and she had very few friends — as Ms. Eugenia.

She got straight to the point — or rather, she got straight to the pretext for her visit.

"Father, I was just wondering," she said, fingering the dreadful fabric of her dress, "what kind of flowers you would like for the altar? For Christmas, I mean."

"What kind of flowers would I —" began Max. Truly, this was unprecedented. For one thing, they were not yet out of October, with the church still decorated for the harvest time with gourds and beribboned clumps of wheat; the church mouser, Luther, was often to be found draped over a large pumpkin. But the women of St. Edwold's Altar Guild chose whatever flowers were in bloom in their gardens, sometimes supplementing them with more elaborate arrangements or filler donated by a florist in Monkslip-super-Mare. Max was never involved in these aesthetic deliberations; his participation went as far as thanking the volunteers for their efforts and no further. Max could say to Eugenia that he didn't care what flowers she chose, but it might sound unkind and it wouldn't be true anyway. He liked the beautiful, sweet scents of nature around him as well as the next person. But so long as he wasn't allergic to the blooms — and so far as he knew, he was allergic to nothing — it didn't matter.

"I suppose," he said, "that Christmas flowers are of particular importance. But I really don't have a preference, Eugenia. You always outdo yourself. Such splendid arrangements! Now if you don't mind, I —" Seeing her face, which had transformed from its usual Anglo-Saxon pallor to a mottled canvas of dark pink and red, he stopped. "Are you all right?"

"Yes, yes!" she gasped. "Quite all right,

Father." He was not to know that the use of her Christian name had sent a tremor up and down her spine, rendering her nearly speechless. For usually, and without really thinking about it, Max addressed her by her full name and title: Ms. Smith-Ganderfort.

That night she would relive this magic moment with Max Tudor over and over in her mind as she prepared her simple meal of tea and toad in the hole, as she did the washing up, even as she watched a quiz show on the telly: "But I really don't have a preference, *Eugenia,*" Father Max had said. "*Eugenia,* you always outdo yourself. *Eugenia!* Did anyone ever tell you how beautiful your eyes are, *Eugenia*?

Of course he had not really said that last, and she knew it, but in the retelling she buffed and polished the moment to mirror her needs. What he *had* said was so different from what she was used all her life to hearing: Eugenia the fool. Eugenia the meddler. Eugenia the busybody. "You always outdo yourself! Such splendid arrangements! *Eugenia!*"

"Well, then, if there's nothing else?" Max picked up his pen and gestured toward the ink-covered pages scattered on his desk, as though suddenly struck by a crucial point he simply must add to his sermon, and straight away.

Eugenia collected herself with a visible effort, although her face was still the oddest hectic mix of colors, as of a woman experiencing a rise in blood pressure, as undoubtedly she was.

"If you are certain," she said. "I thought holly — but that could be dangerous if Luther gets into it. It's not good for cats, you know. Ivy is always nice. But perhaps some roses mixed in?"

Luther, the freeloading lounge cat — was he aware of the loving concern for his well-being that cushioned all his days? Max looked at her as if she might be mad, but he put down his pen and said kindly, "Of course, we have to consider our mouser. Even though, and thank God for it, I don't think he has caught a mouse in years. He used to leave the poor things in the vestry for me to find." He added in what seemed now a non sequitur, "I have always liked roses."

"Red roses?"

"Yes, that would be nice. Thank you. Now, I really must —"

"Of course, of course! I mustn't keep you. I know you're busy. And soon there'll be all the planning for the duck race, too; I know how much you enjoy that. Not the planning.

The race itself." She gathered her parcels and packets and netted bits of things, the contents of half of which now spilled onto the floor, so of course Max had to kneel to help her collect them. Their fingers met over a packet of Ryvita and sparks literally flew — the scuffing of their shoes on the carpet in the dry air of the heated room had produced an electric current. Eugenia threw her head back, looking up into his eyes, a doe transfixed by headlamps.

What on earth was the matter with the woman?

"Oh," she said now, completely undone. "Oh! It's the dark rye, isn't it? It's for feeding the poor on the next Bowls for Souls day. I think the dark rye is so much nicer than the light, don't you? Crunchier. It just looks nicer. They say it's more nutritious, too." Even Eugenia seemed to realize she was babbling by this point. She stood awkwardly, gripping her shopping bags, which stood out from her hips like buoys around a dinghy. "It's for the poor," she repeated.

At this reminder that Eugenia was also a vital component of the free-lunch initiative in Monkslip-super-Mare, Max again stifled his impatience. Really, the Anglican Church ran on the time, energies, and moneys donated by such as Eugenia. Her entire life seemed to revolve around the church, in fact.

That this totality of devotion had started when Max Tudor came to St. Edwold's escaped him.

Just then the door opened, this time followed by Awena. She held the baby, Owen, swaddled in a blue jumpsuit and blanket, leaving only the top of his fuzzy dark head visible. Max felt an access of relief — he was growing increasing desperate at the thought that Eugenia might never leave — and the customary jolt of transcendent happiness at seeing the pair around which his life revolved.

He bent over the sleeping bundle and, with his wife, gazed at their child in rapt devotion. Had any baby's eyelashes ever been that long and dark? Its cheeks that rosy? Even Owen's drool was adorable; Max stopped to dab with a corner of the blanket at the baby's pink rosebud of a mouth. Thea awoke from her slumber by the fire and trotted over to complete the family group.

Awena greeted Eugenia, and added, "I was wondering when you'd be ready, Max." They had planned a visit to the pediatrician's in Monkslip-super-Mare, followed by some shopping and dinner out.

"Just wrapping up here," Max said. He turned to Eugenia, his face still aglow.

And he was taken aback by the look on her face. If he hadn't known better, he might have thought it was a look of the purest venom.

The look was directed straight at Awena.

Chapter 2
Breakfast at Totleigh Hall

Even with only the family in residence, breakfast at Totleigh Hall, Nether Monkslip's manor house, was a surprisingly formal affair. The buffet spread of a full English breakfast, the standard offering when there were weekend guests, would have gone to waste on the small, loosely knit group that called itself the Baaden-Boomethistles. So rather than staggering in at all hours of the morning, in all states of dishabille, they arrived at the large dining room at more or less the same time each morning, and more or less properly composed, to have their individual breakfast orders taken by the hardworking but well-compensated Mr. Hargreaves.

Rosamund, the daughter of the house, was first down. She usually was, for Rosamund was an early riser, unlike her brother, Peregrine, who practically had to be dragged out of bed by the hair each day. But he had gone without breakfast often enough that he had now trained himself to arrive on time.

Rosamund took her seat, reached for the carafe, and poured coffee into the Spode mug at her place. Lacing the coffee with a generous splash of organic cream, she opened the newspaper to the arts and entertainment section; settling her glasses against her nose, she began to read. She wore different glasses to go with each day's outfit. Today it was a pair of rectangular frog green frames to set off her dark red hair and the violet-blue blouse she wore with jeans. Rosamund, being an art student, knew her color wheel.

Peregrine wouldn't know a color wheel if it ran over him.

Rosamund had nothing in common with her brother, a fact she liked to emphasize whenever possible. While they were of similar build — athletic from years of games (him) and horse riding (both) but in danger of running to fat early — they had different coloring and, more important, different temperaments. Rosamund was the bookish one — a proud egghead in a family of hearty, fox-chasing morons, as she saw it. She had a rather desperate need, born of guilt, to separate herself from the life of privilege into which she had been born. She was well aware from her reading that the world was an unfair place — there was, after all, no real reason her family should have easy access to whatever money could buy while others went hungry or died of preventable illnesses in Africa. What she could do to redress the balance, she was not sure. Writing a check to Oxfam every year seemed like a drop in the ocean. But at least she cared. Picture Peregrine caring.

He had become more awkward and gauche as he aged, which did not make her pity him, and did not stop her itch to torment him. Years of public schooling had done little to add to his attractions. Still, he was well liked by his peers, from what she could tell, although well tolerated might be a better description. She thought of him as the human equivalent of the battering ram, for he excelled at various sports, despite the embryonic paunch he carried before him. If he had other ambitions or hobbies apart from drinking, he kept them well hidden, and was usually to be found wandering aimlessly about the manor house or feeding carrots or forbidden sugar cubes to the horses in the vast stables at the back of the house.

And here he was now. Think of the devil and up he jumps — one of their old servants used to say that all the time. But she'd been from one of those places where they had little cults that still believed in the devil. One reason she hadn't lasted long in the position.

Peregrine lobbed his first grenade of the day.

"Do you have any idea how many calories are in that cream?" he asked, casting a significant glance at her waistline. For Rosamund was a big girl, broad and spreading as she grew, like an oak tree.

Not exactly fat. Not really.

Not like Jabba the Hutt here.

She dipped her paper momentarily to glare at him. What a way to start the morning, dueling with Peregrine, the sexist pig. Elephant, rather. With those stick-out ears, her favorite name to taunt him with in childhood had been "Dumbo," but they had rather moved beyond that now. He honestly didn't seem to see the extra stone around his own middle. And why was he wearing his hair like that? When had he started combing it straight down from the crown into a doofus fringe across his forehead? And those glasses! Maybe thick black-rimmed glasses were the hipster style of the moment, but between that and the hair, he looked a complete dork.

55

It was a shame, really. To have to watch her brother ruin his looks through self-indulgence.

She wouldn't say a word to him. She wouldn't. Would not. Wouldnotwouldnotwouldnot. Detachment was all. Detach. Detach. *Detach.*

Not for the first time, she lost the karmic struggle with herself. Self-control was not one of her strengths. Shooting from the hip was.

"If you didn't swill beer all the time with your rich hooligan friends, you might lose that spare tire."

"No one says hooligan anymore."

"Not in the sort of crowd you run with."

"Organic doesn't mean nonfattening," he informed her, continuing the dietary lecture as if she hadn't spoken.

"Is that something you learned in — what is it called? Land Management for Dummies?"

This was a favorite dig of hers. Peregrine was enrolled in a Land Ec course at Oxford, similar to the famous one at Cambridge. It was notorious as an academic refuge for thick athletes and the children of the landed gentry who would otherwise wander the world completely unenlightened. The recent attendance of HRH Prince William at a ten-week course tailor-made for the future proprietor of his father's estate had done nothing to diminish the cachet of the Cambridge course, although if his wife, Kate, had enrolled, it would have caused a mob scene at the admissions office on Trumpington Street.

"Bill Travis could totally rock that course, you know."

The mention of the estate manager/horse trainer seemed to inflame Peregrine, who was generally impervious to any weapon his sister might choose to use on him. At any rate, this snobbish accusation reduced him to the monosyllabic responses of their childhood, endured in a state of armed combat in the nursery at the top of the house. Only a year separated the two of them, Peregrine's reign as king of all he surveyed cut short by the arrival of his little sister, a usurpation of power he never, ever forgave or forgot.

"Could not," he muttered now, turning his attention to his own coffee, which he drank black and free of the offending cream, in the belief it would help a beer hangover. It would not.

"Could too," she said. "*And* he's not letting himself run to flab, even though he's got twenty years on you. You could take a lesson from him. Travis is totally

57

hot, and —"

She was cut short in her commendation by the imperious voice of her grandmother, their father's mother, known to everyone outside the family as the "Dotty Dowager," and to everyone within the family as "Crazy Caroline." She wafted in on a cloud of her expensive Paris perfume, dressed in a fluttery, lacy, feathery number, the sort of thing one of the Gabor sisters might have worn to breakfast.

"We are not," she announced, "going to stoop to talk about that. I have warned you before, Rosamund."

"I was just pointing out —"

"I know exactly what you were pointing out. Am I not a world-famous romance novelist? Am I not a spinner of tales designed to thrill and capture the imagination of every red-blooded woman? Have not my books been translated into forty languages, the better to transform the lives of the lonely and desperate around the globe?"

There was so much in this statement Rosamund felt she could reply to, but wisely, she held her tongue. Granny Dow could be tedious when she really let her megalomania get the better of her, although what she said technically was true. She was world-famous for writing the most incredible Regency dreck, a living testament to the lack of entertainment available to the shut-in, the bored housewife, the toiler in the secretarial pool.

"Your books are a public service, Gran," said Peregrine loyally.

Little suck-up.

"You should use Travis as a model for your next story," said Rosamund, not yet willing to lay down arms.

"What a good idea," said Bree, strolling in wearing her usual outfit for a day spent either in the stables or in the saddle: tan low-rise stretch pants with tall boots and a short-sleeve polo shirt. Rosamund thought she must sleep in those boots; she had seldom seen her not wearing them. Not since the wedding to her father, and a dark day it was, when the newly anointed Lady Baaden-Boomethistle had outshone everyone in the room. Brides were supposed to be beautiful, but Bree was, well, ridiculous, like something out of a Disney cartoon in her perfection. She had even worn a diamond-studded tiara, given to her by her besotted groom. The whole scene needed only mice and small animals holding up her train.

Bree took her seat not at the head of the table but opposite the dowager and poured out a cup of coffee: "Travis would make a *mar*velous hero. Tall, dark, handsome — all the prerequisites." Rosamund watched as she tipped easily a quarter of a cup of full cream into the brew. It wasn't fair that she never gained an ounce. Horseback riding couldn't answer for all the calories burned; Rosamund herself rode frequently. She suspected calories got burned in quite a different way where Bree was concerned.

The topic of Bill Travis seemed to disturb Granny Dow every bit as much as it disturbed Peregrine. But Rosamund didn't believe for a minute Bree would be so foolish as to mess about with the help. That would be suicide, knowing what Rosamund knew of her father's temper, not to mention his snobbishness. He wouldn't kill her as Othello had killed Desdemona. He might sell her horses and throw her out on her ear, though. An outcome devoutly to be wished.

Now the eyes of the two women — the present Lady Baaden-Boomethistle, bursting with youth and vitality, and the former, bursting with strangeness — met over the elaborate floral arrangement, which otherwise acted as a colorful shield during their warfare. Normally, Lady Baaden-Boomethistle, who by any measure had the upper hand in the situation, would not deign to meet the dowager's eyes. This time, though, she allowed herself a tiny smirk, a shot across the daisies, as it were, and the dowager, catching the superior look, flushed unattractively.

The dowager was thinking, *Mixed marriage.* This is what comes of a mixed marriage. The daughter of a groom who meets a member of the landed gentry at a horse show and ends up dragging him to the altar, against the advice of saner heads not addled by unaccustomed surges of testosterone. Heads such as her own. Oh, she had tried to stop him! She had warned him, giving many examples of catastrophic May-December marriages among members of their set. But it had been hopeless. He felt he deserved, he had informed his mother, some happiness.

He deserved no such thing, she had informed him frostily. He was, after all, a Baaden-Boomethistle.

"I saw you," said the dowager suddenly, turning aggressively in her chair to face Bree head-on. She settled her cup noisily into its saucer; there was an unattractive smear of her liberally applied coral lipstick on its rim. "You needn't look so smug. I saw what you did."

Bree upped the power of her smirk to a full-wattage sneer, still managing to look lovely despite a rather cruel curve to her delicately tinted upper lip.

Quite a feat, when you thought about it. Rosamund watched the exchange with some amusement, for she could read her grandmother pretty well and had, in any event, heard many times the woman's opinions of her son's choice of life partner. The dowager refused to admit that in much the same way had Camilla captured a young prince's heart in a castle far, far away and long, long ago: It was not as if there were no precedent. More remarkably, the dowager seemed not to realize that this Cinderella scenario was precisely the same dreck she had foisted on an unsuspecting reading public for years.

Or perhaps that is what she found particularly galling — that the fairy tales she wrote had come true in real life. Rosamund thought it was enough to make a cat laugh, the whole thing, as much as she sympathized with the dowager's dilemma: Bree was a threat to the dowager and her safe little niche here at Casa Totleigh.

Bree was a threat to all of them. It was a wonder no one had tried to set her up for a fall.

Oh, my, thought the butler, entering the

room carrying Rosamund's plate of fried eggs, with a rasher of bacon and caddy of buttered toast. They can't let it rest, not for a single day, can they? I used to think the holidays were particularly bad, but the fact is, every day has been like this since the first wife died. Certainly the children never got over it.

"Thank you, Hargreaves."

At least Rosamund was always polite. The son was another matter. He oozed a sense of entitlement, because he was. Entitled, that is. Richer than anyone deserved to be without working a single day for it. Any sweat that came off that noble brow came from his daily runs about the grounds of the manor house.

The atmosphere shifted noticeably and the butler's thoughts were interrupted by the arrival of Lord Baaden-Boomethistle himself, who took a seat next to his shiny young wife, kissing her forehead and gruffly addressing the rest of the room with a general good morning.

"Morning, Father," said Peregrine, thinking that the old man was looking exhausted. This is what came of robbing the cradle.

Lord Baaden-Boomethistle, in turn, regarded his son. Although he had not for some time been quite certain how to regard

63

Peregrine. Quite often the phrase "pig in a poke" flittered through his mind.

Peregrine was in trouble at University — again. He was probably going to be sent down this time. Lord Baaden-Boomethistle was friends with Peregrine's tutor and, as a result, he knew more about his son's problems than he should do. For once, though, he wasn't certain how to approach the situation. He didn't want to do or say anything he'd have to apologize for later. Not that apology was a big part of Lord Baaden-Boomethistle's repertoire at any time.

That a son of his should read Land Economy at University was all right; it was an honorable calling, traditional for a member of the landed gentry, particularly now that Prince William, the duke of Cambridge and probable future king himself, had jumped aboard that blue-blood bandwagon. And it was not as if Peregrine had the brainpower to do much else; the course offered a light workload for those who wanted it, allowing the sons and daughters of the nobility more time for sports, napping, and carousing. Fortunately, other people had already split the atom and suchlike. But it was distressing nonetheless. As the only son of the house, Peregrine had had great hopes pinned on him from the time he was in diapers. Nothing had been too good for him, no spoon too golden; his mother had doted on his every achievement, however trivial. Now the boy's lack of a life plan for after university was disturbing. He himself, Lord Baaden-Boomethistle, had no intention of shuffling off this mortal coil anytime soon. What was the boy to do with himself for the next thirty years? Comparisons with Prince Charles were inevitable, a man awaiting his chance to do *some*thing, and in the meantime not able to do very much so long as his mother sat on the throne. Peregrine was even less well placed, and less well equipped, to have any kind of impact on world or even local affairs.

And what was the matter with his hair lately?

"We've had a call from someone in the village," Lady Baaden-Boomethistle informed her husband, pushing back a strand of her own dark hair. Today parted in the middle and held by a clasp at the back of her head, tresses framed her face like gleaming satin, reflecting the rays of sunlight through the window. "Eugenia Something-Something, and something to do with a duck race. She said Noah of Noah's Ark Antiques would be in Europe for the duration. Why that's anything to do with us, I can't imagine. I said I'd bring it up with you. So I have. Brought it up." She returned her attention to the horse-racing news. "Grand Red Cayenne won again. I told you we should have bought him."

Lord Baaden-Boomethistle put down the front section of his own newspaper. "I suppose they'll be wanting to use the grounds for their duck race. What a nuisance. Litter and children everywhere."

"Not to mention people in Bermuda shorts who should never be seen in anything less than a tent." This from Peregrine, and he cast a significant glance at his sister as he spoke, a glance that did not go unrecognized.

Why don't you just die, she thought. *Die.*

"I'll have a word with the vicar," said Lord Baaden-Boomethistle. "He's bound to be in touch about it. I am not dealing with some village idiot from the Parish Council or the Women's Institute."

"I don't see why we have to deal with it at all," said Peregrine. "It's a duck race, for God's sake."

"Because," sniffed the dowager, smoothing the ruffle of her blue silk blouse, purchased to set off the blue of her eyes, "it is our duty. You should know that."

"It's for charity," his father informed him.

"And from time out of mind we have sup-
ported these daft little village entertain-
ments. It's expected of us."

Hargreaves took the breakfast order of the
lord of the house, and took the measure of
the temperature of the room, rightly predict-
ing that this would not be a day of fireworks,
but a day of simmering discontent. A day
like any other, in fact. They would sit
around the table, fuming and rehearsing
clever retorts they would never dare utter.
Lord Baaden-Boomethistle would simply
bark his displeasure at any notion he didn't
like, until all resistance was quashed.

Only Lady Baaden-Boomethistle had a
different technique from that of most people, and indeed different from that of her
predecessor, in dealing with her husband.
The current Lady Baaden-Boomethistle
seemed to be secretly amused by everything
the lord did, smiling her catlike little smile,
flicking her catlike tongue at her lips, and
practically purring as he wound himself up
more and more over any- and everything. It
was impossible to say if this secret hilarity
were at his expense or not. Hargreaves
suspected it was. But before any of them
knew it, the lord's anger would have been
dissolved, or diverted into safer channels.
She had that power over him.

A fragment of the famous quotation went through his mind, although he wasn't sure how apt it was. That she was a braver man than he was, Gunga Din.

Which made no sense at all.

Lady Baaden-Boomethistle now made a beckoning gesture with her free hand and her husband obediently took that hand in his. It was a telling move on her part, less a sign of affection than a statement to anyone watching: See how quickly he does as I command.

The dowager, noticing it, too, did not feel she had imagined this. Bree's quick darting look in her direction spoke volumes. It was a tiny power play, one of many in their ongoing struggle for supremacy. For the dowager lived on sufferance in the new household established by her son's remarriage, or at least this was how it felt to her. She had rights by law, of course. They could not just chuck her in the street. But how massive and unseemly a scuffle it would be to assert those rights. How constant the fight was even now. This fear as she grew older was a real thing, a tiger lurking round each corner of the massive house.

The butler leaned over her shoulder to refill her cup. And now Peregrine was whining, letting his unhappiness about something be known — something about borrowing the car — and this unhappiness was framed by a major sulk that was in no way as appealing as Lady Baaden-Boomethistle's little game of sulking, a game to which Hargreaves had often borne witness. In fact, the butler thought the son's mewling was the sort of juvenile performance that was sure to backfire eventually. It reminded the faithful servant that the apples in this privileged family had not fallen far from the tree; inbreeding would one day be the downfall of all the gentry.

They were simply impossible — the dowager, Lord Baaden-Boomethistle, and the children, particularly the son — and Hargreaves could not wait for his days of service to them to end.

As Hargreaves moved away from the table to see to the rest of the food, Lady Baaden-Boomethistle's glance traveled around the room before returning to rest briefly and dispassionately on her aging husband's red face. It was a look the butler could never quite read, whenever the lady looked at her lord. It seemed to contain affection, but there was something more going on.

He, Hargreaves, would not want to be in the lord's shoes. Not for all the rich lands and titles and the privilege and everything that went with it. For the lord did not know whom to trust, and he certainly seemed to be trusting all the wrong people.

Now Lady Baaden-Boomethistle was addressing Peregrine in that exasperated tone she often adopted with him. Hargreaves had not caught the topic, but it didn't matter. She would fillet the boy, regardless.

"You are, I suppose, entitled to your opinions. It would be refreshing if those opinions were original once in a while."

Rosamund stifled a snort as Peregrine, clearly wounded, wrestled to put on a mask of indifference.

"Lay off," he said sourly. "You — I say, you really need to lighten up once in a while." It was a misjudged accusation and it missed the mark by a mile. "Be more phlegmatic." *Phlegmatic* had just turned up, used incorrectly, in one of the papers he was attempting to write for a tutorial. "That means —"

"I know what it means," drawled Lady Baaden-Boomethistle. "If *you* get any looser, you'll dissolve into a puddle of space goop. Oh, wait, I see I'm too late."

Peregrine, now as red in the face as his father, looked as if he might stand and flee the room. Now Rosamund smothered a laugh. She had to hand it to Bree — she

70

could annihilate with the slightest inflection, the merest lift of an eyebrow. She didn't need words, but she was good with them, aiming them like little poisoned darts.

As Rosamund, to her sorrow, knew too well.

"Puh-leeze," said Lord Baaden-Boomethistle. "I thought we had agreed . . ."

Lady Baaden-Boomethistle subsided with a pretty sulk. This seemed to infuriate Peregrine even more. Bree was at her most appealing when she sulked, her glossy pink lips scrunched into a little-girl pout. It was how Peregrine lost every argument on every subject. She was irresistible to Lord Baaden-Boomethistle when she pulled this stuff, and she knew it. She was irresistible, period.

While enjoying the conflict, still Rosamund cursed the day Bree had come into her father's life, cursed the day her mother had died, cursed Bree for being Bree, with her effortless and deadly charm. Her father didn't stand a chance with her in his life, in their lives.

The dowager was thinking, meanwhile: This Bree creature is such a step down from the first wife. Step? Make that a falling off a cliff. She is the daughter of a *groom*. She grew up in a *stable*. Not an ounce of blue blood in her veins, certainly not like her

71

predecessor.

Why, oh why, had her son thrown them all into it like this? He could have had his pick. He didn't have to foist this . . . this *trollop* on all of them.

It was going to end badly. Anyone could see that.

The dowager set down her empty cup and gathered herself to leave. She had agreed to help feed the homeless later that morning in a church in Monkslip-super-Mare. Well, not feed them so much as show up and offer encouragement. Dabbing at her lips with her serviette, she stood and announced as much to the others.

"I wouldn't," said Lord Baaden-Boomethistle, "encourage them if I were you."

"I meant," she said, "encourage the volunteers. Show the flag. Let them know the family stands behind their little humanitarian efforts, however pointless they may be."

"Good," said her son, with a wink at his wife. "The poor we will always have with us. No need to encourage them."

His wife stood also. "I promised to drop by, myself. Perhaps I'll see you there."

"Me, too," said Rosamund. "And I was planning to do more than just show up looking good," she said pointedly. "I shall

72

go in there and get my feet dirty. It wouldn't hurt either of you to do the same."

At a look from her father, she subsided.

No need for Rosamund to ask either woman for a lift. In her grandmother's case, it almost certainly wouldn't be offered.

And Bree Baaden-Boomethistle went almost everywhere on horseback.

CHAPTER 3
LADY BOUNTIFUL

The event the dowager had mentioned at breakfast was the weekly Bowls for Souls luncheon for the poor.

Although people were astonished to hear it, Nether Monkslip had poor people. Well, sometimes just the one: Roger Hayden, who had raised being unemployed to a noble calling, complete with slogans ("Down with Corporations and GMF"). Still, he was what they had, and the mission of the church dictated that he could not be excluded from the table.

Nearby Monkslip-super-Mare had many more poor people, and eventually the food service had drifted and finally settled where the need was greatest, without any ecclesiastical posturing over boundaries.

These occasions were as much beneficial to the volunteers as, one supposed, they were to the recipients of the largesse. The chatter as the volunteers worked, stirring soups and building sandwiches, was non-stop, the sounds of gossip filling to the edges of the room. So dense and excited was the hubbub that only snatches could be overheard:

"She planted her beets during a waxing moon. Anyone could have told her — certainly Awena could have told her — she had it all wrong. They'll *never* thrive now. You plant lettuce during a waxing moon, not beets." . . .

. . . "The Ladies of Perpetual Help have hidden my shoes somewhere again. Lately Maria is more like La Belle Dame Sans Merci." . . .

. . . "Did you say you could volunteer to teach the sewing classes? It's been ever so popular with the women from Pakistan and Afghanistan. It builds their trust, you know." . . .

. . . "Those children and that practically feral mother of theirs. Who's raising those kids is a mystery." This was Suzanna Winship, never one to use the soft-pedal on her pronouncements.

"Tildy Ann seems to be raising herself. *And* her brother." . . .

. . . "Awena is like the Melanie of Nether Monkslip. You know, Melanie in *Gone With the Wind.* Impossibly good. That our dishy vicar fell for her — well, I guess I'm not surprised." (Suzanna again.) . . .

. . . "Have you seen the baby? Is he gorgeous or what? All that dark hair!" . . .

. . . "What on earth was she wearing? A shroud?" . . .

. . . "It was *definitely* not Sandra he was with." . . .

. . . "But Elka needs to take a firm stand. Tell that son of hers which end is up and all. Be strong."

"Like you with your daughter, you mean?" said Suzanna, rushing in to defend. She and Elka might squabble on occasion, but there were times for a united front. And the woman with opinions about Elka had a teenaged daughter who famously ran amok in Staincross Minster the minute her mother's back was turned, although Suzanna diplomatically, for once, forbore to point this out. "Elka is tougher than anyone in the village. And harder working. She just has a soft spot for her son, that's — Step lively, here comes the first round."

Heads turned and faces broke into smiles at each new arrival at the door. The deserving poor were shown into a room where half a dozen large tables had been set for them.

Chanel Dirkson arrived late, running awkwardly on sensible sandals she was not quite used to. Like something a shepherd would wear, thought Suzanna. Clearly, Chanel needed to be taken in hand. She was new to the village, a forty-something writer of self-help books who, like so many lately, had come seeking the bucolic peace of Nether Monkslip. She fell into conversation with Suzanna as they organized sandwiches on trays, for she and Suzanna had become fast friends, despite their outward differences (Suzanna glamorous, and Chanel, despite her namesake, pastoral). Both women had moved to Nether Monkslip from London, although Chanel had arrived there by way of Wiltshire. As she pointed out, "People everywhere have problems, so I can offer advice from anywhere I happen to live. It's just that in London, they tend to have problems with traffic and parking. I'm looking for the real problems, if you know what I mean."

"Parking situations can lead to murder," said Suzanna. "I could cheerfully throttle the next person who cuts me off in traffic. Of course, for real traffic, you have to drive to Monkslip-super-Mare."

"Precisely," agreed Chanel, smoothing the nap of her tunic-style blouse. She always wore all-organic clothing — cotton, linen, and very expensive — and little to no makeup. As Suzanna had observed, this made her fit right in with the granola-crunching, fruit-canning, bean-sprouting ethos of Nether Monkslip. Chanel's features reminded Suzanna of a Madonna in a Russian Orthodox icon. There was a downward curve to her eyebrows when she was in repose that made her look sad; it matched the often-downward curve of her mouth. Whatever wisdom Chanel had to impart, it seemed to have been hard-won.

"What are you working on now?" Suzanna asked politely, not really caring. She got her fill of writerly talk at the legendarily contentious meetings of the Writers' Square, of which Chanel had thus far resisted becoming a member. "Can we get some more cheese over here?" Suzanna yelled over her shoulder. Turning back to Chanel, she muttered, "Typical. Eugenia is never around when you want her. And you so seldom want her."

"They — the publishers — want a novel based on my newspaper columns. A sort of Bridget Jones meets Heathcliff, as it was described to me. But I'm not sure. I'm strictly a nonfiction writer." Chanel's expertise was in sternly removing the blinders from the eyes of the star-crossed lover, for handing out no-nonsense advice of the "get real, he's a loser" variety. Her newspaper columns had spawned several advice books, of none of which, judging by the titles, did Suzanna feel the need to avail herself. Books like *Ten Warning Signs He's a Sociopath* and *Before You Meet His Mother* were, in Suzanna's estimation, for rank amateurs at play in the fields of love. Still, the books sold well; judging by appearances — that organic stuff really did cost the moon — Chanel was comfortable, if not wealthy.

"Sounds interesting," murmured Suzanna. "Are all the tomatoes gone?"

"What I'm working on right now is a chapter about dealing with difficult people," Chanel continued, glossing a slice of whole-grain bread with French mustard and neatly stacking layers of cheese and lettuce on top.

"Hmph. You've come to the right place. But 'Go sit by someone else' would be my advice. The world is full of people, and life is too short."

Chanel laughed. "That's probably a very good distillation of what I recommend. However, sometimes — sometimes people come into your life whether you want them to or not. And stay there. Just leaving them alone is not always an option. Haven't you ever had a difficult boss?"

"Several. I just ignored them until they quit."

Again, Chanel laughed. It was a good laugh that reached those rather sad eyes and made them shine. Unbeknownst to Chanel, Suzanna was already sizing her up for sister-in-law potential. Her brother, Dr. Winship, had been single too long.

"Anyway, you're the expert, judging by your success," Suzanna observed. "We can't be running out of mustard, for God's sake."

"I've been lucky. What, after all, separates the middle-of-the-road writer from the wildly successful one?"

"Talent? Perseverance?"

"No. *No-o-o-o.* Luck, of course. Pure luck. It's a business that runs on luck. Otherwise, I'd still be selling ladies lingerie at Harrods."

"According to our resident best-selling author, Frank Cuthbert, it takes more than that. Frank claims it takes genius. While I'd say Frank is a high-functioning idiot, I'd also say he's right. At the least it takes talent. Don't be so modest."

The chatter continued in a giddy ebb and flow interspersed with laughter; in between could be heard the scrape of utensils on plates or the sound of water being poured into glasses. After a time, Suzanna's voice again could be heard above the rest, asking,

"Where *is* Eugenia? She said she was bringing serviettes. It's not like her to be late."

"Eugenia?" asked a woman who was new in the village. Suzanna thought her name was Bridget.

"You know. The one who dresses like a reenactor, although it's not clear what century she thinks she's in. Seventeenth, possibly."

"Eugenia would have liked the seventeenth century," someone commented. "Lots of rules."

"And punishments," added someone else.

"And public hangings."

Several nodded at this. Under Eugenia's reign at Bowls for Souls, several minor uprisings had taken place, only to be ruthlessly put down. However, if she insisted on X brand of coffee, someone might bring Y in a feeble show of independence — accompanied by a fist pump once Eugenia's back was turned.

Although she put on a brave front, these insurrections were painful to Eugenia. She would paste on a mask of Christian forbearance while nurturing the grudge for weeks. "They know not what they do," she might murmur, in a gross misapplication of Scripture. One and all agreed Eugenia's head was screwed on just a bit too tightly.

It's since her brother died, said some. And didn't she have a son somewhere that no one ever saw? She didn't used to be quite so . . . so. Well, so weird. So particular and driven about everything. But few thought her really sinister or threatening in any way. Simply tedious as a head cold, as Suzanna Winship might say.

Sometimes, when reprimanded by Eugenia, the donor would comment that these were poor people they were feeding, and no doubt those in need would appreciate whatever was given them, and not judge too harshly the brand of mustard being used.

"Are you saying that they should be happy with whatever rubbish we choose to foist off on them?" Eugenia would demand. "That they are somehow less than we are — we who can afford to buy the national brands?"

"Of course not!" would be the reply. "I wasn't saying that!" But somehow the donor felt caught out by the accusation, as if in some way guilty of snobbery or of being a cheapskate, when in fact some of them had a job to scrape together the pennies for the well-intended donation. The whole transaction, meant to be a generous and kind-hearted impulse, somehow had become tainted by this point. Eugenia noticed there were dropouts from the roster of volunteers, but she never suspected she was the cause.

By the time Eugenia arrived fifteen minutes later, the soup soiree was in full swing. She had, she explained, been delayed on the train from London. Not everyone welcomed her arrival, but Eugenia set to work, immediately getting on Suzanna's nerves.

She got on everyone's nerves, but she got on Suzanna's in a big way, since Suzanna frequently also had to deal with her when organizing Women's Institute events.

Eugenia threw herself into WI projects with the same lunatic verve that might have been better applied to resolving a standoff between Russia and the Ukraine. And she was not one to admit failure. A recent theater outing to Staincross Minster she had organized for the women had not been a success, as predicted by Suzanna.

"That's because *Titus Andronicus* was boring when it was first written."

"Was not."

"Was too."

"It's Shakespeare."

"So? Shakespeare had his off years, too. We can't all be Harold Pinter."

"Talk about boring."

"Is not."

"Is too."

Now the perennial argument with Suzanna again had to do with buying supplies for the luncheon. The smart money was on Suzanna to win this time. She had bought half a dozen tins of sliced pineapple on sale, a rare and unusual treat, and she was proposing to make upside-down cakes for a future meal.

"On sale? Are you saying the needy should be fobbed off with stale, low-quality food?" Eugenia demanded.

Suzanna met her steely gaze head-on.

"No, I'm not saying that. I'm saying even I can't afford to eat organic fucking sliced pineapple imported from goddamn Hawaii, for Chrissake."

"Language, please! We are here to set a Christian example."

"Then do a better job of it." Suzanna stared boldly back, taking in the hair, the general air of desperation that she sensed lurked behind the relentless, tireless do-goodery. In charge of feeding the homeless, Eugenia had managed to rile both the destitute and all the volunteers with overly precise instructions ("How many times? I said Ryvita. It *has* to be Ryvita. Where did this CrispAlivo come from, anyway?") and with her constant hovering. Soon many of those in need stopped showing up for their

84

free lunch, heading over to St. Catherine's instead, even though the food wasn't as good and it was a long bus journey out of town to get there. But the nuns fed them, asked no questions, believed their lies, or pretended to, and stayed out of their business. This, to those in need, was much more like it: Just hand over that sandwich and shut up about it.

Eugenia had drawn back at Suzanna's little outburst of profanity. Now she turned the tin of pineapple over and over in her hands, like a grenade she was preparing to lob. "Twenty-two grams of sugar," she read from the label. "Think what it's doing to their arteries."

"Think what going without food is doing to the rest of them," Suzanna shot back. "You know what, I really don't need this." To herself she added, What have the poor ever done for me, anyway? "I should be over at the Village Hall, helping them get ready for the gymkhana on Saturday."

"Fine," Eugenia said shortly. "Why don't you just go do that."

Suzanna, subsiding into a mutinous huff, considered quitting Bowls for Souls altogether. But as she had said the evening before to her brother, Dr. Winship, if she waited long enough, Eugenia might get

85

bored and quit.

"There's also divine intervention," she had added, in what she knew was a lovely, throaty voice — a voice of command she used to good advantage at WI meetings, speaking with a polished and direct delivery that suggested Sarah Palin barnstorming across America's corn belt.

"You're not thinking of how you rose to power in the Women's Institute, are you?" Bruce had asked.

"I was, rather." Suzanna had ascended the throne in time-honored fashion, via the untimely death of her predecessor. Now she reigned supreme and unchallenged. It helped, of course, that no one else, with the possible exception of Eugenia, really wanted the position. It involved a tremendous amount of work. The WI, along with the Altar Guild, constituted a sort of women's underground in Nether Monkslip, the women constantly abuzz behind the scenes, only the results of their efforts showing. And they had fun, too, if the latest wine tasting and photography event were anything to go by. Although it was later suggested they might want to keep these two events separate in future.

"I'd step carefully around Eugenia if I were you," Bruce had warned his sister. "No one has much time for her, but I think she could be a fearless and formidable enemy. There's something not quite right about her."

Suzanna had jumped in before her brother could get atop his favorite hobbyhorse, which she and others had titled "The Killer Amongst Us."

"Yes, yes, of course you're right." But too late. Bruce and his horse had already left the gate.

"Have you seen," he'd continued, "the way she looks at Max Tudor?"

"They all look at him like that," said Suzanna, carefully distancing herself from the charge of which she was equally guilty. Max had been the village's prime bachelor catch until Awena had come along and hooked him.

Without even trying, she thought with an inward sniff. It really was galling. Suzanna was the village's Delilah, a temptress operating at full tilt, a woman who admitted no competition. But even she saw the perfection of the "Maxena" pairing, and was reconciled to its inevitability. Mostly.

Bruce had said, as they continued their conversation over dinner, "Eugenia seems to ignore the fact he's a married man now with a child. It's like it doesn't register with

87

her. Even if she'd ever had a chance with Max, that ship has sailed."

"Don't I know it," said Suzanna. "I mean, yes. You're right."

"That sort of willful blindness, that inability to face reality, combined with a thwarted sexuality — it can be dangerous. Perhaps more dangerous than anything I can name."

"Perhaps you could have a word with her when she comes for a checkup."

"Like she'd listen! Besides, I never really see her in my professional capacity. She's healthy as a horse."

And likely to live forever, worse luck, thought Suzanna now. She returned her attention to the work at hand at Bowls for Souls, which seemed more useful than wrangling any further with Saint Eugenia. The conversation across the table from her had drifted to the whereabouts of the dowager, which soon led to a rehash of the woman's checkered past.

"She came here to help her son out when his wife died," said a plump woman with a topknot. "Devoted to him she was, they say in Nether Monkslip."

"Came over like a shot once the first wife was out of the picture, you mean." Others, seeming to agree with this hypothesis, nodded their heads. "She never seemed to like the first Lady Baaden-Boomethistle all that much — until she saw what the second one was like. But then, no woman would have been good enough for her boy."

"Hardly a boy, although he likes to act like it."

Universal nodding at this sentiment.

"No fool like an old goat," said someone sagely.

"They are very close, mother and son?" Suzanna asked.

"Only in the sense that rich people always stick together."

"The folk at Tot Hall don't have much time for the likes of us," continued the woman with the topknot, who seemed to be sampling as many of the biscuits as she was setting out on plates. There was a telltale smear of chocolate at one corner of her mouth. The biscuits were donated every week by Elka Garth of the Cavalier Tea Room and Garden, and they were always fresh, never day-old, and of the same high quality as the products she sold in her shop. Eugenia definitely approved.

"I hear they live as high on the hog as drug lords in a Mexican prison," said Suzanna.

"I hear they're going broke."

"Wishful thinking."

"But no wonder if they are!" This from a slender dark woman with a pixie haircut. "The new Lady Baaden-Boomethistle sees to that."

"She only cares about them horses of hers. Still, it's an expensive hobby."

"I think the gentry should try joining the twenty-first century. Come down off that high horse and see how the other half lives. That dowager is —"

But this speaker, with her back to the kitchen entrance, was shushed by the others, who had spotted her topic surging through the door. The conversation stilled and polite masks were applied.

Lady Caroline Baaden-Boomethistle smiled at the little group. She was in rare form, reveling in her role as the titular head of various committees, raised like many such to that high estate not because of merit but for the name recognition she brought to whatever worthy cause was in play. In truth, the Dowager B-B, as she was called (behind her back), had trouble telling one worthy cause from another, and frequently would rise to give a little speech in aid of those less fortunate, to the bewilderment of those who thought they had gathered to promote the hunt, save the forests, or protect the dormouse. One thing of which she was certain, however, was her position in the village, which meant she was expected to be on the Parish Council even though more often than not she ended up sending elaborately invented regrets when she could not attend — regrets that generally included a plug for her latest book.

Now Suzanna, also with her back to the door, said, "Viscountess Baaden-Boomethistle is running late. Let's start serving this lot without her."

Eugenia drew back, horrified. Her mouth, generally settled into a straight and unforgiving line, peeled itself open into a shocked O of dismay.

"A viscountess is never to be addressed as such in conversation. It is always *Lady* Baaden-Boomethistle. In any event, she is, since the passing of her husband, the dowager viscountess."

"Who gives a sh—" began Suzanna, interrupted at that moment by loud shushings and throat clearings and eye rollings, and finally noticing the Lady herself.

In she swept, trailing scarves and perfume, shellacked and false-eyelashed and completely out of place at what was, after all, a charitable working environment. The rest of them were dressed casually in jeans and

91

exercise pants or flowered shirtdresses. Possibly to indicate her lack of interest in work or exercise, or in flowers, for that matter, the Dowager B-B wore blue shot silk, black gloves, a strand of matching pearls of incalculable worth, and a great deal of eyeliner. To the further puzzlement of all, she wore a matching blue hat with a bit of netting falling coyly over one eye — a hat at first glance resembling a hedgehog caught in a lobster trap. She looked as Kate Middleton might look in forty years on her way to a royal christening.

Given that the dowager was fresh from her manor house, a homestead of terraced lawns with tinkling fountains, small artificial lakes, and a private tennis court, it was difficult for even the keenest observer to posit exactly what she thought she might bring to the proceedings.

Her daughter-in-law, Lady Baaden-Boomethistle, generally would by now have breezed in and out, wearing pinks and shouting encouragement on her way to the hunt. She would park her horse outside, like a cowboy stopping off for a beer at the local saloon. Actually, she'd leave the horse waiting with a groom or trainer, as it was too valuable a piece of property to be left alone.

But today, despite Bree's stated intentions

at breakfast, she was mysteriously absent.

Now the dowager, pasting on a smile, braced herself to do good in a vague way. Hers was an all-encompassing brand of do-goodery, for she was the type to cut ribbons and make gushing little speeches of hope, flapping her scarves and jangling her bracelets and adjusting her rings, and generally trying to look beneficent, while her eyes rather desperately sought the whereabouts of the drinks tray. Rather to everyone's surprise, she was an avid participant in the whist drive, a key social event of village life. It was assumed the game gave her a safe outlet for the gambler's instincts that were said to run in her distinguished family and to have brought it near ruin more than once.

Suzanna dragged her head around to observe the new arrival. Really, comparisons with Barbara Cartland were inevitable — the Queen of Romance who had also had an uncanny knack for minting coin from the dreams and marital aspirations of women of all ages. One wondered how someone like the Dowager B-B, who had led by all accounts such a cosseted youth, had come to know so much about the wars between the sexes.

The dowager had early on rejected the home-county style of her peers and contemporaries. Not for her the sensible skirt, flat shoes, and padded jacket of the Tory, worn with pearls and a silk neck scarf. Not for her the dogs trotting at her heels as she surveyed her grand estate. She, in fact, made herself very scarce on National Gardens Scheme days, when tourists were permitted into the grounds of Totleigh Hall to be shown about by the head gardener. Even the opportunity to flog her books to the waiting masses could not compete with her innate horror at seeing common folk in cargo pants and flip-flops traipsing about the gardens and parklands of her precious home. Those ill-shod fans (and she did have legions of fans, ill-shod and otherwise) who had purchased a ticket with the hope of meeting the famous dowager in person were regularly disappointed.

Now she gravitated to one corner of the kitchen, where she soon could be heard braying at the one woman in the room reputed to have a drop of blue blood in her veins. The dowager began doing one of her bloodstock tallies: "She was a Witherspoon — one of the Derbyshire Witherspoons, of course I mean, not the other branch, who were something in packaging. Her orchids were magnificent, but she was largely known for her tulips."

"But I mustn't keep you," finished the dowager, and neatly side-stepping any attempts to get her actually to help with the food preparation, she swanned her way into the dining room to mingle with the peons.

She paused in the doorway for a moment before charging in, gushing sincerity and flinging compassion in the general direction of the downtrodden. Noticing a family of three — two young parents and a smiling baby less than a year old — she lobbed herself at them, warbling exclamations of delight in her upper-class drawl. Grabbing the baby (not without a struggle of protest from its mother), she proceeded to dandle the child at arm's length until it began to cry (it wouldn't do to get peasant drool, or worse, on her dress). It was, had anyone but known it, a reprise of her role as mother to Lord Baaden-Boomethistle, a blend of engulfing affection interrupted by very long stretches of bored disinterest. She had not realized her son had learned to walk until one day he escaped from the nanny and, totally nude and trailing his blue blankie, interrupted one of her cocktail parties. She had had to speak *quite* sharply to the nanny about that.

Now she returned the squalling baby to its rightful owners and, literally dusting the talcum powder from her hands, proceeded to dance around the room, chatting at, rather than with, the great unwashed, who were unfailingly polite in their turn. When one of them addressed her as "Old Duck" she smiled bravely, lips atremble, and moved on. Here and there the dowager extended a gloved hand to one of the men, much as if she expected him to kiss the outsize ring on her index finger. It was a queenly act she had modeled on newsreel footage of the Queen Mother touring the bombed-out East End during World War II. In the case of the Dowager Baaden-Boomethistle, it was an act hollow at the core, and was, reflected Suzanna, like watching Gloria Swanson auditioning for a role in *The Song of Bernadette.* The dowager simply could not damp down her fundamental self-interest and self-regard.

Suzanna managed to intercept the dowager's circuit around the room, interrupting the cascade of baroque platitudes and inanities, for she wanted a word about the duck race.

Still in Gracious Chatelaine mode, the duchess inclined her head to listen.

"Oh!" she breathed down into her bosom, ruffling her own feathers. One is so *very* busy, her manner seemed to say, and con-

stantly importuned by fans and other sup-
plicants. Still, she allowed as how this little
duck race was important to the villagers,
who lacked for other rustic outlets. She
raised her eyes to meet Suzanna's, and now
a new mask of condescension was in place:
One must make allowances for the less
fortunate, who wish to bask if only for a
moment in the refracted limelight of a *Famous Author.*

"We also were wondering if we could host
the after-party on the grounds of Tot Hall,"
continued Suzanna.

The mask slipped. "The grounds of —
what did you call it?"

"Tot Hall."

"Oh," the dowager said again, and drew
back, her glossy painted mouth pulled into
a grimace of distaste. Suzanna was wondering how the woman kept all that lipstick
from seeping into the powdered wrinkles
around her mouth, but she rather supposed
the dowager was not one to stand around
swapping beauty tips. "If you mean Totleigh
Hall, my ancestral home, the manor house
where the Baaden-Boomethistles have resided nearly since the time of William the
Conqueror, producing luminaries to domi-
nate the world stage, well, you shall have to
ask my son."

"I was thinking of getting the vicar to ask him, actually," said Suzanna, unfazed by this attempt to shove her down to her place on the lower rungs of the world order. "Since the funds from the duck race are going to help with repairs to the church organ."

"Yes, that would be much more the appropriate thing to do. The Baaden-Boomethistles are always quite happy to benefit our delightful little church, of course. And we have a long history of doing so. Still, I leave all practical matters to the men."

"A recipe for disaster if ever I heard one," said Suzanna.

CHAPTER 4
MAX AND THE
LORD OF THE MANOR

Totleigh Hall, one of the great estates of southwest England, sat atop a swell of rolling parkland south of Nether Monkslip, cushioned side and back by the lush foliage of ancient oaks and sited at the end of a long, stately tree-lined drive. At some distance from the back of the house was a large man-made lake, a lake long rumored to be a source of bad luck to the manor's occupants, although no one alive today could remember why. The legend was as real as Robin Hood to the local villagers.

With views to the lake and to deep forest on all sides, Totleigh was less than a castle, more than a hall, and it appeared somehow enchanted, dozing as it did under the weight of centuries.

In long-ago manorial times, a manor house was often the center around which a village grew — that or the village church or village green. Even now, with the manorial system far in the past, Totleigh Hall drew sightseers who added to the economic prosperity of the village by popping into the shops to buy souvenirs or into one of the inns for a brew and a bed for the night.

The hall was built on land once owned by the monks of the nearby abbey, and its former name was Nunshead. That might explain its reputation for bad luck, as it became vaguely tied into the legends swirling around the mysterious Nunswood, which brooded on a crest overlooking the river Pudmill.

The manor house had replaced an earlier country house, a sprawling, quirky Tudor edifice that had fallen into disrepair and had, in any event, been not nearly grand enough to showcase the ambitions of the family as it took firm root in the area. Later generations wanted increasingly to sweep away any history that suggested humble or tawdry beginnings, and so over the old hall's footprint they erected a much-admired stately home. Private bedrooms and reception rooms replaced the communal areas, where once the lord of the manor and his family had been lulled to sleep by the sound of snoring servants (more about those later). Gilded rooms were made larger and more golden, and glittering windows replaced the defensive stone of old.

Although Totleigh Hall was not a vast, gloomy, chain-rattler of a house in the accepted tradition, it was said to be haunted by the ghost of a woman from the time of King George III, the wife of the then lord. This nobleman had inconveniently found himself to be enamored of a servant girl, despite continuing to father children with the lady of the house, and despite all the social prohibitions surrounding such an attraction, and despite the reputation of his wife for having an evil temper. On the same day each year — legends varied as to which day, but most held the fifth of May to be the day — a woman's voice could be heard, wailing down the corridors of the house. There was disagreement as to whether this voice belonged to the lady or to the servant girl, but what was indisputable fact was that both women had disappeared one night, and as it was unlikely they had run away together, the rumor of course started that they had both been murdered. The lake was deep enough to accommodate both bodies — a thousand bodies. The lord's reputation, never very good, was reduced to tatters, and it was some centuries before his numerous heirs could claw their way back to their places in high society.

Max Tudor himself knew of the legend only from reading the chapter entitled "The Ladies in the Lake" in *Wherefore Nether Monkslip,* an unreliable source if ever one there were, a best-seller written by local worthy Frank Cuthbert. Still, Frank's opinion on what had happened at the manor house had quickly solidified into fact. He'd even given the servant girl a name (Jamaica), although her real name had been lost to history.

Max reflected on all this as he walked to Totleigh Hall on an evening soon after the latest Bowls for Souls gathering. He was going to meet with the lord of the manor, Viscount Bayer Baaden-Boomethistle, and hoped to catch him in a good and generous mood. He wondered idly if the lord were superstitious — if living in a great rambling house of echoing hallways would cause one to believe in ghosts.

It was just after Evening Prayer, and although the sun was still lighting his way, Max took a shortcut to the manor house, where lowering trees shaded his path. The days were beginning to gather in on themselves, and the end of daylight saving time soon would cast the region into gloom each afternoon. By nightfall, the path would be in darkness save for crescent moonlight to guide him back home, where Awena would have dinner waiting for him in a cottage softly aglow with lamp- and firelight.

The family at Totleigh Hall was rarely in residence nowadays, and even when they were, their attendance at St. Edwold's Church could not be said to be regular. They would sometimes attend Sunday services, taking the front pew as if by right, although the tradition of pew rent had long been abandoned. They would stumble through the service, flipping aimlessly about their prayer books and singing from the wrong page in the hymnal. On occasion, Lord Baaden-Boomethistle, in an unusual concession, could be induced to read the Epistle. He would strut importantly up the aisle and make his way to the lectern, where he would massage the passages in his great orator's voice, thundering out denunciations and condemning to damnation whatever group of sinners needed denouncing that week. On first hearing him, Max had thought the man had missed a career on the stage, but then, the idea of career for such as Lord Baaden-Boomethistle was anathema. He simply *was,* as his people had long *been,* and grubbing after money in the common way would be considered, well, common by his peers. Much better to breed horses, ride to hounds, shoot whatever moved, and potter about the conservatory than to be seen engaging in anything resembling a trade. If the rumors were true, the lord had in the past also been something of a roué, but age and his present marriage had calmed him down.

The grand family living among the rolling grounds of Totleigh Hall recognized what was required of them, and had a few years ago entertained carol singers at Christmas, an occasion that was still much talked about. Ancestors of the current residents had provided many amenities for the village, such as the Village Hall and reading rooms for the men, stocked with newspapers and periodicals. A more recent ancestor had provided the railway spur and train that steamed its way to and from the Nether Monkslip station. It was difficult to say what the current lord contributed to the village, apart from a bit of comic relief as he and his horse cantered down the High, but his appearance with his lady was still an occasion for excitement and hushed speculation. They were Royalty, after all, if very minor, and whatever they were, they belonged to the villagers. That the Very Minor Royalty greeted the villagers as they might greet tattooed and barely clad Maori was something most chose to ignore.

Had the St. Edwold's organ not been in dire need of restoration, Max would have excused himself from the entire duck race imbroglio, passing the responsibility to his new curate. Max felt he had learned enough on the esoteric subject of organ repair in the past few months to write a thesis. He was told by the experts that the St. Edwold's organ had speech irregularities and needed its pipes removed and, in some cases, replaced. There were, he gathered, pouches inside the organ that were becoming porous, thus creating dead notes; pipes that were collapsing; and reed stops that would require revoicing. Needless to say, this was not the sort of job that could be left to just anyone with a hammer and screwdriver, but one that required the attentions of the most expert specialist, and it hardly needed to be added that the cost for this specialized and intensive care was astronomic.

The church was flush with cash to keep the roof in good repair, thanks to a surprise bequest, but it had been stipulated those funds could be used for the roof and only for the roof. It was better, as the sexton liked to say, than a stick in the eye, but it did leave Max in constant fund-raising mode to keep the rest of the fabric of the church intact. Thus the need to keep the duck race, as it were, afloat.

And so Max made his way, hat in hand, to see if he could make the lord agree to allow the villagers to trample his beautiful lawns in the charitable cause of revoiced reed stops. The duck race was popular enough that the goal for organ repair was sure to be met.

While Max yearned for the good old days, the organizers had started using plastic windup ducks some years ago when the many and countless problems attendant on using live ducks became apparent. At least this meant that Max could promise Lord Baaden-Boomethistle a reduced level of chaos from the waterfowl kingdom. But the organizer's hope was to establish the finish line for the race at the foot of the Totleigh Hall grounds, and it was the ensuing celebrations that were problematic.

As Max walked, he came upon a paunchy vision in purple shorts and a gray T-shirt bearing the logo of Oxford University. The figure was jogging on a forest path near the house. Max thought this must be the seldom-seen son of the house. The large-eared figure — sunlight filtered through his ears, turning them red as a hare's — lum-

bered past him unseeing, practically staggering; the sweat flew off of him like a lawn
sprinkler. As Max emerged from the trees,
the runner's heavy legs carried him teeter-
ing around the side of the manor house in
the direction of the stables at the back. Max,
a jogger himself, thought there might be a
tipping point where running oneself to
exhaustion was counter-productive.

Max reached the wide stone steps of Totleigh Hall. In answer to his knock, a uni-
formed butler or valet appeared and offered
to take his jacket. Max demurred, not only
because he felt he would need his jacket —
the house was cavernous and probably
impossible to keep heated — but because
he pictured his jacket vanishing down one
of the endless corridors of the house, never
to be seen again. It wasn't as if the place
were designed for the ordinary hall cup-
board under the stairs. No, Totleigh Hall
must have an entire room at the butler's
disposal for the temporary storage of furs
and cloaks, particularly when the family was
hosting one of its glittery parties.

The tall, gray-haired man, having informed Max that "his lordship is presently
at work in his study," led him down one of
the vast corridors. The passage was lined
with various deep alcoves where chairs

designed for either a coronation or an electrocution flanked little tables or glass-fronted mahogany chests full of eye-catching treasures.

Eventually a door was flung open into a sort of antechamber. Max was asked to wait, and presently the man returned to announce that Lord Baaden-Boomethistle would see him now. The butler then drifted out of the room, stopping only to straighten a candlestick that was a millimeter out of true on a side table.

Lord Baaden-Boomethistle sat behind such a vast desk, Max nearly whistled with envy. A dark, shiny slab of mahogany surrounded by three walls of bookshelves, it offered acres of space for books and notebooks and computers, compared with the small, cramped desk at the vicarage where Max composed his sermons and wrestled with invoices. And yet Lord Baaden-Boomethistle seemed to content himself with a laptop computer and a single notepad at his side, from which he appeared to be transcribing notes. The rest of the empty surface gleamed with unfulfilled promise. At one side of the room stood a gun rack; behind the desk, French windows opened to a patio and the parklands that surrounded the house. Wisely, Max felt, the lord had turned his back on the distracting beauty of the trees and flowers outside. At the vicarage, Max was often pulled from his work by the view, but it was the villagers going about their business that distracted him. He told himself the position of the desk helped him keep his finger on the pulse of village life.

The lord, talking into a mobile phone, held up a thumb to indicate he would be with Max in a moment. Apparently listening to a rather lengthy monologue on the other end, he finally said, "I'll get Petherthwaite on it." A few moments later, he rang off.

Since Max had been announced by the butler, he felt it was a bit much to have to sit through the end of this conversation. But at no time in his dealings with the lord of Totleigh Hall did Max feel his collar would entitle him to special treatment. As the vicar of the local church, he was to be accorded some respect, but in a manner finely calibrated to let him know that he was providing a service to the family; as he was not even the younger son of gentry, he should not entertain any ideas above his station.

The lord at last rose to greet him, extending a hand across the shiny wooden plain that separated the two men.

"Good to see you, Vicar," he said. "A rare pleasure."

"The pleasure is mine," Max replied politely.

What Max knew of the family was rumor and idle gossip — "Lord Baaden-Boomethistle was a bit of a scoundrel in his day. The type who might be cast as the playboy spy in a seventies comedy" (Suzanna Winship); "This new wife isn't all she should be" (Miss Pitchford); "The apple didn't fall far from the tree; father and son are like peas in a pod" (Mrs. Hooser) — which Max did his best to cleanse from his thoughts. He didn't want to meet the family, particularly on a mission to ask favors of it, with a mind full of preconceived negative notions. What Max had seen of the father wasn't enough to establish character, and apart from the glimpse just now, he had seen the son only at a distance in the village, speeding past the vicarage on his bicycle. Likewise, Max had met Lady Baaden-Boomethistle too briefly to form any opinion, except that she was an attractive woman and vastly younger than her husband. She was said to be from Cherhill, famous for its hill figure of a white horse.

Max took Lord Bayer Baaden-Boomethistle's hand, taking his measure as he did so. He saw a man very tall, polished, and deceptively youthful in appearance, money having sanded away the lines of care and worry normal to a man of his age. It looked as if his hair might have been dark once, although now it was white and thinning and compensated for by bushy salt-and-pepper eyebrows.

"What can I do for you, Vicar? And how shall I address you?" His manner was courteous, but Max thought it might mask a trace of annoyance at the interruption to his day. Before Max could answer, the lord added, "I knew your predecessor. Sound man, if a bit lacking in imagination. A Cambridge man. One of the lesser Bokelers of the West Riding, I believe."

It was an episcopal version of the dowager's conversation at Bowls for Souls, that litany of the blue bloods of the nation. But the lord smiled and waited now for Max's reply. It was a smile that managed to suggest the recipient was briefly in his lordship's good graces but shouldn't expect to bask in the sunlight for long.

The lord had, however, scored points with Max for asking him how he wished to be addressed. Most people didn't realize that calling him "Reverend" was wrong, if usually well intended. He much preferred to be called "Vicar" or plain "Max" in the case of someone who knew him well.

"Vicar or Father Max is fine," he told Lord Baaden-Boomethistle now, guessing the familiar "Max" was never going to sit well with such as he.

"I'm sorry if our meeting must be brief. I've a train to catch soon. I do love train travel, don't you?" Max nodded, although the question appeared to be rhetorical. "If nothing else, it gives one a chance to catch up on one's reading. And the Chunnel has made it so easy to get back and forth to the Continent. We've used it nearly since it opened, but I do like to wait until they've worked the kinks out of a new project of that size. I'll never forget one summer, the last time we traveled the old-fashioned way — my first wife and I had taken a train out of Spain to catch a plane to England, and we were delayed. How hot it was! How crowded. The sounds — and the *smells* — of crying children the entire time. Merciful heaven. I am one of those who firmly believe children should be seen and not heard."

"Many would agree." Max smiled neutrally. "Fortunately, my son has a quiet and contented nature. Like his mother."

"Ah! That's right. You're a family man now. My congratulations."

Just then, the butler emerged from the murky corridor. He was carrying a tray with silver pots and china cups. He put the tray on a sideboard and went through an elaborate, Geisha-quality performance of preparing and pouring cups for the two men. With a slight bow in the general direction of his lordship, he left the room and the tray behind.

"It's about the duck race," said Max, taking a sip of his tea, an excellent oolong. Under the influence of Awena, Max was becoming something of a connoisseur of teas and herbs.

"Thought it might be," said the lord. "I did hear that Noah Caraway wouldn't be around this year to offer up his grounds. Figured you might want another spot." He patted his sparse white hair, which had been cut short to stand in a small corona about his head. He resembled a larger version of Anthony Hopkins, minus the slicked-back prison hairstyle of *Silence of the Lambs.* The lord's gaze held the same intelligent, speculative gleam as Hopkins's, almost as if Max were being sized up for his potential as an entrée.

"It's one of those traditions that won't die," said Max. "People like it. *I* like it."

"Duck race," the lord said, ruminating as

a catlike smile played at the corners of his mouth. "They've been doing that since I was a boy here at the Hall. The children enjoy it, and I suppose it does foster good-will." But he sighed deeply, as if the thought of all those happy children was more than he could be expected to bear.

Something in his manner added to Max's impression of a man concerned with doing the right thing, but only if observed or certain to be lauded or rewarded for his selflessness. If unobserved, all bets would be off. Max was just following a mental thread to the surveillance cameras that had become ubiquitous in the UK — who could say how much they promoted good or better behavior in its citizens? It might make a fascinating addition to my current sermon, Max mused, when Lord Baaden-Boomethistle interrupted his thoughts by saying, "I suppose we must not let the village children down."

"It's the village adults who would be more disappointed, I think you'd find," said Max. "The villagers make small side bets on the ducks they've sponsored, have a drink or two — all in good fun. It generates goodwill and, of course, it's a most effective means of fund-raising. Does this mean you are willing to allow the use of your land, Lord

Baaden-Boomethistle?"

There was a finely timed pause, the only sound in the room the ticking of a clock on the mantel and the distant roar of a lawn mower — Max looked out the window and could see a man disappearing down a small knoll in the grounds, pushing the machine before him. Lord Baaden-Boomethistle said, "I simply don't know."

Max, fighting down a highly un-Anglican response, gazed with what he hoped was an expression of good-natured earnestness at this potential village benefactor, silently cursing the moment he had agreed to act as village spokesperson. It was really more a job for the chair of the Parish Council, but that eminence was known to be better at ruffling feathers — even plastic ones — than at smoothing them. Under his leadership, Nether Monkslip's government operated according to a hidden, Kafkaesque logic, and many grudges still were held over the "Night of the Long Knives" — the Parish Council meeting on the redesign of the village coat of arms.

An extraordinary meeting of the Nether Monkslip Parish Council had been called over the duck business, with people summoned in haste one evening by the clerk to the council. The ideal had always been to hold the race festivities closer to the river, and Noah's absence this year at last afforded them this opportunity. The only obstacle was in persuading the Great Family at Totleigh Hall that now that they were in residence (for a change), it would be gracious of them to welcome the villagers in this way. The chairman of the Parish Council had, in Max's absence, volunteered him for this task of conversion.

Now the lord smiled icily and said again, "I don't know, Vicar. We hosted the cocktail party after the spring fete one year. Hargreaves still complains about the cleanup involved. Well, not com*plains,* actually" — Max was thinking he wouldn't dare — "but he has his little ways of showing displeasure. The three-minute egg well congealed before it reaches the breakfast table. That sort of thing."

"I do realize the inconvenience, but . . ."

"I have no duck in this race." Lord Baaden-Boomethistle chortled.

"Ha-ha. We can organize volunteers to help with the cleanup. That won't be a problem, I assure you."

Max waited the man out, taking another sip of tea while he considered his options. He really had no compelling argument as to why Lord Baaden-Boomethistle should allow the villagers to trample his grounds and destroy his peace and quiet, and appealing to the man's better instincts seemed a very long shot. Finally, Max played his ace card. "I did hear the Harvest Fayre over at Stelvendore Hall was a huge success. They raised over ten thousand pounds for the church organ there."

Lord Baaden-Boomethistle's flagging interest in the conversation was visibly revived. The owners of Stelvendore Hall were among the noblest and oldest of the land. Max happened to know Lord Baaden-Boomethistle was in an unspoken competition with them, and loathed the very air they breathed.

"Ten thousand pounds," the lord said now. "Really, is that the best they could do? Lord Valleroth was always one to stint on charity. What a tightwad."

"I know," said Max, "that he has that reputation." Max said nothing more, waiting the man out, watching from over the top of his teacup as Lord Baaden-Boomethistle's wish for a quiet life was overcome by this ancient family rivalry with the despised and despicable Valleroths.

"Very well," he said at last. "Let's see if we can't do better than a paltry ten grand, even standing on our heads. Just make sure the noise from the children is kept to a minimum, will you?"

CHAPTER 5
THE HON. SON

Max, as he was being ushered out of the lord's office by his butler, was met by the son of the house, the Honorable Peregrine Baaden-Boomethistle. The young man had showered and changed into artfully torn jeans and a T-shirt, but he was still looking flushed and exhausted. For his age, he is out of shape, Max thought. It might be an underlying medical condition, or it might be an addiction to late-night carousing.

Over the T-shirt he wore a green Barbour jacket, even though the weather wasn't yet chilly enough to justify the warmth of such a garment. Max had the idea Peregrine wore it as a status symbol, for it generally was worn by those who wanted to appear to be posh, and only rarely by those who actually were.

The boy was perhaps nineteen or twenty, dark-haired and dark-eyed, like his father, and while shorter and slighter of build, he was much the same physical type, with an expanding middle. Unlike his father, who looked like someone who might once have won the British Open, Peregrine's sportiness was more suited to a soccer field. Where he differed most markedly was in the doughy, rather truculent set of his face, where his father's was all strong ridges and shadows, like an Easter Island statue.

Max had already noticed Peregrine's largish ears, which stuck out far from his head. For some reason, he had chosen to draw attention to this peculiarity with a trendy style that dictated the hair be shaved close to the sides of the head, allowing the top strands to flop forward. A "hipster undercut," it was called. He would be recognizable even from behind with those ears, but he was otherwise good-looking in a blandly patrician way, portly and genial. He wore trendy black frames that did not add much to his appearance.

On the surface, he looked genial. Max suspected — for there was something rather wary in his eyes — that he was genial until crossed.

"Hullo," Peregrine said politely enough. He stood with arms akimbo and looked Max up and down appraisingly. "You're the padre over at the village, aren't you?"

"Father Max Tudor, yes. I'm the vicar at St. Edwold's Church."

"The spy, right?" he asked, eyes bulging for comic effect from the pudgy face.

"A vast exaggeration," said Max. "I was once employed by MI5."

"Oh, but you would say that, wouldn't you? 'A vast exaggeration'?"

Max resumed walking and Peregrine attached himself at his side, apparently there for the duration and not just headed by coincidence in the same direction. He seemed to want something from him, although Max could not imagine what it might be. He was familiar with the hesitation and the roundabout conversational gambits when a parishioner had something he wanted to share or ask advice on and wasn't sure how to go about it.

"I mean, you wouldn't be able to just come out and admit what you're up to," the young man continued, ambling peacefully beside him, much like a young puppy.

"What exactly is it you think I'm up to?" Max asked, amused.

"Dunno. The vicarage could be a listening station for GCHQ or something like that. If ever I saw a perfect front for undercover operations, it's a man in clerical garb operating out of a small obscure village like

Nether Monkslip."

Again, Max was amused, and busy adjusting to this image of himself as being what he had, in fact, once been: a man who hid behind costumes and beards and false fronts, living assumed lives in borrowed houses.

"I assure you, Peregrine — may I call you Peregrine? I assure you, Peregrine, I am duly ordained as a priest in the Anglican Church, I have the papers to prove it, and I have not been recruited by GCHQ, or MI5, or MI6, or Buckingham Palace to listen in on anyone's phone conversations or to spread rumors and propaganda. We have Miss Pitchford for that."

Peregrine laughed very loudly, a gauche, youthful outburst. Apparently, Miss Pitchford's fame as a living, breathing transmitter of village gossip and disinformation had reached the rarified air of Totleigh Hall. Still, Max was enchanted at the idea of the vicarage being some sort of holdover from Bletchley Park.

"Was there something you wanted to ask me, Peregrine?" As they were approaching the stables area, and he felt anything Peregrine might want to confide might come out more easily where he could not be observed, Max thought to give him the opening while

122

he could. But Peregrine was perhaps not quite ready, had not quite been able to put into a comprehensible form whatever was troubling him, for he said, "I am not sure it's something you would understand, Father."

"I can assure you I have the best-possible bona fides for understanding what might be troubling you. I was your age once, and I remember perfectly the self-doubt that can dog a person at that age. At any age."

"You?" Peregrine was clearly astonished at this admission from Max. "I mean, a bloke who looks like you couldn't possibly have gone through what I'm going through."

So it was female trouble after all. Had to be.

"Why don't you make an appointment with me at the vicarage when you're ready to talk?" said Max. "Better yet, drop in. I'm not usually doing anything that can't be interrupted." In truth, his life was a series of interruptions, but he didn't see how he was to be useful to his flock if he tried to keep office hours like a psychiatrist. People needed him when they needed him, and he didn't want to discourage the conversation that could take place only once the worried soul had reached a fever pitch.

"Will you be around the village much

longer?" he asked the boy. "Surely you'll be going back for Michaelmas term. Hasn't it started already?"

"Yes. Just. I . . . I have a sort of special permission, you see." This was clearly a shading of the truth, but Max decided not to press. "I had wanted to travel to see a girlfriend during the break, but I guess she'll have to wait for next year." He threw the word *girlfriend* into the conversation with a touching man-of-the world swagger that failed to deceive the listener. If he had a girlfriend, it was a new and novel experience for him — not, as he seemed to be trying to imply, just the most recent in a string of amorous conquests. "My father holds the purse strings and my stepmother makes sure he doesn't open that purse very often on my account. Not for 'frivolous' things, as she would call them."

"Where does your friend live?"

"Italy. Near Palermo."

"Ah. Italy is special," said Max, who had lived there off and on for years. He was fluent in the language and Italianate in appearance, which suited MI5's needs well when a suspect wandered outside their usual bailiwick. "Southern Italy I know best, but all of it is special. *Truly* special. The saying is that there is Italy, and then there is the rest of

Europe. Did you know your name means wanderer? Pilgrim, actually."

"Funny you should say . . . I've always loved to travel and I want to travel a lot more once I've collected my degree. If I collect it . . ." His voice trailed off and his eyes drifted from Max's face. Again, Max had the sense of something withheld. "Anyway, I have this feeling that from my first moments, I've been on the move. Probably because my family has one foot in Spain and one foot in England, although we're hardly ever in England these days. Something to do with saving on taxes. No idea . . ."

Peregrine was pothering on about nothing, and he knew it. He found Max's ability to listen with his whole attention very flattering, if unnerving. He was more used to being ignored.

Or he should have been used to it by now. He often felt like an adopted pet — the Easter chick or rabbit that is fought over by siblings for a while and then abandoned when the novelty wears off, particularly when the creature's cute fluffiness starts to fade. He had always felt thus and could not ascribe a reason or a date to the feeling. He simply was not a favorite of his father. This was all the more baffling because he was

the only male child. He could have understood it better, perhaps, if he'd had a handsome, clever older or younger brother to
compare him to. But to be compared to
nothing and no one and come up short . . .
well. His sister didn't count, although his
father didn't seem to have a lot of use for
her, either.

And no pun intended on the short. He
couldn't help it that he was short. And dark.
He felt that parents were required to overlook such things.

Then his mother had died, and the last
person who had had even a passing, token
interest in him was gone forever.

Now Father Max was looking at him as if
he could read his mind on all of this, could
at least sense some of the loneliness he felt.
It gave Peregrine a moment's courage,
enough to say, "I'd like to drop in sometime.
If we could keep the invitation open. I'd
like that very much."

"Perhaps you'll get a chance to meet my
wife," said Max kindly, reacting to that
unspoken loneliness in the boy. "We have a
new baby, a son named Owen. We like
showing him off and we've shown him to all
the village now. In some cases, half a dozen
times. We'd love a new audience to wow."

Peregrine smiled, acknowledging the

welcome and the caring behind the gesture.

"All right," he said, rather gruffly. "I'll be heading off back to the house now. Thanks."

And with a wave of his large square hand, he was off.

Max, continuing on his way, saw two figures in conversation by the entrance to the stables. One was a well-set-up man — muscular, broad, and tall. He had the plaid sleeves of his woolen shirt rolled up to ensure no one could overlook the fact. The woman he was talking with wore a large scarf covering her hair, in much the style of Queen Elizabeth II touring her own royal stables. This woman was large, on the plump side, and decades younger than the monarch, and her gaze up at the man before her was doting and adoring. Even from a distance Max could see the attraction. In a cartoon panel, there would have been thunderbolts of electricity zapping in the short distance between them. But was it mutual?

They spotted Max, and he felt it would have been churlish to pretend not to have seen them, as well. Did he imagine it, or was there a swift change of topic as he approached? As a vicar, he was somewhat used to this. People tended to sanitize their speech in his presence. He was less used to people nearly jumping apart at his approach. It was a rather instinctive, surreptitious move they both had made, and he wondered what, if anything, it meant.

"I'm not sure about tonight. Tomorrow, perhaps," the man had been saying. Now it became, "Of course, the foal needs watching and I'll stay with her tonight — make sure she's all right." A slight switch of topic and yet, Max was certain, a switch that had been made for his benefit.

The man turned to him with a smile. In line with recent Hollywood trends, his face showed a day-old stubble of beard.

"Bill Travis," he said, holding out his hand. His grip was predictably strong, the grip of a man used to hauling tack about and reining in wild horses. The powerful grasp did not come across as showing off, but as an unconscious display of innate power; he exuded command and presence, and from the young woman's happy and enthralled expression, this fact had not escaped her. "You probably know Rosamund," the man added, indicating the young woman at his side.

Rosamund, Max thought, was rather pretty, as plump and rosy as a Renoir maiden at a country dance. Standing near Travis, who was about six feet tall, made her appear dainty by comparison, but she was muscular, with what looked to be an athletic, sturdy frame beneath the fleshy surface. The tendrils of hair escaping from her scarf were corkscrew curly, and she wore enormous purple glasses with green temples, behind which her eyes gleamed with a keen intelligence as she turned her gaze to meet Max's. She would not, he sensed, have been the same person without those glasses, which clearly were not cosmetic, but composed of a strong prescription. She was one of those people who would peer about like a mole without them.

Max heard a mewing sound and turned to see a marmalade cat squeezing itself out from beneath the stable wall. She did not stay to be petted, but seemed to be on a mission. Max heard behind her a chorus of small mewling voices.

"That is Marbella," Rosamund informed him. "She's just had her kittens — we've no idea exactly where or how many. Three or four, from the sound of it. She won't let us near, of course. She comes out to find her own food and they carry on until she returns. Cook has been leaving out leftovers for her. I don't suppose you'd like a kitten when the time comes?"

Max shook his head. "I love cats, but my

dog has had a lot to deal with lately, already. We've just introduced a baby into the household." Max never missed a chance to insert this news into the conversation whenever he came across someone who might not know the glad tidings. "But Thea's really been lovely about it. Concerned and protective."

Rosamund made satisfactory cooing sounds to express her pleasure at this update. Bill Travis looked as if he might want to guy-punch Max on the shoulder but thought better of it.

"Anyway, I didn't mean to interrupt," said Max. "You were talking horses, not a subject on which I am any sort of expert."

"Yes, I was saying we have a foal, close to being a filly now, who seems to be going off. I've had the vet by to look at her. I don't dare leave her for long. . . ." He turned his head, as if he might rush off right then to look in on the animal.

No, thought Max, that was not what you were saying. That was not the topic at all. But aloud he said, "That's too bad."

Bill Travis nodded. "She's an expensive piece of horseflesh."

"I meant," said Max evenly, "that it's especially difficult for us humans when animals suffer. They can't tell us where it hurts."

As if realizing how callous his statement may have sounded, Travis said, "She *is* a nice creature and I don't like to see her suffer, of course. But she's losing rather than gaining. We will soon have to take a decision on what to do.

"We can't," he added, "afford to let sentiment get in the way of progress."

Chapter 6
Murder in the Woods

Max was to remember these conversations a week later as late one evening he retraced his steps to the manor house. He had come in answer to a summons from Lord Baaden-Boomethistle; as it happened, he had been planning a walk with Thea to clear his head at the end of a long day, and the woods around the manor house provided an attractive venue. Awena had settled the baby in for the night, and when last seen, she was shelling English peas for their dinner. They would start the meal with pumpkin soup, she'd promised: while the rest of England had seen much of its crop rotted by the damp, the southwest of England had enjoyed a bumper crop.

Whatever the lord wanted, it did not seem to be an emergency, and probably it could have waited. But the man sounded unlike himself on the phone — unsettled and subdued, and he could not be induced to say what the matter was.

"I'll tell you when I see you," Lord Baaden-Boomethistle had said. "I'll have Hargreaves set out the good whiskey, shall I? I'm taking Foto Finish out for exercise — I ride every evening — but I'll be back in good time to share a drink with you. There's something I'd like to take your mind on."

The blatant bribery made the summons all the more intriguing, so Max agreed he would see him in a few hours. He was told to come around the back of the house (which he understood to be an honor meant for family, rather than a demotion in status) and to find his own way to the study, as it was Hargreave's evening off.

In the end, it was a fruitless visit. Max arrived at the house a few minutes early and, leaving Thea by the steps with a command to stay, made his way down the hallway, taking the turns as he remembered them. But there was no answer to his knock at the study door.

"Hmm," he said aloud, thinking, *This doesn't seem right.* The lord was abrupt in manner and used to having his way, but standing up an appointment would not, in the world in which he lived, be the done thing.

Max tried the door handle, a polished

brass affair probably copied from something at Buckingham Palace. It turned. He gave the wooden door a push.

There was the promised whiskey on a tray, with two clean glasses waiting.

And the massive polished desk, a desk on which to plot wars and takeovers and strategies.

But there was no Lord Baaden-Boomethistle, a fact Max found curiouser and curiouser. Rudeness just to be rude was not in the man's makeup.

Max spent fifteen minutes cooling his heels, taking advantage of the unlooked-for chance to admire the artwork, the paintings and statues and cabinets filled with exquisite curios of porcelain and jade. But he was impatient, wondering what had gone wrong, why he had been summoned in the first place, just to be stood up.

Finally he gave up, leaving by the back entrance, through which he had entered, collecting Thea, and making his way back home.

Nether Monkslip nestled at the base of Hawk Crest, which overlooked the same river that ran past the base of Totleigh Hall. From the top floor of his vicarage, Max could see the river sparkling in the sunlight on good days, carrying its cargo of diamonds to the sea. The tang of seawater from the south often floated on the air, mixing with the scents of cultivated soil and pastureland and the flowers of carefully tended gardens. Max thought it was as close to heaven as one could hope to find here on earth.

It was past the hinge of the day and the sky had lost much of the light; only dying rays of the sun had shimmered through a curtain of falling leaves as he and Thea ambled away from Totleigh Hall. It was getting cold, and he wore his heavy woolen coat for the first time that season. Its collar smelled of a scent Awena often wore, a smoky herbal fragrance.

The forest's evening rush hour had been stilled. There was only the occasional scuffling in the undergrowth to signify his presence had been noted. Thea, hearing something that only dog radar could detect, tore off down one of the forest paths winding its way back toward Totleigh Hall and the lake. It had been some time since she had been on an extended walk, so Max decided to let her enjoy herself awhile longer.

Eventually she came back, bringing with her a small branch of just the right size and shape for games. Obligingly, he began to throw it for her, watching with pleasure as she bolted away, her silky ears flying. He had always thought Gordon setters were one of the loveliest of the breeds, with their shiny black-and-tan coats, their intelligence, and their loyalty. He thought Thea to be outstanding on all these counts. Of course, he acknowledged, he *would* think that; a rescue dog, she had been his companion for so long, he could not imagine life without her. He had wondered if the baby would make her feel displaced from the center of the universe, but she had welcomed Owen as a sort of added bonus to her life, an additional, if shockingly small, human being to love and defend. She had fallen immediately into her new role of protectress, glancing from Max to Owen and back to Max again, as if to say, Yours, right? Okay, stand back. I got this. And she never willingly left the baby's side from that day forward, sleeping at the foot of his crib at night and beside his bassinet in Awena's shop during the day. She would come to fetch either Awena or himself a moment before the baby started to fuss for food or comfort.

The moon made a fleeting appearance from behind the skeletal trees, and Max idly watched its sliver of light come and go through the partings in the overhead canopy. Earlier in the year, they'd had an enormous supermoon, but now it was only a small silver crescent in the sky, like a coin that had been clipped too often. Gray threads of cloud were woven through inky blue as the day deepened past twilight, but even though the smell of rain was in the air, Max thought it might be some hours before a storm reached Nether Monkslip. Rainstorms had been frequent in recent weeks, and the scent of wet earth and composting leaves surrounded him.

The trees' branches rustled softly in a quickening wind, throwing off their leaves, but still they managed to shield the manor from what the Dowager Baaden-Boomethistle no doubt thought of as the vulgar gaze. Thea returned to Max, who again threw the stick for her, this time deeper into the forest; he continued on the rough footpath as she went off the track to find it. A thin fog lay low to the ground; even though they were some miles from Monkslip-super-Mare, traces of sea fret often crept inland. Max knew that from a distance he would appear to be walking on air, an image that pleased him. He heard the river tumbling in the distance and imagined a gleam of moonlight frosting its surface.

Thea's game had brought them nearer the lake, where a chill coming off the water hinted at the winter to come. Max thought he could hear the sound of crickets; surely they would have but days to live now. Through an opening in the trees he glimpsed the formal gardens surrounding the house, with evergreens shaped into symmetrical forms. In the shade and darkness, they looked like giant human figures. This imposed civilization seemed barely to hold back the untamed forest surrounding the estate. Where Max walked might in ancient times have been part of a green path, a wide track used for herding animals. He had a sense that the cloak between the prehistoric and modern worlds had worn thin here, as Awena would have it; that he was walking in some forgotten holy place, perhaps a burial ground, or a place of sacrifice. Nether Monkslip, as he had learned, was dotted with places like that.

The shortest way to the village from here would be to cut through an opening in the hedgerows, some of which dated to Anglo-Saxon times. While the lord of the manor might have the right to restrict access to his land, in practice the bad feeling this engendered made active enforcement not worth-while for the old family. Sheep and cows were driven across any available opening, as had been done for centuries, and schoolchil-dren found their way home in much the same way.

It was getting dark, and he wished briefly he'd thought to bring a torch with him. All he had was a small promotional torch at-tached to his key ring, something he'd picked up at a religious conference. "Shine a light," it read, beneath part of a verse from John 8:12.

He called for Thea, no longer wishing to meander, but now in haste to get home to his wife and child. At the thought of them, a breeze stirred, carrying that heady mix of sea and forest smells, and joy coursed through him in one of the many exquisite moments of grace he'd been granted since Owen's arrival.

Which was why he jumped and turned, heart pounding, when Thea sent up an unearthly howl, a sound he had never heard from her before. It was a sound that startled birds from the trees and scattered whatever small wildlife had been in hiding, waiting for her to leave.

What in the name of —

Max fumbled the small torch out of his

pocket as he broke into a run, leaping into the forest in the direction of the sound, jumping over rocks and tree branches fallen in the winter storms long past. He plunged into an area where the trees grew closer together, impeding his progress, as no moonlight could penetrate here. All he had to go by was Thea's unearthly howling, reduced to a fretting whine as she heard him approach and realized help was on the way to sort out this event, unprecedented in her experience. He skidded to a halt on a mat of wet fallen leaves that nearly tipped him on his backside.

Thea had found Lord Baaden-Boomethistle, or a significant part of what remained of him, which was his decapitated head. Its eyes, thank God, were closed.

Of all the things Max might have expected to see on this serene evening, it would never have been this.

He called Thea sharply to his side to keep the area undisturbed, for surely where a head was, a body would be nearby. He pulled her lead from his pocket and attached it to her collar, for in her agitated state he didn't entirely trust her not to run from him, to start helpfully looking for the remains of this poor human.

The canopy of tree branches parted at this

spot where the head lay, giving Max a moment's clear view of the area. Looking around and craning his neck, aiming the small torch upward, he saw a worn spot on the tree trunk nearest him, a rubbing away that exposed raw wood, looking exactly as if someone had used a garrote on it. Training the light directly across the narrow path, he saw a corresponding cut.

Someone had tied a sort of trip wire across the trail, and then later removed it, for there was no sign of the wire now that he could see. Whether they had done it in recent days or hours could not be said, but what were the chances? This exact spot where Lord Baaden-Boomethistle had died showed signs of a recent booby trapping. Since he had to have been traveling at some speed, it was natural to assume he had been on horseback, taking the exercise he had mentioned to Max. The question was why the killer, whoever it was, hadn't just left the wire in place, but perhaps the thinking was that it might contain evidence, DNA or whatnot, and that it was safer to remove it than leave it to be tested.

As Max turned away, his torch chanced upon the gleam of a gold object at the base of the same tree. He hunched over for a closer look. It appeared to be an engraved hair ornament of some sort. He left it undisturbed for the police.

It was a ghastly crime, suggesting a villain with an iron, if reckless, will, someone waiting, and plotting, and, having seen the success of his or her reprehensible deed, coolly removing all traces. Certainly this death was no accident.

Max had the inconvenient and unwelcome thought that his bishop might see this as the last straw, for wherever Max Tudor went, the bishop could not help but notice, murder was sure to follow. This just seemed a bizarre escalation of the crimes the priest had witnessed to date. The bishop appeared in his mind's eye as Max had last seen him, racing across the courtyard of his magnificent palace, flushed by the exertion, red hair flying about his face and purple robes billowing around his legs. The man had been marvelously patient and understanding, but surely . . .

There was nothing for it now but to call the authorities and worry about the bishop's reaction later. If Max were some sort of murder magnet, after all, sending him away from Nether Monkslip would surely be to send the problem of murder along with him.

CHAPTER 7
DCI COTTON TAKES THE CASE

"Another body, Max? It's like you're becoming the grim reaper of Nether Monkslip — and parts beyond." DCI Cotton, impeccably suited, looked around him at the forested area, over to the forensics team going about its grisly business, and added, "Where's the horse got to, then?"

"He's probably headed back to the stables. Isn't that what you would do in his shoes?"

Cotton glanced down at his own Italian leathers and said, "I'm not really a mind reader when it comes to horses. If I were, I might take up betting at the races."

It was some time after Max had called the station in Monkslip-super-Mare, asking to be put straight through to DCI Cotton, wherever he happened to be. Cotton had been interrupted at his dinner in front of the telly in his spartan apartment, a place of polished chrome and gleaming bare surfaces. Max had done a preliminary search while waiting for the authorities to arrive, finding only a summerhouse nearby. At first glance, it had looked forgotten, frozen in time, like something from a children's tale, a Victorian relict of days when ornate follies were all the rage.

The decedent's body, its hands bagged and accompanied now by its head, had been removed by the mortuary attendants, and the chorus of the experts in the art of death also had vanished, taking with them the usual accoutrements for investigating an untimely passing — in this case, a messy and unseemly one. It had taken the videographer and photographer, for example, much longer than normal to document the scene, and the blood-spatter expert much longer than usual to document the carnage. Scenes of crimes officers, even with their search aided by artificial light, were hampered in finding evidence or samples by the dense undergrowth around the trees. They were further hampered by not knowing what, if any, evidence they were looking for. Even though the ground was cooperatively moist, given all the leaf fall there were no footprints, only the horse's hoofprints to show them the path he had taken home.

Now a lone constable stood watch, waiting for what, it was not clear. He represented some sort of swipe at the concept of crowd control, Max supposed.

The police doctor also remained behind. He was packing up his paraphernalia at a safe distance from the crime scene area, and he had begun carefully removing the outerwear that had shielded him as he went about his job. He was a man who looked ridiculously young to be responsible for such a momentous task, one with so many large responsibilities. He wore glasses and the supercilious smirk of the know-it-all, made more aggravating by the fact that he did, usually, know far more than his police audience.

Now returned to his usual civilian attire, jogging pants and a black T-shirt, he walked over to the two waiting men, one blond and one dark-haired. He was used to seeing Max Tudor at scenes such as this, and had early on begun treating him as part of the investigative team.

He nodded to each man in turn. "Hullo, padre. Howdy, Chief." Max thought the doctor's name was Sprottle, but before he could confirm this, the young man had moved on past the niceties. "Before you ask, no more than three hours dead. Closer to one hour. I'll know more when I've got him on the table."

Max told him about the planned meeting with Lord Baaden-Boomethistle, for which he had inexplicably — until now — been stood up.

"And you're quite certain this was he? The corpse's head, I mean."

"Yes," said Max curtly. It was not a sight he'd soon forget.

"Someone really wanted to send a message to this guy," said the doctor, "but God alone knows what the message was. *'Sic semper tyrannis,'* maybe, or whatever the peasants shouted as people were taken to the guillotine. I can tell you this, you're not looking for an animal lover."

"How do you mean?" Cotton asked him.

"Too risky: The animal could have been injured if it had lifted its head at the wrong moment, or been frightened by something and reared up entirely on its hind legs. It's also a very dicey way to kill someone. Even though — and this is what is interesting here — even though I'm betting the wire was arranged to strike precisely at the neck of a rider of the exact height of the victim. His height as he sat, I mean. He had a rather long torso, so he was, you could say, riding high. And the wire was strung precisely at the spot where the path started to slope steeply downward, mitigating the risk *some-*

what. The risk to the horse, I mean."

Max nodded. "The path up to that point was wide and clear for some length, so the rider would have been getting up some speed."

"It was probably an old green path used to drive cattle, sheep, what have you."

"Yes, I was on a similar path that runs almost parallel."

"But at the spot where the path narrowed, the rider would have been forced to slow down from a full gallop. There's a bit of a turning there, too, so you wouldn't see what you were headed into and you wouldn't have time to pull up if you did. Then there's that dip in the road there where it slants downward."

The three men were silent, picturing the unthinkable.

The doctor continued: "So the rider's body and head would momentarily have been angled back — no longer at a ninety-degree angle as he sat. It was finely calibrated to work and it seems to have gone off like clockwork."

"God," whispered Max.

"I doubt he even knew what hit him, if that makes you feel better. I'm just going to see if they found the horse. I need to take his measure, too. But I think I'll find my hypothesis is right. This was planned down to the half inch."

"It's like something out of a spaghetti Western," Cotton observed.

"Yes," said the doctor. "Very dramatic, and as I say, outside of the cinema, a very chancy way to do away with someone."

"Could the horse have been the target?"

"You mean for the insurance or something? Well . . . same problem. You'd be as likely to kill the man as the horse. Which is what did happen, of course. But there's no way any insurance company would see this as an accident. With horses, that is much easier to arrange without the neon sign of a wire across the path. I should think you'd want to avoid the sort of lengthy insurance investigation this would cry out for."

"So it's murder — the willful taking of a human life. And a coldly calculated murder at that. Okay." Cotton turned to Max. "It's all *so* dramatic. Maybe we're looking for a film fan."

"Maybe we are," agreed Max. "Some people believe whatever they see on the screen, putting aside all sense of what it really takes to kill someone. Unstable people, that is."

"So this unstable person got lucky, in a manner of speaking."

"And the victim did not. By the way, I had a look around, well away from the crime scene, while I was waiting for your lot to arrive. There's a grove over there with a sort of summerhouse — a garden temple in the middle of it. A clearing in the trees with this small stone-and-wood structure tucked inside. It looks like a nice spot for an endezvous of two like-minded people."

"A temple?"

"Well, as I say, a summerhouse or gazebo of some kind, but with a small altar and a statue of a Hindu goddess inside. A goddess of love — Parvati. That's what made me think *temple.* It's well-hidden, private, if you take my meaning."

"I believe I do. Are you suggesting Lady Baaden-Boomethistle . . ."

"I'm suggesting nothing, really. But it's not abandoned, as I first thought. It looks clean and well kept up, not overgrown, as you might expect. And it was built with luxury in mind, rather than being a site of worship, to my eye. The statue is window dressing, with no offerings or candles before it. The structure itself is rather difficult to find if you don't know where to look for it. Even then, if I hadn't been wandering, rather at a loose end, I might never have found it. It's hidden in a dense thicket of trees, with only the narrowest footpath to it. The path has, however, been used often enough that it is well trodden."

"Got it. We'll have someone take a look."

"There was also some sort of small golden object near the crime scene. A hair ornament, I thought."

Like a conjurer, the doctor produced a paper evidence bag and opened it for them to peer inside.

"Do you mean this? It's engraved with initials — B-B. You're right in thinking it's a hair ornament. There's a strand or two of dark hair caught in the little clasp — you see? — that might help us by providing DNA, but only if the root of the hair is intact."

"Useful. Do you need me any further tonight?" Max had rung Awena after he'd called the police, to let her know he'd be delayed, but that had been hours ago. He had not given her the terrible details, except to let her know there had been another death in peaceful Nether Monkslip and that he had been the one to discover the body. That seemed enough for her to know, although by early morning the news would be everywhere, as the folk of Nether Monkslip tended all to be early risers. There was no way all the commotion would go unnoticed for long.

Cotton shook his head. "Show Sergeant Essex where to find this temple of love, and we'll have a closer look tomorrow. There's not a lot of point in everyone's tripping around out here over fallen branches in the dark. We're just getting started gathering and analyzing evidence, and it will be a while until we've got anything to go on — *if* we're as lucky as the killer was. Of course, it is a case for the coroner, and we'll have all we can manage gathering everything we need in time for the inquest.

"But where I'll need you, Max, is in providing background on the family. Talking to one or two of them, even. What do you say?"

"I don't honestly know the family that well," Max demurred. "They've scarcely been a presence in the village in the time I've been here."

"But you can tell me something about the family?"

"Well, I've spoken with the son recently."

"So there's a son. Do tell me more."

Max hesitated before speaking. Then he sighed, as if having decided where his duty lay. "Not a towering intellect, I would say," he began at last. "Genial, quite young for his age, rather awkward around adults. I

151

don't know how well he does with his peer group at university, but I gained the impression he was uncomfortable around me, at least at first. To some, I'm an authority figure, you know. I also rather got the impression he was lonely and wanting someone to talk to, so I let him know my door was always open.

"There is also a daughter, but I've only spoken with her briefly." He hesitated again before adding, "I think she is rather fond of the estate manager. But I wouldn't read a lot into that if I were you. I'd say it's puppy love on her part and not reciprocated. He's too old for her — not in years perhaps, but in experience. He is a man used to the company of women. That was my fleeting impression."

Cotton was staring in the direction of the house as he listened, his expression inscrutable.

"You have such a quaint way of putting things, Max. You mean he's a bit of a lad, correct?"

Max nodded. "He knows he can have his pick of women and is a bit spoiled in that department."

"I see. Well, brace yourself for the media circus. It's a well-known family, of course. Which fact generates more interest right there. Your average drug deal or pub brawl that ends in death can't hold a candle. Whenever I try to interest the media in helping us catch a suspect, I can find them chasing after Prince Harry's latest girlfriend. Still, it's understandable, human nature being what it is." Cotton turned to face him. "What do you know about our victim, Max?"

Max shrugged. "He wasn't too interested in the village duck race for charity — but of course that's not what you mean. He distinguished himself overall by not taking much of an interest in local affairs. People say he wasn't a patch on his grandfather, who kept the village going for years: He made sure poor children had porridge and milk in their bowls, and he paid to get a railway line in to the village — things like that. Again, to be fair, I didn't know Lord Baaden-Boomethistle — the present lord — all that well. The family stayed away for tax reasons, leaving the place in the care of a handful of loyal retainers."

Cotton took a deep breath, peering up at the night sky as though it might hold the answers. "Look, I really am going to need your help on the local angle," Cotton said at last. "I'll square things with your bishop if you need me to. I'll tell him you're essential to helping me solve the case and restore order to the parish, which will be torn apart by this appalling crime. The villagers may even revert to pagan sacrifice in their shock and distress. A sort of cry for help. You know, the usual."

Max laughed. Cotton could be relentless: if he'd thought bribing the bishop would work, he'd probably try it on. Besides . . . "I do know the butler, but slightly," Max said. "He's a member of St. Edwold's."

"See? If anyone knows anything about the family, that's the man who will."

"But a good butler would never gossip about his employer."

"It wouldn't be gossip" was Cotton's ready reply. "It would be more like confession in this case. An opportunity to get things off his chest."

Max just smiled: *Nice try.*

"But for now, just you go home to Awena and the baby. I'll be in touch."

CHAPTER 8
MAX AND THE BUTLER

Several days passed before Max heard from Cotton again. The forensic tests, even though logged in with a note citing Cotton's pleas for haste, had run up against the usual bureaucratic backlog and the competing demands of other crimes in the area. Still, given the prestige of the family, and the spectacular way in which the head of the clan had lost his head, this was a matter of some urgency. ("We have *got* to stay in front of the media on this," as Cotton put it.)

And so Cotton managed to get what he wanted out of the coroner's inquest (more time to investigate) and out of all the forensics specialists (faster test results) through a combination of finesse and a calling in of favors owed. And while he never bullied, he did, as he liked to put it, persist until he got results.

Which in this case did not amount to much. The wire used as a murder weapon had eventually been found after a brief search, not far from the body; it had been taken down and thrown into the undergrowth around a large oak tree. The speculation was that this had been done to prevent any further catastrophe for anyone unlucky enough to decide to ride a horse on that same path, following after Lord Baaden-Boomethistle.

"We are dealing with a considerate murderer, in other words," Cotton explained to Max over the phone. "And someone who knew he rode on that path at that time every day, which was not a well-kept secret, apparently. But there are no prints — impossible on such a narrow surface. No DNA, either — the chances are the killer wore gloves, anyway. The wire seems to have been cut from a supply that had been sitting around a storage area in the stable for an undetermined amount of time, although long enough for rust to have started to form on it."

"The tack room, no doubt," said Max. "We're looking for someone with access to the stable, then, obviously."

"Yes, and that could be anyone in the area. The buildings are shielded by trees from the house, and sited far away, so nipping in, taking what you wanted, and nipping out

156

again would be easy. While there are stable hands and people like that running about with ropes and saddles and other horse accessories, there aren't enough of them that someone's comings and goings would necessarily be noticed. And if the perpetrator concealed the wire about his person, under a coat or sweater, say, wrapped around his waist, there would be nothing in particular for anyone to notice."

Cotton's reference to "horse accessories" rather than "tack" reminded Max that Cotton was even less in his customary environment of mean city streets than usual, and that he knew even less than he, Max, about the world of horses. They might need to take expert opinion on this case before it was through. Unfortunately, the nearest experts to hand were all suspects in the case.

"Does the butler ride?" Max wondered aloud. "Hargreaves?"

"I don't know. Why don't you go ask him?"

The butler occupied a nice little living quarters within the house. As tradition held, it was near the kitchen and it no doubt was a major perk of the job to have an on-site living arrangement included. Max knew, as he had in his MI5 days impersonated a butler on more than one occasion, that the position also often came with a decent salary, paid vacation time, a mobile phone, and, in remote spots like Nether Monkslip, a car. The downside was that the job generally required a sixty-hour workweek, since the modern butler was often a jack-of-all-trades, including bodyguard.

Hargreaves looked, however, as if his bodyguarding days might soon be over. He was in his mid to late sixties and probably looking forward to retirement. His lodgings, while pleasant, were more like a private suburban bedsit than a suite of expensively wallpapered, tufted-satin rooms, as might be found in the rest of the house. It was warm and cozy, with plaid fabric on the chairs and sofa contrasting in a pleasing, old-fashioned way with floral prints and narrow-striped pillows. The overall effect ought to have been ghastly, but it was more as if the fabrics had accumulated over time, each butler from the past having left behind a cherished possession or two to mark his occupancy. Hunting scenes and inspirational quotes hung on the walls, a quote from *Henry V* being the most stirring ("I see you stand like greyhounds in the slips,/ Straining upon the start. The game's afoot:/ Follow your spirit; and, upon this charge/ Cry 'God for Harry, England and Saint

George!' " A fire burned in the hearth to take the chill off the air, and the butler offered Max some tea and homemade oatmeal biscuits "made by the cook early just this morning, special for your visit." Max, who had come to accept that murder investigations were fattening, especially in the environs of Nether Monkslip, took a biscuit from the proffered plate. Had he been in London, he realized, he'd have been lucky to be given water, and then only if he appeared to be suffering from heat prostration.

The butler handed him a cup with the requested one lump, no milk, and then sat down opposite him in the riot of color that was his sofa. Max shuffled the selection of pillows at his own back and settled in, taking a sip of the excellent tea and a bite of biscuit, delicious enough to rival anything Elka Garth might produce.

"It's the murder you want to talk about, of course, Vicar. If it were the funeral arrangements, I imagine you would be talking with Lady Baaden-Boomethistle."

Max acknowledged this was true. Lord Baaden-Boomethistle would be buried out of St. Edwold's, as had all the Baaden-Boomethistles who had come before him, and he would be interred in the family

159

vault. It was normally not a matter in which to involve the household staff, although as a matter of courtesy Max might keep them informed of the family's decisions, particularly if it seemed communication had broken down somewhere along the way. There would always be extra arrangements involving relatives come to stay, a gathering after the service, and so forth, on such an occasion.

"You have been with the family how long?" Max asked him. He was trying to avoid licking the crumbs from his fingers, as he had not been provided with a serviette. Hargreaves noticed instantly and flung himself off the sofa to go and rectify the omission.

"Eighteen years" was the reply on his return from the pantry. The butler went on to explain that his former employment had been at a famous grand old house in the north of Scotland. "I could not endure the winters any longer," he told Max, resuming his seat. "I am not a young man, and when you start thinking in terms of your bones actually freezing and snapping apart like sticks . . . well. Either that or being blown clean off a cliff, which could easily happen. Anyways, when this opportunity opened up — well, I gave a good long notice. Lord

Rosefield was nice enough about it — it seems it had happened before. I heard my replacement was a hale and hardy Scotsman who lived nearby. Too bad. Too bad I had to leave, I mean. They had two wee bairn who were the nicest children."

"Ah," said Max, wondering if this were in any way a comparison with Lord Baaden-Boomethistle's children. Was the butler trying to say they were *not* the nicest children? Was he using a sliding scale — not quite as nice but pretty decent kids overall? As Max contemplated exactly how to phrase this, the butler returned his cup to its saucer and saved him the trouble.

"They were not spoiled, those two up in Scotland. They knew the value of a pound, for one thing — I know, I know: It's a stereotype, the thrifty Scot, but I mean that they were instilled with character, not with an inflated sense of entitlement. I blame the parents when that does happen, and I try not to fault the child. Of course, *these* two here lost their mother at a very young age, so perhaps there is no comparison. Lady Rosefield was a paragon. Lady Baaden-Boomethistle — the first lady — was likewise an absolutely lovely woman, long-suffering though she was. So for the children to lose her at a tender age — well . . . You do see."

Max nodded sagely, as if this rather rambling discourse were all he could have hoped to hear. He was well aware the man would not be talking about his employer like this to any outsider — stating opinions as to how the children were turning out, and who might be to blame if they were not turning out well. The fact that Max was a priest — his confessor, in fact — made Max's place in the grand investigative scheme of things rather ambiguous.

The lyrics of the song "Our Lips Are Sealed" came into his mind just then. Rather a theme song for priests, it had been a running joke during his training at St. Barney's in Oxford. The sacrament of Reconciliation, commonly known as Confession, meant that he could not relay what was told to him in confidence by a penitent.

"You are friends with that DCI, I know," said the butler. Perhaps it was that servant's ability to anticipate problems — missing serviettes, a wine cellar that needed restocking, a conflict of interests — that made him sensitive to Max's position.

Max acknowledged that this was true.

The man sighed. "I wish I could tell you something that might help, but the fact is, I can't. I mean I know nothing about the

162

murder and I have no inkling of who could have done it. *None.*" Did he protest too much on that last word? Max thought it a possibility. "I have indicated the children are not all they could be — the usual bun fights at meals, you know the sort of thing — but they are not murderers. I would bet anything I own. They are spoiled and headstrong — the boy especially — but this is another arena. I wouldn't think them capable of it."

"I wouldn't think anyone capable of it," Max pointed out, "but someone did it. And it required a certain amount of knowledge of the lord's habits." Indeed, Max had reached the conclusion some time ago that whoever had done this had had ample time to observe, to plot, and to plan. The trap was so nicely calibrated and measured.

"I know. And Peregrine did quarrel with his father — but that was the usual sort of father and son thing. Nothing out of the ordinary."

"Any idea what the quarrel was about?" Max asked him, all ears but feigning nonchalance.

"No, Vicar, I've really no idea. I heard only the end of the quarrel, anyway."

"What was said?"

"Lord Baaden-Boomethistle was quite

angry — what about, I don't know. He said, 'You're no son of mine. You're unnatural, that's what you are. No son of mine could do what you did.' And Peregrine said something like 'I wish that were true! I wish anyone but you were my father! Then I might be happy.' Then he sort of flounced away, slamming the door. Young Peregrine does tend to flounce and pout when he doesn't get his way, I'm afraid. The entire family just missed a career in the theater."

Max said, "We have to return to the fact, painful as it may be, that Peregrine knew his father's habits well. He had to have done."

"That's true of almost anyone who has spent any time with the family," said the butler loyally. "Any member of staff — myself included. Or a weekend guest, perhaps."

Max nodded, saying, "All right. We also have to consider that this murder was committed by someone with a knowledge of the sort of horse Foto Finish is, I should think."

"Smart, you mean. Responsive and easy to train, so I heard Lady Baaden-Boomethistle say once. Unspookable. Biddable. Unlike the young lord, of whom most of the staff have despaired at one point or another."

"Funny you should say that," said Max softly, remembering. "That Foto Finish is so biddable." It had been Awena who had reminded him of the story that had been nibbling at the edges of his mind. The story of Brat Farrar, a story with a murderous horse wanting to rid itself of its passenger.

They had been at breakfast, reading the news coverage, when Awena said, "Somehow the horrible method of this murder has me thinking of that old book by Josephine Tey. *Brat Farrar?*"

Max looked at her over the top of his section of the newspaper. *"Brat Farrar,"* he confirmed. "I've read it, but it's been years ago now. She's one of my favorite mystery authors."

"It's one of her best stories, although it's hard to beat *Daughter of Time.* It's probably been on my mind just because of the theme of horses and wealthy families. In the story, someone tries to kill Brat, using a rogue horse named Timber."

"It's something to do with an inheritance, right?"

Awena nodded, stirring a teaspoon of chia seeds into her cereal. Owen nestled against her shoulder. "Yes. Brat is a foundling who gets talked into impersonating an heir, partly so he can inherit a stud farm. He

165

loves horses, you see."

"Just as Lady Baaden-Boomethistle is said to love horses."

"Right. Horse-mad she is, or so I've heard. Anyway, in Tey's story, there is a strong family resemblance and Brat takes advantage of it to pretend that he is the twin of a man who disappeared. The missing man is thought to have committed suicide. So Brat's a criminal, you see, although horses and people seem to like him. But he uncovers a far worse crime during his impersonation."

Max nodded. "It's a good story. I remember I read it all in one go on a long train ride."

"And it's a real psychological puzzle. The reader is never quite sure which criminal to follow . . . if you follow. And you join with the family in suspecting Brat, then accepting him. Tey just pulls you along where she wants you to go."

Max, sitting now with the butler, thought that the horse in this case, unlike Timber, was not known for its bad temper. Cotton had said this at some point and the butler had just confirmed it. It was a beautiful and high-spirited animal, and it had raced for home the moment it was free of its rider, as horses are wont to do. It was hard to see further parallels in Brat Farrar to the current real crime.

Max returned his full attention to Hargreaves, who was saying, "She'd be nearly forty now."

"I'm sorry, who is this?"

"The nanny. The woman hired to take care of Peregrine when he was a baby. I told you most of the staff despaired of him at one point or other, but it was the nanny spotted trouble early on."

"Do you happen to know where she is now?" He had so little real insight into Peregrine or any other member of the family. But servants saw what was hidden from the world. It might not pay off, but he wanted to get a better sense of the family and its history. And certainly a nanny would know the innate character of her charges better than most.

Hargreaves shook his head. "It was before my time she left, of course. I've only seen photos. Lovely girl she was. Scandinavian in her background, one side or the other, by the look of her. Pale hair, blue eyes. But I don't think she was from there. Or from here."

Quelling Max's disappointment, the butler added, "I do know she stayed in the UK and didn't return home, as so many do. I overheard Rosamund say she got married to an Englishman."

It might mean her name had changed, but surely there would be enough to go on in the immigration records. And Cotton's people could find out more from Rosamund, perhaps.

"I'll just have a look-see in the household accounts for that time frame, shall I?" Hargreaves asked, again anticipating Max's need, like the good servant he was. "Her name as it was — her maiden name — is sure to appear. Your DCI can take it from there to find out what her name might be now, and where she's living."

CHAPTER 9
SECOND NANNY

Awena's reminder of the Josephine Tey book had sent Max to his study shelves that evening to retrieve his copy of *Brat Farrar,* but he'd had time to skim only the first chapter. Still, with its theme of imposters, the book made him think it wouldn't hurt to look into the history of those who inhabited Totleigh Hall. Cotton and his people would tick the usual procedural boxes, but Max felt he needed a broader understanding.

The butler had come through with a maiden name and an address where the nanny's last check had been sent. Cotton's team had quickly been able to locate her.

Fortunately, she lived not far away. It was less than an hour's drive to Fugglestone Parva, a hamlet at no great distance from Glastonbury. She no longer was raising other people's children but had two of her own. They were at school until four, she

169

informed Max once he had, with an assist from Cotton's Sergeant Essex, established his bona fides.

The former nanny turned out to be Afrikaner by way of the Netherlands, her family part of the great wave of immigrants into and out of South Africa. Her name, rather improbably, was Candice Thor St. Gabriel. Over scones and coffee, she told Max her mother had been Scandinavian, confirming the butler's memory of her appearance.

And if Max had been Lady Baaden-Boomethistle at the time Candice was at Totleigh Hall, she might never have been offered the job. He knew it was sexist, he knew it was many small-minded things, but Candice fit every stereotype of the young woman destined to stir storms of jealousy and family discord, often in all innocence.

She still looked impossibly young to have been the nanny at the hall two decades before, and surely could not have been much more than a child herself at the time. Supposing she was eighteen when she took the job, she was thirty-eight or so now, but looked a decade younger. She had the dense, creamy skin of many Scandinavians, and the pale, farseeing eyes that gave the nation its reputation as home to seers and sages. The dark-haired Awena, for that matter — dark-haired apart from a streak of white at the temple — had the same sort of eyes, but this woman was a white-chocolate blonde, a walking embodiment of the cliché of the Nordic temptress. She was youthfully dressed in a tank top and jeans deliberately torn at one knee. She wore cowboy boots and colorful dangly earrings; there was an air of last-minute chance to her ensemble that seemed to Max both authentic and rather endearing. The house showed every sign of having recently been vacated by youthful brigands with a fondness for color-ful plastic toys and chaos.

Her English was lightly accented with what sounded German to the ear but was, Max knew, a remaining trace of her native Afrikaans. The mid-nineties had seen a significant emigration out of Africa to the UK, most of it in response to a rising crime rate. She was, as she told Max, a descendant of missionaries to South Africa, which pos-sibly explained her willingness to talk with him. Different religion, same hymnal, he thought.

She further said it was a point of honor with her that she had not been an au pair, and she corrected Max when he slipped and used the term. Perhaps she was herself all too aware of the stereotypes.

"I never did domestic work. I looked after the children and that is all I did." There seemed to be another unspoken emphasis behind the words. Max waited.

"It's an enormous responsibility," she said.

"Yes, I know that well. My wife and I have just had our first child. You never quite sleep from that day forward, do you? And you never feel even the most trusted and qualified person can do the job as well as you can."

Mrs. Hooser had offered to watch the baby when he arrived. Max, who could think of few people less qualified to watch a baby, since her own children's having survived infanthood seemed like an instance of God's amazing grace, had smiled wanly at her well-intended kindness. Mrs. Hooser was blissfully unaware that in any practical sense of the term, she was an appalling mother.

"Thank you all the same, Mrs. Hooser, but we'll be hiring a childminder for the occasions when Awena and I aren't around." He had thought of the solution on the spot but knew something of the sort would have to be arranged.

"I've heard all the jokes about foreign au pairs," Candice told him now. "Men can be so silly. It is unfortunate, because even the most repulsive of employers come to think they are expected to make a pass. That we all must live our lives as part of some grand farce in a television sitcom."

"Ah."

"So looking after the children, that is all I did," she repeated. "If you have heard rumors to the contrary, you are wrong. They are wrong."

Max considered pretending he didn't know what she meant, but just as quickly, he dropped the pretense.

"Lord Baaden-Boomethistle is known to have had a roving eye," he said. "In his youth."

"Yes. And roving hands. I quickly put a stop to all that. I didn't need the job. *They* needed *me.* I was a highly trained nanny with outstanding references. And Peregrine was a handful."

"Put a stop to it, how?"

"I told his wife."

Max had to admire the girl's spunk. How many in her place, with a possibly precarious immigration status, would have been afraid to make waves?

"And she kept you on? Even though she must have seen you as a threat?"

"First of all, every woman with a pulse was a threat to that marriage. Second of all,

173

she didn't care anymore what he got up to — you could tell. I was safe as houses so far as she was concerned — so far as my working for her was concerned."

"And he?"

"Meek as a lamb once he realized I wasn't having any."

Max would never have given the lord high marks for likability. Still, he'd been murdered in such a spectacular way: It had to suggest a highly personal motive. And sadly, that suggested involvement by his family. Or was it possible he'd had a mistress — someone carrying a grudge because he wouldn't leave his present wife for her? Not out of the question, Max supposed.

"Besides, she was a lady," Candice was saying. "I mean, not just the title. She was a real class act. Nice. I liked her. The chances I would hurt her like that, with him? Less than zero."

"You haven't met the current Lady Baaden-Boomethistle, have you?"

She surprised him with her reply.

"No, but I've heard an earful. From the daughter. From Rosamund."

Really. "And how is that?"

"Rosamund can't stand her."

"Not unusual, is it, in a stepmother and stepdaughter relationship?"

Candice shrugged. She had no opinions, apparently, on whether it was unusual or not. But she added, "I think Rosamund is a little highly strung: Her dislike seems excessive to me. She feels her father married too soon after her mother's death."

"You have met Rosamund since you left Totleigh Hall?"

"Yes, I met up with her and her brother in London on a few occasions. The women of the family belong to some women's club there — she took me to tea once. It was so grand, a nice treat for me, you know? We took a liking to each other from the first. She was a serious little girl. Highly intelligent. I found her charming."

Max considered: Rosamund would not be the first child who felt displaced when parents died or moved on following a divorce. The loss, emotional and financial, could have an impact that lasted decades.

"Of course I remember the family well," Candice was saying. "I was with them until the children left for their schooling. I heard from Peregrine for a while. It was one of his school assignments to compose letters, and I would get these awful stilted things, which I treasure to this day. I don't think . . ."

"Think what?"

"Well, I'm guessing now, but I don't think

he had anyone else to write to. Family, I mean. It was the same story with the girl, with Rosamund. Lonely children they were — they really only had each other. And unfortunately, they did not get along that well together. Even from when they were tiny. Even though he was said to be sickly at first — he outgrew that. But she never seemed to make allowances for him."

"And he?"

"Oh, the jealousy and spite cut both ways, to be sure. He was always on her about her weight."

"You say he was sickly as a child? He shows no signs of it now."

Candice nodded, telling him that Peregrine had been kept in hospital for a few months with some sort of medical complication. She had been hired shortly afterward to care for him.

"Wouldn't it be more usual for a nanny to be hired ahead of time? So the parents would be ready and trained in what to expect, and the nanny get to know the family?"

"Not really," she replied. "Maybe *slightly* more usual." She wiggled her hand in an equivocating fashion. "Come to remember, they said something about having hired someone before me who did not work out

— that I was a replacement. They said she was a religious nutter — that's right. That was it. Another scone, Father Max? I must say I've grown to love the scone. At home, my mother made *stroopwafel,* but I can't duplicate them here — every experiment has failed. The ingredients just aren't the same here, or the oven. Or maybe it's me. . . ."

"Do you recall her name, the nanny who came before you?"

She started to shake her head sadly, no, she did not recall, and then she stopped. "I was friends with someone in Nether Monkslip who ran a bakery there. She would know. She took me under her wing, made things like *stroopwafel* for me when she had time, because she knew I was homesick. Such a kind woman. Her son was useless, as I recall. He sponged — is that the word, *sponged?* — off of her all the time. Before I left, I asked her to keep in touch. She didn't, not really, but I understood why. I never saw anyone who worked so hard."

She had to be talking about Elka Garth of the Cavalier. He supplied the name and she nodded enthusiastically.

"I really should pay her a visit. See how she's doing. Take the children to meet her . . ."

"She'd like that. And so, they stayed in touch, the children of Totleigh Hall?"

To his unspoken doubt, she said, "When I left, I left behind for them many children's books. But only Rosamund read them, she told me. She was always going to be such a great reader, you could tell. I put my name in the books — I had used them myself, to help with my English, you understand — and I told her to keep in touch, that if she forgot me, she could always look at my name and remember. I told her I was a bit alone here in England myself — which was certainly true, at least before I met my husband.

"I wasn't surprised when she wrote me. We met several times over the years when we were in London shopping or going to the theater. She belonged to her mother's club there, as I mentioned . . . some women's thing. We would meet up there.

"She is a bit of a lost soul, that one. More coffee, Vicar?"

178

CHAPTER 10
FIRST NANNY

It was a simple matter of ringing Elka Garth to track down the first nanny in the Totleigh Hall household. He could hear the hubbub of the shop in the background; Elka had a thriving business catering to the neo-hippy, gluten-free, granola-munching clientele of Nether Monkslip, but she did a fair side business in decadent offerings, like delicate pastries dripping with chocolate and caramel.

The gurgle of conversation was suddenly shot through with what he recognized as Suzanna's raucous laughter: "Chanel, you are the limit!"

To which came the reply, "I'm serious! I am so glad I wasn't here. What can it be like to be a suspect in a murder?"

"It's loads of fun, actually. I've been a suspect on many occasions. Stick around the village long enough. You'll get used to it."

Max also heard what sounded like Eugenia in the middle of another conversation, baying, "I told you. Just like Hester Prynne."

Someone had dared mention Hester Prynne when Awena's pregnancy first became evident. That person had quickly been rounded on and shushed. That person had probably been Suzanna — it was a typical Suzanna sort of joke. But apparently the thought had become embedded in Eugenia's brain. Such a tiresome woman. Max thought he might have to deal with it one day, the apparent jealousy, although ignoring her for now seemed the better course. Maybe it was the coward's course, but it all seemed too petty for a flat-out confrontation.

Elka asked Max to give her a few minutes to look up her address book, then rang back with the phone number he needed. Happily, the other former nanny at Totleigh Hall lived in Staincross Minster, no great distance from where Max was now, and a short tree-lined drive back home.

The woman he now thought of as First Nanny — Elspeth Muir — answered the phone on the first ring. He quickly gained the impression she was one of those people who in their loneliness or general chattiness welcomed interruptions, including the attentions of telephone surveyors, people dialing wrong numbers, and anyone who was not a prank caller. When he arrived at her house, a neat two up/two down in the suburbs of Staincross Minster, she greeted him with a plateful of scones. Inwardly, he sighed: Extra running time and exercise were in his future.

Elspeth proved to be a rounded, spritely body with short gray hair, in her mid to late seventies. She fussed about with a tea set in a routine that was familiar to him from his visits to Miss Pitchford, first shooing an enormous tabby named Helena away from "his" chair. Helena narrowed her eyes at Max and stalked from the room. Max, who was as resigned to cat fur as to extra calories on his pastoral visits, sat down and smiled with every evidence of pleasure, knowing his dark clothing was already attracting hair like a magnet. At least with a tabby, one out of approximately four hairs would match his slacks and jacket.

Elspeth Muir, with a final rattling of teaspoons against saucers and a proffering of paper serviettes with the slogan "Keep Calm and Drink Tea," settled comfortably into the armchair opposite. Her battery finally having run down, she sat alert and solid as a statue and trained her beady eyes on him expectantly, rather like a hen waiting for the eggs to hatch.

"You're here about the murder, of course," she said. "There's been nothing else in the news since it happened. I knew no good would come of the secrets in that house." She pronounced it *"say*-crits" with her heavy brogue, but Max knew what she meant.

"Secrets?" repeated Max, suddenly alive with the hope that this was not all a colossal waste of time.

"*Dark* secrets," she assured him.

Are there any other kind? He leaned forward, smiling encouragement.

"I kept their secrets for them," she told him, setting her teacup into its saucer so she could focus all her attention on her story. His reaction had been that gratifying. Usually, Elspeth liked to spin out a tale and gradually snare her audience, but this time she had gone in for the quick kill. Really, *most* gratifying it was. *Such* a fine-looking man, too. Too bad he was not a follower of the true religion.

"Although," she continued, beaming, "you can be sure it was only after many hours of prayer I agreed to go along with it. I didn't, truth be told, want the bother. And I knew

182

that made it a sin, in your religion and mine, Father. It weighed on my soul so much, I finally had to leave. 'Tell the truth and shame the devil,' my mother used to say. But I thought to myself at the time, you see, What would it gain anyone for me to go blabbing? The wee bairn needed a home, and he got a good home, or at least he wanted for nothing money could buy. Schooling, clothing, a beautiful house."

"Peregrine," he said. "Peregrine was adopted."

She wasn't asking for forgiveness or for anything resembling it; she was not appealing to him as a religious in any formal way, for he batted for the wrong team as far as she was concerned — he could see that. She might take it up with someone whose opinion she valued in the Church of Scotland, a thought she confirmed in the next breath.

"Now you've reminded me, I'll take it up with my minister." She eyed him. "I believe you've been sent, I do. God works in mysterious ways. True enough, He sent me an Anglican vicar — now there's a mystery for you. And even though those exact words are not in the Bible, He does His best work in ways that mystify us mortals." With Elspeth, the capital *H* was apparent, even in speech.

Max nodded his agreement, in case she was setting him some sort of test of his knowledge.

He was thinking he didn't want any deception over Peregrine's adoption derailing the case. What if the media got hold of it somehow? He must, as Cotton would have it, stay ahead of the story.

He thought he must have looked concerned, for she added, "There's no need to worry. My minister is a sound man and not a bearer of tales. I won't be naming names, either. I worked for a lot of families in my time, so he won't have any idea who I mean exactly. I'll present the situation to him as a moral puzzle, like. A — what do you call it? — a quarry."

"I believe you mean a quandary." Max smiled, looking at her. "A moral quandary." The picture he'd been painted of her as a religious nutter was fading. She was a churchgoer and a moral person; in trying to do the right thing, she had stopped at being asked to carry out a deception that would stretch over decades and have God knew what ramifications.

The family expecting her to take a salary to help them maintain the deception had chosen wrong, that was all.

And of course with the next nanny, the

family had learned its lesson. Candice was hired after they had brought the child home and he was already in place. Perhaps in need of good help by that point — help who would not need to be entrusted with any secrets — Lady Baaden-Boomethistle had been even more inclined than usual to overlook the fact of Candice's centerfold good looks.

"Stepping back for a bit, what do you recall of the household of those days?" he asked.

"Well," began Elspeth. She might just have been waiting for this opening. "The lord was not above a bit of draughty senior, if you follow my drift."

From the gentle blush that bloomed across her face as she said this, she could only mean droit du seigneur, a feudal lord's supposed right of sexual access to any woman subordinate to him.

"I'm interested in Lady Baaden-Boomethistle, the lord's first wife, particularly."

"Oooo, she was lovely. Frail. Yes, I would call her frail. Not physically — she was a great athlete, loved riding horses and things. Do they still keep all them horses at Totleigh?"

Max nodded.

"Lovely creatures. My father used to raise them."

Max prompted: "You were saying she was frail."

"Mentally frail, I meant," she said. "Not a lot of stuffing to her, and of course he was such a bully, and a lot to stand up to for any woman. She did want that baby so. . . . I suppose she didn't see the lie for what it was and would have told a million lies to have that child be hers. That was part of what made it so difficult, you see. She really did want him and, as I say, he would want for nothing with a mother who was devoted like that. But I did hear she died. I read it in the papers. Horse threw her off, didn't he? Wild creatures. We only think we can tame them. I suppose Peregrine was nearly grown by that time?"

"Yes," said Max. "More or less. Peregrine was a teenager when it happened."

"Peregrine," she repeated with a sniff. "Fancy name. I dinna care for it."

"I gather it's a family name."

"I had a cat named Pellegrino once," she said. "I'm teetotal, you see."

"Ah," said Max.

"He was Italian. The cat, I mean." Max decided he was not going to follow her down that path by asking her how in the

186

world she knew the cat's heritage.

"Was there anything else you'll be wanting to ask? My ladies' group meets here this evening. Please take a scone or two with you if you'd like. They are all slimming half the time and I end up making too much for them."

Max held up his hands, refusing the offer and saying, "I don't know if you're aware Peregrine later had a baby sister."

"There was mention in the paper, yes. I don't recall the name."

"It was Rosamund."

"Ah. That sounds like it. You're wondering if Rosamund came from the same place as Peregrine? I wondered, too, when I saw the notice. It . . . disturbed me. Put me in mind of Cain and Abel, for some reason. Yes, it did. Still, it's so often the way — the adopted baby is followed soon after by the child the couple thought they couldn't have."

Max had been thinking much the same thing.

He also had been wondering if Peregrine had found out about the circumstances surrounding his birth. If so, could the shock — the rage, even — at such a deception be a motive for murder?

"It's stirred it all up again," she added. "I

do think I've been careless — not asking my minister's advice, I mean."

Before driving away from Elspeth Muir's house, Max stopped to look for messages on his mobile phone. It was something he'd gotten more and more into the habit of doing with Awena and Owen in his life.

There was a message from his bishop, the Right Reverend Nigel St. Stephen. Rather, it was from the person in the bishop's office who organized his calendar. Max's heart sank. The bishop no doubt had seen the latest news. And he no doubt was alarmed and wondering if and how Max was involved in this latest incident of carnage in otherwise-peaceful Nether Monkslip. Max had been expecting the call, but he had not rehearsed what he might say. The bishop had been understanding thus far, almost viewing these horrendous homicidal incidents as somehow divinely sent, if such tortuous theology could be admitted.

Max himself had come to wonder — *was* he a catalyst for murder? Had he been sent to Nether Monkslip to root out evil in the village?

And if so, was this ever going to end? Was there a bottom to it?

During his years of training for the priesthood at Oxford, Max had stumbled across a few corpses, and had been involved in solving many of those crimes. He still remembered with a shiver of distaste the clean-cut murderer he'd helped put away his first Michaelmas term. He had never quite realized until now how much crime had dogged him, not just in Nether Monkslip but throughout his adult life. He supposed crime solving might be some special gift or calling, like tap dancing or harmonica playing. Somehow things had gone from no murders happening in Nether Monkslip, at least not in recent memory, to variations on *The Murder at the Vicarage.*

Max had one further uneasy thought: The bishop also might ask about the baptism for Owen, a question for which Max had no ready answer. He and Awena had not worked out yet, as they had for their marriage, what sort of ceremony might encompass and honor their differing beliefs.

Oh, and there was the further problem of the face that kept reappearing on the wall of St. Edwold's Church. A man's face, reputed to have miraculous healing properties, a face that bore a strong resemblance to the bearded face of Jesus on the famous Shroud of Turin. As well as to the face recently discovered — by Max — at the obscure nunnery of Monkbury Abbey.

Coincidence?

There was certainly no shortage of things for the bishop to be concerned about.

Whatever. It was better to get the call over with. Max took a deep breath before punching the reply button, thinking as he did so that he might as well put the bishop on speed dial.

CHAPTER 11
SUZANNA AND THE WI

Back in Nether Monkslip, Suzanna was rallying the members of the Women's Institute in preparation for the Harvest Fayre. "Rallying" in Suzanna's case involved a sort of scorched-earth diplomacy delivered with heavy-handed flattery and exhortation. Now talk of the Totleigh Hall murder had, of course, derailed her agenda, and Suzanna was having a struggle to keep her squadron of forty or so women in line. The harvest and even the looming duck race were minor diversions on the village calendar; the shocking murder was what was happening now. She made eye contact with Chanel Dirkson as she entered in a silent plea for help. Chanel, even though she was a *self*-help guru, was used to being enlisted in this way — she spent much of the day reading letters pleading for outside assistance. She cooperated now with a loud shushing noise.

"All right, ladies! The Fayre is almost

upon us and we've a lot of ground to cover today. If you could shut the hell up about the murder, please, we'll get through this a lot faster."

There was the usual horrified gasp from Miss Pitchford as she dropped a stitch in whatever fleecy item she was knitting for one of her grandnieces or grandnephews. The rest of them were, to a greater or lesser degree, used to it.

Miss Pitchford was always threatening to resign from whatever group Suzanna was involved with, but she could never bring herself to do so. It would shut her off from everything going on in the parish, and compromise her cherished role at the center of the village grapevine.

Unfortunately, Suzanna enjoyed fanning the flames. She had recently run a photo in the parish bulletin of Miss Pitchford peering out from behind lace curtains as she spied on passing villagers. The fact everyone did this on occasion made no matter; Miss Pitchford had elevated the pastime to a full-time career.

"Put yourself in her shoes," Max, brought into the fray as peacemaker, had said. "Think how you would feel."

Suzanna thought for a full minute, then said, "No can do. I cannot for the life of me think my way inside that woman's shrunken head, nor do I want to be in there."

"You'll have to print a retraction. Or something."

"You can't retract a photo."

"An apology, then. Suzanna, she's elderly, and she has no one. Her status in the village is all she has."

"She has no one because she's an insufferable pain in the ass."

"Suzanna," said Max, his voice carrying, unusually, a warning note.

"Very well, then. I still don't see why just because you're elderly you should expect all this special treatment. You're the same person you always were, just more wrinkly and in general ten times more obnoxious."

"Let's pray you live a long time, Suzanna. Perhaps you'll change, or you'll change your mind about your expectations. Anyway, a retraction?"

Some more grumbling, followed by: "I'll try to think of something. I suppose I could Photoshop her into a scene where she's actually contributing to the common good. Feeding the poor or hugging Mother Teresa or something."

Now Suzanna took a deep, calming breath as she surveyed the chattering group before her. There was no question she had lost

193

control of the situation for the moment. Only Lily, the village textiles expert, was paying attention. The shepherdess, as Suzanna called her. Lily's stall at the Fayre, where she sold hand-knit scarves, hats, and jumpers, was always among the most popular, so these meetings were important to her. She was a purist when it came to her profession, dealing globally now in wools and yarns, and raising her own sheep for their wool, dying the resulting yarn using fruits, vegetables, and plants. She gave each of her sheep a name, for they were more like her pets, and named each of her designs after its former "owner." Last year she had created the popular Anjelica Ray jumper, which she wore now — an airy confection in harvest shades of greens and dark oranges and brownish reds.

Lily tended to dot her conversation with mystifying terms like *backstrap loom, weft,* and *tabby ground weave.* She had recently branched out to create silk slippers with stylized words of inspiration like *Love* and *Hope* woven onto narrow strips sewn together to create the shoe face, an idea inspired by an exhibit she had seen about the Silk Road. For a while, her only regret had been that she didn't have time or resources to cultivate her own silkworms and plant the mulberry trees to feed them. Then she had read a PETA article that informed her that "1,500 silkworms are killed to produce 100 grams of silk," and that had been the end of her slipper enterprise.

She sat next to Tara Raine on one of the Village Hall's hard plastic seats. Tara wore her usual yoga ensemble: leggings with batik stripes, and a loose-fitting top in all colors of the rainbow. With her curly red hair tied into a knot at the top of her head, she, and Lily beside her, looked like an ad for New Age herbal supplements. Tara's mind, characteristically, was not on the murder, for she struggled to banish negative thinking from her mental landscape, but on the wholesomeness of the CleanMind Clean-Body retreat she would be offering with Awena next summer in Monkslip-super-Mare. It had become an annual event, drawing people, many of them celebrities with a newly discovered spiritual inclination, from as far away as London.

These thoughts Tara was having were, however, swimming against what she called "a wee tide of worry" about the sudden long silences of her boyfriend.

She felt a presence beside her and opened her eyes (she had been sneaking in a quick mini-meditation, as advised by Deepak to counter anxiety), to see Chanel Dirkson had quietly moved into the seat to her right. There was a soft rustle of organic fabric, a choice of which Lily heartily approved — this time Chanel wore a tunic of soft yellow over flowing gray wool trousers. Her hair shone from what looked like a recent visit to the hairdresser's; she wore it tapered to rest on her shoulders in a flattering bob.

Tara smiled, for she liked the older woman, finding her sympathetic but not intrusive. The smile was warmly returned.

Tara decided on the instant to turn the question in her mind over to the expert, for it had to be good karma that had brought Chanel to her side. Tara's boyfriend of long standing, who lived in nearby Chipping Monkslip, had been showing a distinct cooling of interest in their relationship.

Chanel, much like a doctor at a social occasion, was often asked to take the patient's pulse, metaphorically speaking. Inwardly, she sighed — why did they always come to her when it was nearly too late to save them? Women — and men, too, of course, but mostly women — could make such messes of their love lives, when a little common sense was all that was called for.

"My best advice," she said, once Tara had

described the symptoms, "is to vanish for a very long time."

"But I —"

"But you're busy working with Awena at Goddessspell, I know, and you can't just leave. I didn't mean you should actually go somewhere else. Here's your concern, right: You think he might forget you if he doesn't hear from you every day?"

Tara hung her head and, with a sigh, unloosed the luxuriant red curls from the top of her head, as if it would relieve the pressure she was feeling.

"Something like that."

"I would actually block his number on your phone for a while, in case he does try to call."

"What? But —"

"You heard me. He won't be able to text or ring and leave a message. And you won't be checking your phone every ten minutes to see if he *has* rung, which will help break the spell. He can't get in touch, and for the next few days or weeks, that's fine with you. You are busy. You have a life. You're not angry with him; you just don't *care.*"

"But what if he needs me? He's awfully sensitive. I don't want him to think I —"

"What is he, eleven years old? Trust me, sweetheart, he thinks right now he doesn't

197

need you. Maybe he does; maybe he doesn't. Maybe he's met someone else." Tara gasped, for this was the one possibility, and the obvious one, she had not allowed herself to dwell on. "But the best — the *only* — way to find out the truth is to make him wonder where in hell you went to. Hey, maybe *you* met someone else! You need to find out where you stand before you waste any more time on him, and confronting him about his absence is not the way to go."

"But . . . if he needs me . . ."

"Does he have a car?"

"Sure, he has a car."

"Good. If he needs you, if he's worried, he'll get in that car and drive over here. I wouldn't be at home, if I were you. Go to the cinema or something." She held up a forestalling hand. "He'll probably do whatever it takes to make sure you're all right. Why would you want to be with someone who wouldn't show that basic concern for you?"

"It seems like playing games."

"It is. That's exactly what it is. It's the oldest game in the world, and remember, he started it. Tara, he knows he should have called by now, better than you do."

Lily, who had been eavesdropping, leaned in.

"She's right, Tara. It's basic common sense."

Tara looked at her. Lily was, to put it mildly, no raving beauty, but half the men in the village seemed besotted with her — Major Batton-Smythe, a kindly, if clueless, widower in particular. It was a fact of which Lily seemed completely unaware.

"My stock-in-trade," said Chanel, "is common sense. Try it for a week. Cold turkey. No phoning him, and no calls from him allowed. Bury the mobile if you have to, or give it to me for safekeeping."

Tara sighed. "You're right. I know you're right. How did you get to be so smart?"

A rather sad expression came over Chanel's face. She said, "It's easy when you are not the one in the thick of things. It's easy to see the answers when you're alone, looking in from the other side of the glass."

Lily nodded. She also liked Chanel and didn't want her or anyone to be alone, although she, Lily, was not bothered by solitude. She lived on her farm outside the village, with only her sheep for company, and was content with her designs and ideas to occupy her.

She had once had the thought she might die out there one day and no one would know. Caring only that the sheep might starve, she had set up an agreement with Awena that they would ring each other every day before ten, just to check in.

"Have you ever been married?" Lily asked her now. "Lived with anyone?"

Chanel shook her head. "No," she said flatly. "I never have. Always free as a bird, that's me. Ironic, isn't it? And here I am dispensing advice to people."

"You don't have to live it to know what's right, do you?"

"I think it helps, rather. You have to stay detached in my business. To keep your head while all around you — oh, sorry. I forgot about our local murder. How awful."

"I know," said Tara. "The most appalling turns of phrase keep popping into my mind since the lord was killed. It's too horrible to think about."

"So the brain keeps pushing it down, which of course makes the thought pop up at the most inopportune times," said Chanel. "I hope they find whoever did it soon. It's creepy, the whole thing. And really, so sad. He was a kind man who welcomed me to the village with open arms."

"He did?" said Lily, amazed. "That was never my experience of him."

"Mine, either," said Tara. "To be honest, I thought he was full of himself, *and* a bit of a lech. Still, he might have mellowed with age. And his wife was perhaps a calming influence."

Hearing a frantic shout from the podium, they quickly shushed and turned expectantly toward Suzanna. But not before Chanel had time to murmur, "Somehow I doubt that."

At least, thought Suzanna, eyeing them, these three are paying attention. Not like Elka Garth. Still, Elka got special dispensation because she always provided biscuits for the after-meeting coffee. And Elka, it was rumored, might be in love. Suzanna always made allowances for that.

She had seen Elka and Adam Birch, of the Onlie Begetter bookshop, walking together on more than one occasion. This had happened often enough to cause Suzanna to delicately raise one perfectly waxed eyebrow and get on the wire to notify those most likely to be interested, which was everyone. Even, in a special concession, Miss Pitchford, who had ruined everything for Suzanna by claiming to know all about it already.

A further major indicator was that Elka Garth had gotten the bean in her slice of cake during the Twelfth Night party at the Village Hall, and Adam Birch had gotten the pea. These were major portents to those in the know. The pair had thus been crowned queen and king for the evening, and glasses of wassail had been lifted high, and speculation that they might one day become an item ran rife. It was a development of which the villagers much approved.

A further bonus to this budding relationship seemed to be that it helped Elka get her son, Clayton, sorted. Strangely enough, from the moment Elka had stopped focusing on Clayton, wringing her hands over his many moral lapses, he had begun taking stock of himself. He weaned himself off the minor drugs that had almost certainly been a part of his leisure activities, and started taking a course in Monkslip-super-Mare on holistic medicine. He had become a habitué of Awena's Goddessspell shop, and a regular at Tara Raine's yoga classes. It was, Elka had been heard to say, like getting her son back: like seeing someone washed clean of the mud that had obscured his face from her for years.

The pairing of Elka and Adam, quickly christened Elkadam, seem preordained somehow, particularly since they had played Cupid with Max and Awena (Maxena) in their courtship days. Maybe the dart "backfired" a bit, thought Suzanna now, and got aimed at them, as well. What do they call it — blowback? Yes. Served them right, and it could not happen to a nicer couple.

If only her lover, Umberto, could be caught in the same tender trap . . .

She got them all through the meeting somehow, managing to convince a satisfyingly large number of women to persuade their husbands to help set up the booths. "Remember," she said, "Stonehenge was built one megalith at a time. We can do this." At which exhortation, Chanel nodded approvingly, wondering if she could adapt it for a chapter of her book.

Despite the murder up at the mansion, the duck race for charity must go on, she reminded her listeners. Suzanna corralled a few "volunteers" and began to describe how each mechanical duck must be labeled with a number tagged to the name of its sponsor. Individual sponsors paid ten pounds sterling to participate; "corporate" sponsors — shop owners — paid fifty. Sponsorships were down this year, and Suzanna began to say that heads would roll for this, and caught herself just in time.

The minds of her audience began to wander; they were looking forward to the refreshments. But when she mentioned Bill Travis as the man she had put in charge of the race, there came a small gasp from somewhere among the women — an audible intake of breath, possibly from more than one source. Suzanna, who had had a good look at Travis, could understand why. A hunk of burning love if ever there was one. But she scanned the faces before her and could not see whose pulse it was that had quickened at the very mention of his name. Surely not plain little Nancy Braddock, who wouldn't say boo to a ghost and was miles out of Travis's league anyway, in Suzanna's assessment. Confidently smoothing her pencil skirt over Spanxified hips, she thought she herself was very much in the running, if his smile and body language as she had explained to him the rules of the duck race were any indication.

Eventually, she brought the meeting to a close. There was the usual crush of people toward the table at the back of the room — such a crush, Suzanna barely noticed that Destiny, the new curate at St. Edwold's, had made her appearance at last, pushed now into the center of the throng of arms reaching for the peanut butter biscuits. Better, thought Suzanna, late than never. She strode over to welcome Destiny — really, what sort of name was that? — and accept any apologies due. It was as well to stay on

the good side of the clergy. You never knew
when you might need a blessing.

CHAPTER 12
NOAH'S ARK

Max called Awena before leaving Staincross Minster for home. He relayed what Elspeth Muir had said about Peregrine's being adopted.

"Ah," she had said. "That explains some of the rumors."

"Meaning?"

"Well, he doesn't really look like any of them. Father nor mother. The rather mean village tittle-tattle should not be repeated, but it does get around."

He should have known, Awena was not one to pass along unsubstantiated gossip.

"What do you know of the family? You've been here much longer than I have."

"Not much, really. Only hearsay. Old tales about how the son was supposed to have been in hospital but emerged as hale and hearty as you please, and far too big for the age they claimed he was. Nothing that amounted to fact, you see. Just silly conjecture. You know how people can be. Especially since the family was seldom around and had not made itself popular, there was a lot of room for speculation."

Max thought, Awena would have been a very young woman, newly arrived in the village and busy establishing her shop, when the young lord came on the scene. So what she knew would be hearsay not only at secondhand but from a long time ago.

He thought, Who else in the village would know the family at all well? And the name that came to mind was Noah Caraway, purveyor of fine antiques.

A marble gray sky held the promise of rain as Max parked the Land Rover in Vicarage Road. Noah waved to him from his shop, almost as if he'd been waiting for Max to arrive. Max ambled over to the Old Vicarage, now home to Noah's Ark Antiques.

As Max came into the shop, Noah was busy polishing antique silver, using, as he explained, a mixture of baking soda and vinegar.

"No chemicals. It ruins silver."

"Good to know. The only silver I'm ever likely to own is my mother's tea set, which I hope very much she will give away to someone else before the time comes."

207

"I hear you," said Noah. "It's work, but worth it. Sorry about the duck race this year, by the way. His round face creased in an expression of concern, like a worried man in the moon. "I simply got the dates mixed up, and when I realized, it was too late to scratch my plans. And now . . . it's all a bit awkward, isn't it?"

Yes, with Lord Baaden-Boomethistle's death, it was difficult to say what might happen. Perhaps the whole thing still would have to be canceled, despite the best efforts of Suzanna and the WI. What a shame, thought Max. On so many levels, what a shame.

Max was never sure if he were interrupting Noah in the middle of something important, or if he were giving him something to do. Noah sat surrounded by the luxurious and opulent trappings of his trade, the very picture of a potentate with reams of time at his disposal. But someone had to dust and polish, and someone had to catalog, and someone had at least to pretend to be running the shop. Even though Noah, by his own admission, found it difficult to part with any of his treasures, which were, in theory at least, on sale. He didn't have to sell so much as a teaspoon, of course; he was quite wealthy as it was. The truth was,

Noah collected beautiful things because he loved beautiful things and there was no more room in his house to hold them all.

Max looked around the shop, with its furniture, lamps, and sets of glassware and dinnerware, each item lovingly curated and displayed. His eyes alighted on a pile of thin paper, brown and curling at the edges with age. It looked to be an old typescript done on an early machine.

"What's this?"

"I'm transcribing an old diary with a view to publishing it," Noah told him. "I found it in a desk I bought from the estate of the widow Barnes. It's my contribution to the Writers' Square, which I recently joined. Frank said he'd help me get it published."

Ah. Frank Cuthbert — Nether Monkslip's single claim to literary fame. Well, notoriety, more like. For what Frank really wrote were potboilers disguised as history. According to Awena, who was a member of the Square, which met regularly at the the Onlie Begetter, Frank was working on a sequel to his book, a development the members of the group viewed with a sort of resigned horror. Especially given the revelations about the village's ties to a miraculous object in a nearby nunnery, Max joined them in feeling trepidation as to what the Great Author was up to now.

For, to the astonishment of all, Frank's *Wherefore Nether Monkslip* had made the best-seller lists. What was basically a glorified pamphlet had been seized on by Arthurian legend enthusiasts, crackpot historians, and assorted fans of village life. There was talk now of interest from the BBC — talk started by Frank, to be sure. All that was known for certain was that Frank was frequently interrupted during meetings of the group by calls from his publicist.

Adam Birch, the bookshop's owner, had been spurred by Frank's success to finish his own novel, and was often to be seen working by lamplight at the window of his shop, scribbling at a furious pace.

Frank had taken to wearing a scarf year-round as part of his authorly persona, and a velour tracksuit of dark green — his "good luck" writing outfit, like something worn by an off-duty Robin Hood. He was often seen typing away at the Coffee Pot, taking advantage of the free Wi-Fi, or at the Horseshoe, reviewing fresh pages over a pint, a red pencil at hand, his steady progress only occasionally slowed by a tiny cloud of self-doubt.

As Suzanna Winship said, it seemed to be asking a lot of them to listen to a goddamn sequel, particularly when Frank's first book was still fresh in everyone's mind. Suzanna had high hopes for the time-travel romance she was now writing, although the others had encouraged her to try her hand at erotica, which seemed to be selling well lately. ("Why should I write it? I've lived it" was her reply.) But she would distract the group with real-life tales of the glow-in-the-dark underwear she wore, to some avail, for Umberto, an unrepentant workaholic. (There was a lovely new chocolatier in the village who was giving Suzanna cause for concern. The woman and Umberto had so much in common, like food. Suzanna, uncharacteristically, felt at a disadvantage.)

Overriding protests, Frank would regale them with as many as three or four chapters at a time of his WIP. (WIP, he explained condescendingly, stood for work in progress.) In addition to the scarf, he had taken to carrying a pipe about with him, and this he would wave around, punching the air with the stem for emphasis as he read. Suzanna privately hoped he would set the scarf on fire, but somehow it never happened. What with the beard and the scarf and the rose-tinted glasses, it was as if he were channeling Hemingway but had gotten a few of the details wrong, like the velour. He'd just begun offering writing workshops, driving all about the countryside in his Aston Martin to sprinkle literary fairy dust on aspiring authors.

His wife, who ran La Maison Bleue, was still fuming about the author biography that was appearing on his dust jacket copy: "Frank Cuthbert lives with his wife Lucie, a bichon frise, and two cats in Nether Monkslip." Lucie had quickly grown tired of the ribbing about being a dog. And she did not believe Frank's protestations that he had not been consulted about the jacket copy, although Max believed him. No one would dream of consulting a pedant like Frank on a point of comma placement or grammar.

"It's quite interesting," said Noah, indicating his typescript find. "And I enjoy transcribing. I'm not really a writer, you know. Not like Awena. Now, I believe she's really onto something with her recipes and folk remedies. They're all doing something quite original. Even the Major."

"Yes, I know. Awena fills me in." Major Batton-Smythe, who was writing a military history, would arrive at the meetings of the Writers' Square with an enormous sheaf of pages, all cross-indexed and color-coded, the important pages (most of them, apparently) indicated by colorful tabs bought from the office-supply store in Monkslip-super-Mare. How many usable pages of manuscript his fastidious methods produced was debatable, but no one could deny the sheer volume of pages alone was impressive.

"Have you heard the latest rumors, Father Max?" Noah asked him now.

"Erm," said Max, wondering which of several dozen rumors swirling around the village at any given time Noah might have in mind.

"You haven't heard, then! A statue of the Virgin Mary has been found buried up on Hawk Crest, in Nunswood. Just past the menhirs. It's a beautiful piece of stonework, wrapped in an embroidered cloth — probably an altar cloth. The cloth is falling to dust now, of course. The statue was part of a treasure trove: a golden chalice, a paten, an altar cross, and so on. They brought it here for safekeeping — because I have a safe big enough to secure it for the time being and they understood what they were looking at was rare and valuable. Big discussions are afoot now as to who it belongs to — or should that be whom? Anyway, there must be a finder's fee that the village will be entitled to, don't you think?"

"That rather depends on who found it,

don't you think?"

"It was Tom. Little Tom Hooser."

"He was up there by himself, I suppose. He's too young for that climb — it's dangerous."

"I think so, too. Anyway, he went to fetch his sister when he saw what he'd got. The pair of them kept the find from their mother, which is just as well. She's useless in any situation requiring, well, intelligent thought or action. You know how it is with those children."

Yes, and it absolutely figures, thought Max, that Tom would be the one to find such a treasure. The young boy roamed around unsupervised half the time. If it weren't for his slightly older, very bossy sister, Tildy Ann, he'd have had no upbringing at all. Max let them both hang about the vicarage after school, doing homework while their mother pretended to housekeep.

It figured on a different level, too. It was Tom who had first noticed the mysterious face that kept appearing on the St. Edwold's Church wall — the face that still resisted all attempts to obliterate it. Max wondered if vinegar and baking soda would work, the way it did on silver tarnish. He, the sexton, and the church handyman had tried everything else.

The site Noah was describing — near the prehistoric stone menhirs — had been rumored for centuries to be haunted, as haunted as the lake at Totleigh Hall. It was a legend that had gained traction since a villager, most sadly and unnecessary, had died up there not long ago.

"Show me," said Max.

Noah opened the old-fashioned walk-in safe and led Max inside. He put a cardboard box on top of a table and with a ta-da gesture stepped away to let Max have a look.

Max was no expert in antiquities, but at a glance it seemed to him a treasure trove indeed.

"I've not attempted to clean the dirt and mud off of it. I'm leaving that for the experts. I just left it all in the same box Tom and Tildy Ann dragged in here."

"Any theories on what it is and how it got there?"

"It has to be loot from the time of the Reformation. Things the monks at the abbey tried to save from destruction. Nice to see they got away with it. If they'd been caught . . ." Noah made a slicing gesture against his throat. There seems to be a lot of that going around, thought Max. "Oh! Sorry," Noah said. "That was in poor taste, given what's going on up at Totleigh Hall.

It's just been on my mind, you know."

Max, still trying to make out the contours of the gleaming treasure, waved away the apology. Even given the centuries of grime, he could see these were beautifully crafted artifacts, valuable not just for their gold but as works of art. Each seemed also to be embedded with precious stones and jewels. The statue of Mary was carved out of stone and was a little over a foot high. She held an image of a tiny Christ Child in her arms and around her neck was a cross on a gold chain that glimmered as it caught the light of the overhead lamp in the vault. Are those diamonds? Max wondered. If so, the value of the trove was probably incalculable.

"That's garnet there," Noah said, pointing. "And around the base of the chalice, those are pearls. The condition of everything is remarkable, considering."

Did this have anything to do with that reappearing face in the church? It seemed impossible it did not. It was almost as if the . . . the *holiness,* the sacredness of the place was emerging from the ground, making itself felt. The sanctity that seemed to encompass the whole of Nether Monkslip.

Max recalled the map he had discovered at Monkbury Abbey. Carved in stone in bas-relief, it hung suspended by two golden chains from the base of a painting — a depiction of what the nuns called The Face. Nether Monkslip, most improbably, had appeared on this map, indicated by a star. Max had concluded it was a sort of treasure map, his own village, many miles from Monkbury Abbey, the key to some hidden puzzle — a puzzle he was only now beginning to fathom.

His heart sank. Once word of this newest find got out, the size of the masses already crowding St. Edwold's Church seeking a miracle cure would only grow by leaps and bounds. Good news, in a way, to reignite the hopes of the faithful. But wouldn't it also bring the treasure hunters? The religious maniacs? The just-plain crazies?

"There seems," said Noah, with admirable understatement, "to be a lot going on in our little village." He said it in such a disapproving tone, Max felt compelled to say, "Well, don't look at me." But the truth was, all this — well, this *fuss* — had started with his, Max's, arrival in the village.

Fuss, meaning murder.

And miracles, rumors of.

"What," Max asked him, "do you make of the situation at Totleigh Hall?"

"What do I make of it? I've no theories, if that's what you mean."

Max imagined it wouldn't do to say he was full up with theories and that what he was really after was gossip.

Noah seemed to read his mind. "I suppose you and the police already know," he continued, "so I'll not be spreading tales, but the present Lady Baaden-Boomethistle — well, she is rumored to be rather free with her favors."

"What exactly are you saying, Noah?"

Noah tore his eyes away from the box of treasures to look up at him. "There has been talk for some time she's been having an affair with one of the grooms over there. Or maybe it's the estate manager. All very Lady Chatterley, you know. Well, who would be surprised if she were? Lord Baaden-Boomethistle is an old tyrant, and she's — well, you've seen her."

"Hmm."

"And of course Peregrine. Well. He may have been found under a cabbage leaf, for all I know, but it would appear he was not born into that family. At least, that's another rumor that's gone round. But until the lord was murdered, well, everyone felt it was best kept under wraps. A local matter, a family matter, you do see. And really none of our business. Now . . . well, now it's agreed that it's gone beyond being a family matter."

Clearly they'd all been discussing it, at length. Max should have realized — sometimes he felt all he had to do to solve a crime was hang about Elka's tea shop. "How and when did this particular rumor get started?" Max knew the village grapevine too well. It was correct half the time. But one never knew which half.

"The gap in time became evident right away," said Noah. "I mean, the timing for the pregnancy of the first Lady B-B did not add up. We could all count to nine months as well as the next person. I remember it well. A six-month old, at least, was brought home and passed off as newborn. Biggest sumo wrestler of a newborn you ever saw. Villagers assumed it was to cover up an out-of-wedlock conception, an affair, something of the sort."

"And Lord Baaden-Boomethistle, ever the gallant, conspired in this deception to protect his wife, and to adopt an unknown man's child as his own?"

"I know, I know. It doesn't sound much like something he'd do, does it?"

"No, it does not." And now he was dead. He and his first wife both. There was possibly no one alive who knew the whole truth.

Except maybe Peregrine, the giant newborn, who had been too small to remember.

■ ■ ■ ■

At the Writers' Square later that evening, the aspiring authors agreed not to talk about the murder. *"We're here to work!"* they reminded one another repeatedly.

Of course they spent the next two hours talking of nothing but, arriving at no conclusions except that the butler almost certainly did not do it, and that Suzanna might try her hand at an erotic crime novel based on the case.

"Too much of a cliché," said Frank. "The butler, I mean."

For once, the rest agreed with him. The good money was on Lady B-B, but the rumor mill had already discovered she had an alibi.

"She had to have been with that hunky estate manager," insisted Suzanna.

"Nope. Too easy for them to alibi each other. Too suspicious, I mean," Frank replied sagely.

How annoying, thought Suzanna: He was almost certainly right.

"She was with a friend — an entire family in Monkslip-super-Mare. No way she could have done it, and no way they'd all lie for her."

No one asked where Frank got his information, but undoubtedly it was from his wife, who plied the local bobby by stocking his favorite French wines in her shop.

So undoubtedly Frank was right.

Suzanna crossed her legs and studied one pointed toe of her new Louboutins.

Most annoying.

CHAPTER 13
DESTINY REMEMBERS

"I just heard the news."

Destiny, in full curate regalia, bustled into the vicarage study, her cassock ballooning behind her. Max had noticed it was the women who liked wearing cassocks, more so than the men. Perhaps because their right to wear them had been so hard-won.

His mind still grappling with the implications of Noah's newfound treasure horde, Max wondered what particularly struck Destiny as newsy at the moment.

"I've been in Monkslip-super-Mare, checking supplies for Bowls for Souls," she said. "I have family there, so I stayed over — as I told you I was going to." Max nodded. "And I come back to this . . . this incredible story." The "Why didn't you tell me?" was implied but not spoken.

The village grapevine had exploded with the news while Destiny had been away, but of course she was not yet plugged into Miss

Pitchford's network. That would come in time; anyone at the center of village life, like a curate, would be central to the Pitchford mission of disinformation and misdirection, but for now Destiny was still the newcomer, still being monitored and assessed. She remained, in other words, a topic of conversation, not its conduit.

"Totleigh Hall, you mean?" Max asked.

"Of course Totleigh Hall," she said with measured emphasis. "How often do you have a murder around here? What else could I be talking about?"

"Well, actually . . ." Max hesitated. He wanted his new curate to be happy here, not frightened out of her wits. "It doesn't happen all that often."

"It doesn't —" Good Lord. *It doesn't* happen all *that often*? "Max, listen: I have something to tell you. Something that might be relevant to the death of Lord Baaden-Boomethistle."

"Pull up a chair by the fire. Tea?"

"The thing is, I know at least one of the players in this drama. It's just that I don't know who it is I know."

They were settled over a nice cuppa, the fire burning low, just warm enough to chase away the October chill. Destiny's gaze drifted to the rowing oar Max had hung atop the seascape over the fireplace. He had rowed as an undergraduate at Oxford, but St. Barney's, where he'd done his graduate study, did not have a rowing team — at least not officially. The sort of manic roughhousing in rented or borrowed skulls didn't count — those thrilling weekend displays of machismo and show-offmanship.

How I miss it all, thought Destiny. The last-minute revisions; the moments of sheer terror as the clock struck midnight, wondering how I'd ever pass my exams; the bitter cold of my little room at the top of the college, a cold that seeped into the bone with a promise to stay forever. She had been certain she'd learn firsthand the meaning of chilblains if she didn't graduate soon.

How little I appreciated it while I was there. It was *grand.*

Most of all, she missed the hours spent in the Bodleian, turning the pages of some old leather-bound book and reveling in the rustling sound made by its stiff, thick pages, imagining the hands that had turned the same pages centuries before. Time would never stretch before and behind her as endlessly as it had then.

She and Max had been theology students together at St. Barnabas House — she an undergraduate, if a "mature" one, and Max a graduate student. She had gone on to graduate study herself, and to ordination as a priest in the Anglican Communion.

The Major persisted in calling Destiny "a Vicarette," a fact of which Destiny was aware despite Max's desperate attempts to keep it from her. She was resigned to that sort of thing, suspecting that any attempts to correct the old soldier or drag him into the twenty-first century were doomed to failure.

It was at Oxford over a pint (for him) and a club soda (for her) at the White Horse pub, next to Blackwell's, that Max had asked her how she had come by such a name.

"My parents were hippies, and highly impractical hippies at that, pure-minded and well-meaning. Wonderful people, if a bit vague in the parenting department. I don't think they realized that when I grew up, people would think I was a porn star."

She looked across at Max now, this preposterously handsome priest, the man she had known way back when. Unlike herself, Max had had a perpetual star beside his name, in everyone's book. She had never kidded herself that he would give her a second glance, not in a romantic way, although hundreds more in his orbit had not seemed to be as practical. Prince Harry had nothing on Max in the chick-magnet department. He had, however, adopted her as a trusted confidante, and this in itself had astonished her. It amazed her even more to come to realize Max was prone to most of the same self-doubts as any mortal. Who was he, Max would wonder aloud over those drinks in the White Horse, to dare to think God had called him? Had some special plan for him? Was he quite mad to think it?

Now here he was years later, sitting in his own cozy vicarage, married to the marvelous Awena, a woman who stayed on her own spiritual path while remaining completely in harmony with her husband's beliefs. Max, the proud father of Owen, that smashing baby born with his mother's eerie, preternatural gaze and a full head of shaggy dark hair like his father's. He is a child destined for great things, thought Destiny, who seemed to share with Awena an affinity for being able to glimpse a sacred world beyond the veil, and for being perpetually alert to signs and portents. It was *there,* that other side: she knew it, she could feel it, and on days when she was feeling replete and happy and at one with the world, she could almost see the Presence that helped guide and protect her.

"Why don't you start at the beginning," Max suggested, dragging her attention back to this world, which held, truth be told, little interest for such as Destiny. Awena was completely practical and down-to-earth by comparison, a rare combination of bohemian laissez-faire and transcendent awareness of the metaphysical world.

"That's a good idea," she said, "except that there are at least two beginnings. I'll start with where I was when I overheard a conversation that, if nothing else, proves this murder was brewing for a long time. At least since the spring."

Max leaned forward, nodding encouragingly. He took a sip of tea to mask his impatience. Destiny was a solid-gold person, and whatever she had to say might be important. It often took her a while to get to the point — her sermons were exhibit A — but get there she did.

"I went to the Women's Institute meeting on my return, you see," she told him. "In the Village Hall — their usual monthly meeting. Although I was late getting there, Suzanna had especially asked me to attend. She said it would be a good chance for the other women to get to know me better, since undoubtedly some of their projects for charity would overlap with church missions. When I got there, though, what they were really doing was talking among themselves about the murder — of course. Suzanna was rather stridently trying to keep it together. I take it that is part of Suzanna's management style."

"Tyranny shot through with bribery and sarcasm," said Max. "Yes."

"Well, as I say, I was late anyway. Traffic leaving Monkslip-super-Mare was a snarl. So the meeting was just breaking up into a scrimmage for the refreshments table. I overheard a woman talking and I recognized the voice, you see. That's what did it — stopped me in my tracks, it did. She sort of brushed past me, part of a knot of women heading for the back of the room. I had stepped aside to let them pass.

"I heard this woman talking, and I was sort of transported back to another time when I heard a disembodied voice talking — the same voice. *The same voice,* Max. And at first I could not remember who, what, why — it was just this nagging feeling. Like when you try to remember a song or lyric, you know?"

"Mmm-hmm."

"So. I heard the voice just as the meeting

was breaking up and I could not figure out in the surge of bodies who it was who had been speaking. I'm not tall enough to see over a crowd is the problem. They were all talking a mile to the minute. Someone said the butler at the hall had shifty eyes, and someone else said she'd trust her life to that butler, and shame on anyone who suspected him. Anyway, if this one woman in the crowd had not said 'suspected' in a particular way — 'I always sus*pec*ted,' she said — I might not have picked up on it. I'm very good with voices and accents, you know — part of my stage training from when I was an undergraduate. It was a low voice, a Lauren Bacall voice."

"But you couldn't see who it was."

She shook her head. "A *low* voice," she repeated. "It might almost have been one of the men come to pick up his wife from the meeting. They'd all started to pour in by then, grabbing a share of the refreshments while they were at it."

"Okay. And this is important *why*?"

"Hold on. I'm getting to that."

And she related to him the conversation she had overheard in the steam room that day just before she took up her duties at St. Edwold's. Word for word, as much as she could remember.

"I'd never have paid much attention, but they said 'Nether Monkslip,' or one of them did, and of course I came wide-awake."

So she'd been drowsy, nodding off in the heat of the room. Still, there was no reason to discount what she thought she'd heard.

"They talked about *Strangers on a Train*?"

"That's right. But it was brought into the conversation more as if to say, 'Isn't it a shame we can't do a switch?' Rather than to say, 'Let's do a switch, what do you say.' If you follow."

Max asked her to repeat the conversation again, word for word, as much as she could remember.

"I can't be sure of a lot of it," Destiny said. "For example, when one of them said, 'They all do, once the courtship is over,' the other one said, 'Not yet. I don't believe that.' Which doesn't really make sense."

"Might it have been 'And yet, I don't believe that'?"

She shook her head. "Maybe . . . Sorry, Max, I just can't be sure."

"And whom was this phantom woman talking to?"

"That's the part I don't know, either! But given what's happened, what are the chances it wasn't Lady Baaden-Boomethistle?"

"Was Lady B-B at the meeting?"

"Almost certainly not. I asked Suzanna afterward, although it seemed unlikely to me she'd be there, given she's recently been widowed."

"The names of those present would be in the meeting minutes."

"Yes." She nodded. "Or at least the members who sent regrets, so those who were present could be extrapolated from that."

"How many were there?"

"There must have been thirty-five or forty women. When the men started to arrive — say fifty people."

She paused, thinking. The logs had burned so long, they'd acquired the look of snakeskin and would soon crumble into the hearth. Max, following her gaze, stood and replenished the wood.

"But it couldn't have been a man," she told him. "A man trying to get anywhere near that sauna would have been shot on sight. If you'd ever seen the Ladies' University Club, you'd know I'm right."

How maddening it was, not to be sure which of the two women she'd overheard was which. They'd have been easier to identify with their clothes on, somehow, clothes being very distinguishing. But the combination of the steam and the ubiquitous white towels on their heads and wrapped around their middles had rendered them anonymous.

She recalled the looks of shock or surprise from the other women when she'd put on her collar in the changing room. Yes, clothes were very distinguishing indeed.

"And she didn't recognize you from the steam room? The woman at the WI meeting?"

Destiny shook her head slowly.

"Are you sure? This could be important." He didn't want to say, "your life could be at risk," but he was thinking it.

"If I couldn't see her, I doubt she could have seen me in that crowded Village Hall — remember, I was swamped by a sea of people all taller than I am. I didn't think she saw me in the steam room, either. I was sitting on a lower shelf, beneath them, my back to the wall, with only my legs and feet sticking out."

Max thought for a moment. "Is it possible they knew you were there? That they were hoping you'd overhear?" It seemed a long shot, unless for some perverse reason the women had wanted to play games and send her on a wild-goose chase. But perhaps what was simply idle talk had later gelled into reality — into a real murder plot. In part because they'd assumed they were anonymous, voices rising as if out of the steam — that even if overheard, no one could ever trace who they were.

"That is was staged somehow?" Destiny asked. "Well . . . It's just possible, I suppose. But they are awfully good actresses, if so. And when they realized I could overhear, they shushed up very quickly."

"They *could* be good actresses. That's what a good actress would do."

"Oh, really? Well, wait until you hear this." She settled her empty teacup on the table in front of her and leaned in conspiratorially.

"There's more?"

"There's more," Destiny said.

And she told him of her near-miss accident, how she was nearly run over when she stepped off the curb near St. James's Square. How it had happened so fast, she didn't see the make of car and couldn't even be sure of its color.

So maybe she had not been as invisible in the steam room as she'd thought.

Maybe someone had followed her from the club. They'd have had to lie in wait to seize their chance — not easy to do on crowded London streets, small wonder they'd missed.

They must have been very worried about what she might have overheard.

Aloud she said, "But what bothers me about that is this: how could they know I had any connection to Nether Monkslip?"

Max was thinking a quick peek in the guest registry at the club might have clued them in.

"When you signed into the club, what forwarding address did you use for mail or things left behind?"

"Oh, I see what you mean. Nether Monkslip."

"It's possible they saw that. Or that they overheard a conversation of yours while you were in the club library or at dinner."

She thought back.

"I suppose."

But, thought Max, it didn't matter where she was from. If they realized someone in the steam room had overheard a burgeoning murder plot, they would have recognized that person was a threat. That person would have to be eliminated, wherever she was from.

And if one of the women had followed Destiny out . . . The wonder was that there had been no attempt on her life in all these months. Perhaps the fact she'd never told anyone what she'd overheard had assured her safety. Until now.

"It was a dark color is all I can tell you," she was saying. "I was flat on my face. Not so long ago, there would have been a different explanation for that. But I was stone-cold sober."

Max nodded his understanding. Destiny was an alcoholic, a fact she had shared with Max when the whole issue of being his curate had come up. Although she had been sober for years, it was still a crucial fact of her life.

"I've come to believe the reasons I drank aren't important," she had told him. "Which is a good thing, because I don't know what the reasons are or were. It was — it is — the centerpiece of my life. If you take me on, you have a right to know. I can only promise you that I wrestle with this demon every day and so far, I'm winning."

"How are you so sure?" Max had asked her. "*Alcoholic:* That's a difficult word to apply. A harsh word to apply to yourself." An AA group met weekly in the Village Hall, but it was full of people from Monkslip-super-Mare. They wanted to be truly anonymous and so were willing to make the drive to help ensure it.

She had laughed. "Oh, there were little clues. For one thing, I had bottles hidden

235

all over the house, and I lived alone. We need a new word for crazy. After hours of therapy, it was decided I was trying to hide the problem *even from myself,* a behavior Freudian in its obviousness. Or obvious in its Freudianness. Whatever. Everything about it was interfering with my life. I couldn't think beyond when I could have my next drink. It was measured sorrow — sorrow measured out in the number of empty bottles put out in the rubbish bin each week. A good week was only one bottle of my favorite whiskey. A bad week — well.

"So one day I joined a group, and I found I was far from alone. And I wasn't crazy. And I wasn't lost, not anymore."

The one thing she had learned from those meetings was that treating yourself well was the only key to being of help to anyone else. And it was the desire to help others that drove her. It was often said that the best comparison was being on a plane when the oxygen masks were deployed. You made sure your own mask was on before trying to help anyone else. Otherwise, you were all going to go down.

She had told Max all this, knowing she was still a risk. One day at a time, she was still a risk who might embarrass him in the highly political world of the Anglican Communion.

Max had not hesitated. He'd said, "The position calls for a human being, not a saint. Saints are of no use to me. People of compassion and hard-earned wisdom are."

Max said now, smiling, "So, even stone-cold sober, and even though you were nearly run over, you didn't make the connection with what you'd overheard?"

"No. Would you? Drivers in London are insane. Much worse than ever they used to be."

"Would you recognize *both* voices if you heard them again?"

She nodded her head, but doubtfully.

"They were plummy, upper-class voices is all I can say. Throaty and somehow privileged voices, if that makes any sense. Thick as cream, but rather braying — you know what I mean. One younger and one maybe slightly older, at a guess, but not *old.*"

"Do you think it was a woman connected with Totleigh Hall?"

"Had to be, don't you think? Knowing what we know now," Destiny replied. "Unless there's been another murder in Nether Monkslip I know nothing about."

Max shook his head and smiled bleakly. "Not recently."

"But it's really too bizarre to imagine, isn't

it? They could use Totleigh Hall to film a remake of *Brideshead Revisited.* All grandeur and gilt-edged glory. But you're thinking one of the women must have been the wife. Lady B-B. I've never met her, so no — no idea."

"But if you heard her voice?" Max thought nothing could be easier than to arrange a meeting. But if Lady Baaden-Boomethistle really were a deranged killer, what kind of danger would he be letting Destiny in for, then? Possibly a spot of prearranged eavesdropping was called for. . . . Destiny hidden behind a tapestry or within a stall in the stables . . . But he was forgetting: Cotton had told him Bree had a clear alibi, with multiple witnesses to prove it. The anxiety that had gripped him relaxed its hold, but only for a moment. Alibis could be faked; witnesses could be bribed.

"Maybe I'd recognize her voice," Destiny was saying. "It's been so long — I doubt my testimony would stand up in court, but at least *I'd* know. It was just a fluke I recognized the voice in all the hubbub at the meeting. Worse luck I couldn't on either occasion see to whom the voice was attached."

She paused, pushing back her thick auburn hair with both hands. She wore it

238

chopped short at the neck, as if she'd taken the scissors to it herself. She would push the curls back when she was beset by a problem, which created a most unfortunate mushroom-cloud effect: Einstein on the verge of a great discovery. Today she had applied gel in a last-ditch effort at controlling what the moist sea air creeping in from the coast would destroy. The result looked somehow inflammable.

"I am reminded of a similar situation," she told him, "in the village where I grew up. A widower who owned a small chain of shops married a much younger woman. Since he was considered to be a catch, there was a certain amount of talk, particularly among the ladies who had tried and failed to catch him. He had a son, a bit of a layabout, who didn't adjust well to the new situation, as so often is the case. As seems to be the case there at Totleigh Hall — I have heard the stepmother and the son don't get along at all. It is easy to think in clichés — older man, younger woman. The son in my village was sure the new wife was after the money. Gasping to get her hands on the pearls and the silverware. Nothing could have been further from this woman's — Betty's — true north. She was not interested in *things*. That is what people were too hidebound to see. She and her husband had fallen in love — she respected him enormously, perhaps as a father figure, but whatever. And that really was all there was to it."

"The son may have felt it was necessary to guard his mother's memory by rubbishing the woman who had taken her place. That is a very common reaction to that particular sort of grief."

Destiny nodded, adding, "The boy clearly had too much time on his hands, and a head stuffed with grievance and guilt. He used his anger to justify his failures, of course — as if his father's remarriage were the reason he never achieved anything."

Max was mulling over everything she had told him. What were the parallels to the situation at Totleigh Hall? Would grievance and guilt — anger at Bree's quick assumption of power — have led Peregrine to exact a horrible revenge against his father?

Max needed some time to focus on the case. But time was what he never seemed to have. Unless . . . "Would you take the service for me on Sunday?" he asked her suddenly.

"Of course," Destiny replied happily. "Any particular topic I should dwell on? 'Thou shall not kill'?"

He shook his head. "I think they know that already."

"All but one or two of them, perhaps."

"I'm afraid you're right about that. Just keep it short. The congregation has a limited attention span."

An hour later, one of the sudden squalls that could beset the coast sprang up, lashing tree branches against the vicarage windows and rattling the fragile panes. Destiny, watching the storm from her cottage window, decided her hair was better than a barometer — she could always tell when rain was on the way. A great crack of lightning disguised the creak of the gate leading into her front garden, a gate designed more for keeping stray animals out than for keeping the cottage dweller safe from intruders.

Fortunately, Destiny could not linger; she had promised to visit a shut-in parishioner. Stopping just long enough to throw on a coat and rain hat, she went flying down the garden path and out the gate to her car, eyes scrunched against the pelting rain. She never saw the dark figure that stepped back off the path to hide from her in the shadows.

In the same way, a roll of thunder soon disguised the creak of the gate leading into the nearby vicarage garden, and the sound of someone lightly tapping an exploratory rap at the door — a door that proved to be unlocked when that same someone tried the handle.

Max returned from securing all the windows against the storm to find Ms. Eugenia Smith-Ganderfort standing in his study, looking like the proverbial drowned rat. A man with nerves of steel, he actually jumped back an inch at the sight.

Lord help me.

"Eugenia, please — if you'd not walk in unannounced. That is what Mrs. Hooser is for."

Actually, what Mrs. Hooser was for was anyone's guess, and the skeptical look on Eugenia's face seemed to confirm the absurdity of Max's assertion. But she merely said, "I'm sorry, Father Max. It *is* a vicarage, and thus I thought it was open to all who need your help."

"Of course it is, just not . . ." *Oh, what is the use?* "What is it you wanted, Mrs. Smith-Ganderfort?" he said, distancing himself with the formal address. Her disappointment at this change showed in her crestfallen gaze. The wind set up a howl just then beneath the eaves. He imagined he could feel the roof lifting, as if the old place might take flight, with him and her in it.

"Oh, nothing, really. I was . . . I was just wondering how the murder investigation is coming along."

Really? "I don't know a lot about it —"

"Oh, but that's not true. Everyone knows you are at the very center of things. You always are."

"— at least, nothing I'm at liberty to discuss," he concluded firmly. What did she imagine as she stood there, water from her slicker dripping onto the vicarage carpet? That he would invite her to sit down and pick over the clues with him?

"That wife of his is not all she pretends to be, you know."

Another country heard from. Unfairly or not, while he would be inclined to give credence to whatever Noah or Destiny speculated, he would doubt any contribution of Eugenia's. If Bree reminded Destiny in some Miss Marple–like fashion of a situation in her old village, an innocent accused, there might be something to it. This, however . . .

"She's unfaithful to him, you know."

Masking his annoyance, Max said, "If you know anything for certain, you must tell DCI Cotton. I'm not at lib—"

"He'll think I'm just guessing. I'm not

guessing. I know. I understand the human heart! I hear its cries. Just because I live in a small village doesn't mean I don't know anything of life. Oh, I know about *life* all right!" She paused, looking at him intently, willing his eyes to meet hers. "Don't you feel it, too, Father Max?"

"Hmm?"

"The electricity. Don't you feel it, too?"

Max, listening with only half his attention — really, he wanted to get back to his work while he had five minutes to himself; Awena would be closing the shop in a few minutes and they had little enough time alone as it was. So he said, "The rug shock the other day, you mean? That was just —"

"You must have felt it, too," she told him earnestly. "That current that runs between like minds — minds thinking alike. *Being* alike. From the beginning, I've felt it — that . . . that awareness, like being drawn to like. Soul to soul."

Oh my Lord. He reached blindly for his chair and sat down, hard. This was worse than anything Max could have imagined. He felt he was staring, not for the first time in his life, straight into the face of madness. Only this time it was not the egomania of a drug lord or the paranoia of a terrorist steeped in religious mania, but a harmless woman of middle years who was undoubtedly too much alone in the world.

The recent words Destiny had used echoed: *Too much time on her hands.*

Was she harmless?

He debated with himself what was best to do. How to extricate himself without harming or alarming her. In the end, he reminded himself that arguing with a delusional person only gave credence to their beliefs, allowing them to set the agenda. Much better to change the subject.

And better still, to leave the conversation, as gently but decisively as could be.

"I am afraid I must visit Miss Pitchford today," he told her, pulling his jacket from the back of his chair. "Mrs. Hooser will have to show you out."

And then, as always, his unfailing kindness kicked in. He could not bear to injure someone so fragile.

"Thank you for stopping by," he said.

CHAPTER 14
ST. EDWOLD'S

Outside, the storm had become an insistent drizzle shot from a lowering sky. Max grabbed his mackintosh from the row of hooks by the vicarage door and pulled it on over his jacket, tugging the collar up against the wind.

He had told Eugenia the truth about his planned itinerary — but he was headed first to the church, *then* to check on Miss Agnes Pitchford. She had an increasing tendency to fall — a particular worry with her fragile, aging bones, according to Dr. Winship — and so Max would often look in on her.

God would have to forgive him for the almost-white lie — he didn't feel it was wise to give Eugenia a minute-by-minute account of his plans. The topic of his sermon mocked him, but the ends must sometimes justify the means. Must they not? Or was everything to be put in God's hands while mankind stood passively by?

As he set out, Max could see the Cavalier, alight like a beacon against the darkening storm. In springtime, the seductive aroma of hot cross buns would fill the High, a temptation to anyone trying to lose that extra half stone before swimsuit season. The ever-enterprising Elka, who had started her business serving customers on her mother's old wedding china, would also offer egg-shaped Easter biscuits and marzipan bunnies with near-transparent ears. Max's favorite Easter treat was the simnel cake, a tradition believed to have originated in the Middle Ages, with its eleven marzipan balls representing Jesus' disciples, minus the one who had betrayed him.

At this time of year, with Hallowe'en approaching, Elka's shop would be filled with the aroma of bread pudding and plum and blackberry crumble and apple pie and hot spiced drinks, with a bit of rum-soaked cake thrown in to keep her customers warm.

The early church had tried to stop the Samhain practices that welcomed the return of the dead, along with other pagan customs like the sacred springtime cakes, but in the end the church fathers had decided to pick their battles more wisely. As Samhain became All Souls' Day, so the pagan celebrations of the spring equinox had morphed into the Feast of the Annunciation. The date for Easter itself was not fixed and unchanging, but tied in a most paganlike fashion to the phases of the moon. There had been various other Christian fiddles designed to win converts. It was overall a better plan than annihilating people outright, Max felt.

As his steps took him past Miss Pitchford's cottage, he threw a glance over his shoulder to see if Eugenia had followed him to catch him in a lie. She had not. He did see the telltale twitch of Miss Pitchford's lace curtains. She must be feeling better if she was spying on the neighborhood again. "Keeping tabs," as she called it. "For security's sake." At least, she had the sense to hang curtains to hide behind, but then she had her standards. Those curtains, to his certain knowledge, were washed and starched every month. That was how she had suffered her last fall, rehanging them from a stepladder. But she would suffer in steely-eyed silence rather than allow the white lace to yellow.

Miss Pitchford would sometimes lure Max to her cottage with the guilty pleasure of a Battenberg cake, a checkered edifice glued together with a hardened sugary frosting. These were special occasions, when Max had a bit of information she was anxious to pry loose, generally having to do with a murder investigation. The fact that Max remained incorruptible despite these blandishments did not stop her from trying. She would sit before him, her black skirt primly tucked over her support hose — pink industrial-grade stockings that looked as if they could be used in bridge construction — and prod and insinuate until Max was forced into a defensive posture, attempting to save her latest target from social ostracism. He was quite certain that given recent events in the village, one of these cakes awaited him, threatening to spoil his dinner. His biggest debate with himself for the moment was whether to allow this to happen.

The sight of Miss Pitchford's curtains returned him to a rare memory of his MI5 days, when he had helped crack a case of corporate espionage. The corporation had been housed in one of those glass monstrosities ubiquitous in London, and Max quickly realized the spy had only to rent a flat across the way and use binoculars to watch through the plate-glass windows as workers logged in to their computers. A search for the flat most recently let had led straight to the culprit.

But his days with Five were long over, put on the shelf with a sigh of relief.

Max passed the churchyard, on the look-out for dormice; Awena had told him a family of them was nesting there. She had come into the vicarage carrying a hazelnut, announcing that she was going to mail it to the Dormouse Officer at the People's Trust for Endangered Species.

"They can tell by the teeth marks if a dormouse has nibbled it open. The hazel dormouse is vanishing and they've started a project to monitor where they live."

"The Dormouse Officer?"

"Officer. That's right. I'm sure they mean it as a little joke, but it's tremendously serious. The mice are dying out because we've destroyed their native habitats. The Trust has resorted to catch-and-release programs."

"They must be rather easy to catch," said Max.

"How, easy?"

"They're generally asleep. It must be a matter of just scooping them up with a spatula and relocating them to a nearby woods. If they're anything like my church mice, they can sleep through anything, even organ and choir practice. Not to mention my sermons."

Awena smiled. "Dearest, no mouse would think of sleeping through a sermon of yours.

Anyway, they generally hibernate between October and May. I understand they do snore a bit."

"But quietly. Unlike some of the parishioners."

In the middle of his reverie, a black cat seemed to drop from the sky, landing at his feet. A startled Max realized it had jumped from the top of the church's lych-gate. A pair of yellow eyes stared at him briefly, dismissively. He was reminded of the irredeemable Luther, whom he had often been tempted to excommunicate, as the eccentric poet and vicar of Morwenstow had done to his cat, allegedly for mousing on a Sunday. Unsettled, Max looked behind him to see if the cat was following, or Eugenia, but the cat had vanished. He saw Eugenia slipping into the Cavalier.

He shook off his feeling of unease. What was the superstition about black cats anyway? It had looked a perfectly nice cat, well fed and loved.

Max passed the Plague Tree on his way through the churchyard. The tree was believed to have been planted centuries ago and was said to mark the final resting place of dozens of Nether Monkslippers, who had been deposited there when there were too many corpses to bury and too few people left alive to bury them properly. Max could not walk by the tree without an inward shudder at their fate. Even in a time when medicine could seemingly cure anything, there remained the threat to mankind of the rogue virus that no vaccination could prevent and no treatment cure.

St. Edwold's was as typical an old village English church as could be found. But everyone agreed it was a special place, preserved in an amber glow of rare tranquility. Its very air seemed permeated with a calm that cloaked the visitor on entering.

Max had often thought the building resembled an illuminated manuscript. Skilled masons had chiseled the stone surrounding each of its windows to encase the precious glass; the wood had been embossed at each point of intersection in the roof, the designs picked out by colorful paints.

As Max entered, shutting the door on the wind at his back, a small group of women was emerging from St. Eddie's, the church's coffee shop. Located in a corner of the crypt, it had begun as an experiment, opening after Morning Prayer to give people a place to gather and chat. Max had given Elka Garth the concession, limiting the coffee shop's open hours so as not to cut into her tearoom profits. St. Eddie's was soon a great success as a meeting place for young mothers and pensioners, and had expanded into an evening gathering spot for village youth. Elka welcomed the new revenue stream, once she was able to hire reliable help to man the coffeepots and serve fairy cakes from behind the small counter. That this reliable help took the form of her formerly lackadaisical son was a source of wonder to all who knew them and their fraught history.

Max stopped to shake the rain from his mac. Unusually, the church had a small fireplace built into the wall of its porch, near the entrance door, and a stone bench protruding from the adjoining wall. In times past, before the Village Hall had been built, the village worthies would hold their meetings there. He tried and failed to picture today's villagers draped in old-time costume, something grayly medieval with intricately starched collars, or perhaps looking like characters sprung to life from *A Christmas Carol.* Would they have gathered to discuss the duck race? The Harvest Fayre? A sighting of witches?

Max stepped into the jewel-like interior of the nave, anticipating the peace he knew would descend on his spirit. St. Edwold's

was a still and holy place, hushed and waiting for the centuries to pass. It always
seemed to Max as if God had just left the
space for a moment and that if one waited
patiently enough, God would return. Can-
terbury Cathedral, a sort of hub for Angli-
cans, might be awesome, a place Thomas à
Becket had made holy by having been
murdered there. But St. Edwold's humbled
and lifted the spirit as no grand cathedral
could. It spoke immediately of centuries of
worship, of its centrality to village life — an
intimate place of baptisms and weddings
and burials of members of the local families.
Lord Bayer Baaden-Boomethistle was simply the latest Totleigh Hall noble to be laid
to rest from St. Edwold's.

Max walked past a stall where jars of
donated jams and chutneys were displayed,
there to help raise funds for the church.
There had been a significant uptick in these
sales from visitors in recent weeks, so he
had been told by Mr. Stackpole, the church
sexton.

Someone had left a Hansel and Gretel
trail of Cheerios on the floor of the fourth
pew from the altar. No doubt these spores
had been left by the Rancine child, who
seemed to require constant bribery and attention from his parents. Not like Owen,

thought Max complacently, who fusses only when an undeniably good reason presents itself.

Max paused in front of the altar, making a reverent bow. The altar wore the prescribed green of the church season, for through October they were in Ordinary Time. The lessons and hymns followed their set rotation, as well. Each cycle of the year told a different story, the symbolism and routine as comforting to Max as the return of the harvest moon.

A woman was praying in a pew near the face — the image that stubbornly reappeared on the wall of the north aisle, near the Lady Chapel. If anything, the visage of the bearded man with closed eyes practically shone from the wall, now outlined with a startling clarity. The woman — middle-aged and smartly dressed in cotton slacks and a colorful print blouse, a scarf around her neck and gold at her ears — was not anyone he recognized from the village, but that was becoming a common occurrence. She may have been visiting, one of the many being drawn by the stories of the face's miraculous properties. She may even have been one of the weekenders from London; although Nether Monkslip was too far away for anything like daily use of one of the cottages, the trade in second homes was booming. The distance did not stop people from buying up any of the charming thatched cottages they could, for a price that no elderly pensioner could refuse.

In a corner of the church, nearly hidden behind a pillar, sat Ana Cutler, one of his parishioners. The sight of her sent a rush of pity through him, along with a sense of how prideful he was — Owen, the perfect baby! — and how delicate was the foothold these fragile lives had on this life.

He called up the small face of the Cutler boy from his memory. Not all babies are by definition cute, although all are adorable. The Cutler baby had been born looking like a wizened old man, with a prominent nose and gooseberry eyes. His saving grace, and every baby had one, was his calm and quiet demeanor. Nothing upset him. If he was hungry or wet, he waited patiently until someone remembered to feed or change him. Nothing seemed to excite him, either. He regarded the world with that pop-eyed, good-natured but detached stare and seemed to have no comment to make on it.

By the time he was four years old, it was evident something was seriously wrong with little Bruce. He began an ordeal of specialists and hospitals — "trial by doctor," as his mother put it.

Max visited him in hospital as often as he could. The boy seemed to sprout more tubes and wires each time Max saw him. Finally, his immune system completely compromised, he was moved to a sterile hospital unit where only his parents, shrouded in space-age high-tech gear, were allowed their too-brief visits. The visits finally became about saying good-bye.

"I've told him I will see him in heaven," his mother had told Max. "And he's starting to fret about that. 'When will I get there? How will you find me?' I don't know what to tell him. I don't want to lie, but I don't want to frighten him, either."

Max had thought about it overnight, and called on her the next day.

"Has he ever been in an airport?" he asked her.

"Several times. We visit my mother in Portugal whenever we can."

"Then tell him this. When he gets to heaven, he is to have a sign made up with your name on it. Like the drivers do at the airport. Your full name: Mrs. Ana Marie Regis Cutler. Then he is to wait at the entrance to heaven, where the new arrivals disembark, and where you are sure to see him with the sign. If he asks, tell him he won't have to wait but a few minutes. Time is different there."

Ana Marie had smiled a rather wobbly smile and said she thought that would work. Then she had burst into uncontrollable floods of tears.

It was the maddest sort of improvisation on Max's part, but it had worked, easing the child over the roughest spots.

The hardest parts for Ana, of course, came after.

The well-dressed woman from "away" had left now, a gold-bedecked stranger who had come seeking solace. Praying for a miracle cure? The theme all around the village of Nether Monkslip seems to be healing, Max reflected.

He thought he saw Bree just then, leaving the church. Was it she he had seen kneeling in prayer in one of the pews? Perhaps her husband's death had affected her more deeply than she was being given credit for in the village — more deeply than he or anyone knew. Just because she had never been a regular at services did not mean she wasn't a believer.

He stood before the face, the face "painted," or whatever it was, on the wall. Steeped, somehow, into the very fabric of the wall. Noticed first by Tom, still so small that when he knelt in church beside his mother, he disappeared from Max's view at the altar.

How often Max had requested the stain be painted over, because of its potential to draw media attention — which it had done, slowly and surely. It wouldn't be long before television reporters descended on the village, shirttails out and microphones blazing.

Max had often reflected that it might be a first, trying to whitewash a miracle.

If it were a miracle.

According to the sexton, it was. And if ever there lived a man not given to fanciful ideas, it was Mr. Stackpole. Dry and humorless, literal-minded and punctilious. The melancholy, rail-thin Mr. Stackpole would no more dream up a miracle than he would file a false report with Her Majesty's Revenue and Customs Office. It was unthinkable.

Mr. Stackpole emerged daily from his uncluttered cottage with its neatly shorn thatched roof, regular as clockwork, to attend to his duties at the church. These duties were carried out with military precision and a minimum of fuss, for which Max was grateful, even though anything like ebullience and human warmth were sadly not in

Mr. Stackpole's repertoire. Where others might feud over the interpretation of a passage in Isaiah, Mr. Stackpole did not stoop to feud — not he. What he knew to be true was right and incontrovertible and any suggestion of a different understanding of the facts was preposterous.

As he undoubtedly would have said at one time, miracles were for those of the Roman persuasion. The Anglican Communion had not been tested in the fires of the Reformation only to revert in the twenty-first century to popish ways.

So if he said they were living in a time of miracles, no doubt they were.

It was little Tom who had walked into Max's study just the other week and announced, "Jesus is back."

And Max's spirits fell at the news. Because he knew this was not news of the Second Coming, but a statement of fact. The Christlike visage that kept appearing on the wall of St. Edwold's Church, despite repeated lashings of whitewash by Maurice, the church handyman, had somehow once again managed to emerge.

No one could guess the cause of this apparition, and Max had had experts in to look. Leaks had been ruled out: The roof was brand-new, thanks to the unexpected legacy, so that wasn't the answer. There were no pipes to burst behind that wall, and no strange mold was growing, although bleach also had been tried.

There was no answer for it. Most of all there was no answer for the fact that the face did not just sort of look like a face — the kind of image that might be imagined on a slice of toast in some online hoax. It looked like a very good negative image of a man's face, the eyes closed in death. It looked exactly like the face on the famous Shroud of Turin. An image some scientists claimed had been created by ultraviolet lasers, in an age without such a thing. A negative image, created by a sudden flash of light.

Created using a technology that did not yet exist.

Max now stood staring again at this apparition, this source of such consternation. The draw for thrill seekers and cure seekers. Today was a slow day; generally, there would have been a dozen or more people here, staring and gawking or devoutly praying before the image. Tomorrow there would be more. And probably exponentially more after that. For adding to the cult of fascination that was forming around this image at St. Edwold's was the fact that news of his find at Monkbury Abbey had now hit the airwaves.

There had been a slow trickle of curiosity seekers at first, then a flood, for Suzanna in her capacity as editor of the parish newsletter had chosen to write an article about the face, and she had put the newsletter online before Max could stop her. From there, it had spread like wildfire. Like a plague of locusts. Like — whatever was unstoppable.

He looked again at the image. Surely its eyes were not beginning to open, just slightly? Mentally, Max shook himself and the illusion wavered and disappeared.

Max closed his own eyes in brief prayer, and when he opened them again, the face was back to the way it always had been. He thought, *Let it stand. Just let it be.* He would give up all attempts at whitewashing the face on the wall. It was increasingly pointless to try. The face kept coming back, showing through, now shining through.

Maurice, when asked, had professed to be as baffled as Max.

"It's good-quality paint I've been using. No cheap stuff," he told Max.

"I know. I believe you."

"There's no good reason for this."

"I know."

Max was overwhelmed by it all. He had

first roped off the area to keep the curious at a distance; then he had had to institute opening and closing hours for the church itself. For the first time in its history, St. Edwold's Church was closed and locked at night. The fear was that someone would damage the face, try to steal it by cutting it out of the wall, plaster and all. Why they should do this, Max couldn't say, but there was an element of crazed frenzy growing. The halt and the lame came to pray, and most particularly, those losing their sight came to pray before the face.

For that was its legend, that it could cure blindness.

And many had reported a cure. They would return from a doctor's visit with documentation that their eyesight was clearing, all without medical intervention.

Max was glad for them, even as he assumed a placebo effect was at work.

He was also frightened. How to maintain the pristine serenity of his church once it became a focus of international attention?

The face may have struck him initially as more of a Catholic relic — a hangover from the days of miracles and wonder. But he had also thought, pragmatically, it might bring people back to faith — to believing in something outside themselves, to asking the age-old questions of why we humans are here in the first place.

All of Nether Monkslip, he realized now, gathering all the threads in one hand, was awash in this theme of healing. Awena herself was a healer — of that, he was sure. A healer of souls, a healer of bodies; Awena with her salves and herbs and potions.

There was also the healing spring by the menhirs on Hawk Crest, where holy relics had been buried.

And now the healing attributed to St. Edwold's, with its miraculous face.

Was all of Nether Monkslip a holy place, a sort of spiritual nexus in one of the world's thin places?

He remembered a conversation back in his student days. The conversation over several beers had drifted to Joan of Arc and her Cross of Lorraine, and to her miraculous pipeline to heaven, and the question had been, first of all, whether God had involved Himself in a matter that amounted to local politics.

As for Joan herself, was she delusional? Schizophrenic? Or was she simply a superior sort of teenager, endowed with perceptiveness and courage beyond her years? Certainly she deserved better than she got, to be left to her ghastly fate by the man she had been sent by her God to save.

He turned at the sound of a heel scraping against the stone floor, and somehow he was not surprised to find Eugenia standing there. He kept the irritation he felt from his expression. How had he not realized she had followed him? But he had seen her go into the Cavalier with his own eyes. His MI5 training was wearing thin if Eugenia Smith-Ganderfort could outsmart him.

"Oh, good evening, Father Max," she said brightly and a little too loudly in an unconvincing show of surprise, as though Max were the last person she expected to see in a church, his own church. Her hand flew up to tame the untamable hair.

Max realized with full force that he was facing a situation that did not lend itself to logic. A glance at her face, scored with harsh lines of distress and permanent displeasure, was all he needed to convince him of that.

"You said you were going to see Miss Pitchford," she said accusingly.

He remembered now that look she had given Awena, and his heart seized for a moment. At all costs, this situation had to be contained. Resisting the rash impulse to ask her what business it was of hers, he said very softly, in his hostage-negotiator voice, "I remembered I had some other business to attend to first. Oh, and look." He looked with elaborate, exaggerated care at his watch. "I'm late for my appointment with her now."

Half an hour later, Max left Miss Pitchford's, setting his steps toward home and Awena and Owen. Tonight, Awena had told him, they were having lentil soup, garden salad, home-baked bread, and pumpkin panna cotta for pudding. He had looked forward to the meal all afternoon. It was a sign of his contentment he had forgotten how thoroughly he once had disliked lentils. Had not, truth be told, been certain what a lentil was.

The fuss over the face would ebb, he told himself now, and the villagers would go about their normal routines. It would all be forgotten as common sense prevailed. It was probably dying out already, and — oh no — His eye fell on a sign outside the Onlie Begetter bookshop.

Tonight Only! Frank Cuthbert, world-famous, best-selling author of *Wherefore Nether Monkslip*.

The wildly popular book critics rave about — in which the miraculous secret of Monkbury Abbey was revealed, for the first time, to an astonished world!

Only at the Onlie Begetter. Tonight at 7:00 P.M. sharp. Tickets 30 pounds — includes the price of a copy of the book, SIGNED BY THE AUTHOR!!! LIMIT: 1 COPY!

Oh good merciful God in heaven, thought Max. In a just world, no one would attend. Just as people of good sense had scrupulously avoided Frank and his blasted book for years, now they would shun this renewed publicity push with its strong whiff of snake oil.

He supposed he should be happy for Adam Birch, owner of the Onlie Begetter bookshop, and he was: This kind of megaevent with Frank, the Sun King, would keep the beloved little shop running in the black for a long time. Adam had stuck by Frank from the beginning, hosting signings back in the day when even Frank's bichon frise had to be dragged to the poorly attended events. But the throngs — and Max had no doubt there would be throngs — would only increase the crush to visit the center of all the to-do: St. Edwold's itself, already becoming something of a shrine.

Max supposed he wouldn't mind as much if people stayed for the service, and some of them did. But most just came to gawp, and to drip candle wax all over the floor, and to leave little petitions tacked to the walls of the church. Rarely if ever did they think to leave a donation to the church, and Max resolutely refused to charge admission.

He wasn't, as he would tell Awena that night, running a sideshow.

His thoughts clouded in the day-to-day, he almost failed to notice Eugenia standing beneath the eaves of the church, watching his progress toward home.

It shook him. Again, it was not something he would have missed in his MI5 days.

CHAPTER 15
THE DUCK RACE

The day of the duck race dawned clear, cool, and sunny, the sky scrubbed blue by the recent rain, with only a light breeze to ruffle the water of the river Puddmill. Max led the Morning Prayer service with a heart alight with gratitude for the day, sped through his routine parish chores, and headed out quickly so as not to miss the beginning of the race. He himself had two ducks in the race, Suzanna having pestered him relentlessly to "set a good example." Awena had painted his ducks black and put a small clerical collar around their necks, while hers wore a crown of miniature autumn leaves.

Once these entries had been duly numbered and recorded, Max walked through the growing crowd of villagers, greeting and being greeted in turn. It took him half an hour to walk a few yards, as he had to stay and chat with so many friends and parishioners. Awena had told him she was running late but would join him later. She'd arrive with Owen, which would mean they'd soon be enveloped by a group of cooing villagers.

He was surprised to see Major Batton-Smythe and Lily Iverson in attendance — rather, he was surprised to see that she had apparently allowed the Major to escort her to the festivities. The pair had been engaged in a would-they or would-they-not dance for ages now, but the good money said Lily, now rumored to be a self-made millionairess, either preferred her single state or was holding out for someone a little less stodgy than the Major.

Max saw Chanel, the self-help expert, flirting rather tipsily with Bill Travis, the estate manager, horse trainer, and more — "so very much more," as Suzanna would put it — from Totleigh Hall. The "more" was only if one were inclined to believe the rumors of his amorous exploits, and Max was rather inclined to, even granted his very slight acquaintance with the man. Bill Travis, he realized now, reminded him of someone from his university days — someone to whom Max had taken an intense dislike, someone who had proved to be, in fact, untrustworthy. An embezzler, as it turned out. Travis stood talking with Chanel, rather looming over her, flexing his biceps and clearly enjoying himself. Max remembered he'd looked much the same when talking with Rosamund, also an attractive woman, but of a completely different type. He'd marked Rosamund down as bookish, rather the sort to try to gather her experience via books and films; Chanel struck him as more a woman of the world. Perhaps the chase was all, so far as Bill Travis was concerned. He probably flirted just to keep in practice.

Chanel was looking particularly autumnal, dressed in earth tones: She wore a brown polo-neck jumper under a flowing rust-colored tunic, and dark slacks tucked into expensive-looking boots. She held a glass of white wine, from which she drank freely, even though it was not yet twelve, but she was not alone in this. Most people saw the duck race as a chance for a bit of a knees-up, and since this year the race was so near the harvest celebration . . . Well, why not, thought Max. Everyone looked happy in the Edenic garden that was Nether Monkslip, despite recent tragedies, and he was grateful for anything that helped them forget, if only for a few moments. Max himself bought a half pint from the stall set up for the purpose, and a Cornish pasty from Elka

271

Garth. She was swamped with customers, so Max didn't pause to talk, but she handed him her duck and asked him to enter it in the race for her. It wore a doll-size version of a cavalier's hat. Max began to think this time of year was much better for a duck race, as it allowed a sort of dress rehearsal of Hallowe'en costumes.

They had come through some tough times together as a village, he thought, what with the odd cluster of murders and all — not just the death by beheading of their liege lord. Surely all that was past now. If he could solve this crime at the very heart of village life, wouldn't that be enough to placate the ancient gods that seemed to have been stirred up since his arrival? Max shook off the fancy as both silly and self-centered. Not to mention somewhat un-Christian. It was purest awful coincidence that so many had been done to death by murder most foul since his arrival.

It seemed as if the entire village was there. Destiny Chatsworth was not at the race, though; she had told Max she'd be visiting an ailing parishioner in Chipping Monkslip, a woman with whom she'd formed a fast friendship, but that she'd try to get back to the village in time for the festivities. She was to have dinner with Max and Awena that night. Destiny had quickly become one of Awena's favorites, not least because she, too, was an accomplished vegetarian cook. The two women could engage for hours over whether to use tarragon or coriander for roasted carrots and parsnips.

Adam Birch would join them after he'd closed the bookshop, making a fourth for dinner. Although Max knew that he and Elka were rapidly becoming an item, Elka had to work at her tea shop this particular night.

Max entered Elka's duck in the race and continued to stroll around, savoring the crumbs from the delicious pasty and wondering whether to buy another. So many people gathered! If Eugenia were one of them, she had made herself invisible for once. Oh, wait — he had spoken too soon. She was there, standing apart, her lips a slash of deep red lipstick, and her wild hair tied back in a black scarf like a nun's. The lipstick looked experimental, haphazardly applied. He averted his eyes, as if that would make him invisible to her. He actually stepped back, and in doing so, he bumped into Rosamund. From her flustered reaction, Max was the last person she wanted to see, perhaps apart from Cotton.

The accidental meeting seemed almost to

force something out of Rosamund, much as the jolt had momentarily forced the air from her lungs. She looked at him, galvanized. It was nearly the same look he was getting used to seeing from Eugenia. Rosamund gasped and her eyes actually welled up with tears.

"Father, there's something I need to tell you. It's been bothering me. A lot. I need to tell — I need someone to tell that DCI what — what I've, well . . . what I've —"

"What you've done?" Max prompted. He took her arm and gently led her outside the crowd to a stand of oaks farther from the riverbank, where he continued. "This wouldn't have anything to do with your stepmother, would it?"

She hung her head, not able to look at him. The gesture made her glasses — today they were purple frames with yellow bows — slide down. Roughly, she pushed them back up to the bridge of her nose, wiping away a tear that had escaped the rim of one eye while she was at it.

"It was in the stables and I picked it up," she said. "I only meant to return it, really. Honestly. Even though it had been my mother's. Bree had no right —"

"The hair ornament, you mean. Gold with the initials B-B on it."

She sniffed. "Yes." Her voice was barely audible; she was still talking to the ground, unable to face him.

"And not just initials, either, but strands of hair caught in the clasp. Rosamund, look at me."

It took her several seconds to do so, but finally she lifted her bright red face to him and said, "I feel so foolish. It was stupid of me. Bill is crazy about her, you see, and I — I guess all I could think was that I wanted her out of the way. I found my father lying there like that and I think — I really think I lost my mind for a few minutes. I *knew* she'd done it, you see. I just knew it. There was no question in my mind. And I wanted her punished. She had to pay. I couldn't let her get away with it. I felt that thing in my pocket and . . . Don't you see, for her to have anything of my mother's, anything at all — the thought was just unbearable. You do see, don't you? Can you tell Cotton for me, maybe not mentioning me in the telling?"

Max shook his head. "You know I can't do that. It is just lucky for you she has an alibi for the time in question."

"She does?" Rosamund's shoulders slumped with relief.

Max nodded.

"I'm sorry I told you, then."

Max nearly laughed. "If confession is good for the soul, it is much better if it brings no repercussions. I get that. But if the DNA from the hair points to Bree, as it likely will do, I will have to set the record straight. I'm obligated to do that anyway."

"I don't see wh—" she began.

"But I'm not obligated to ask Cotton to do anything official. You could be charged with perverting the course of justice, you do realize? But I can have a word. I do think finding your father as you did may have caused you to lose all sense of reason. It would do so in the strongest person."

She nodded eagerly. "It was just an impulse. The thing was still in my pocket and I just threw it there. And I ran. As fast as I could. I was thinking of going back for it, but I couldn't — I just couldn't bring myself to do it. Then your dog — I heard her. My God, I don't think I'll ever forget that sound."

Neither, thought Max, will I.

The shouting nearer the river had intensified; the start of the race was at hand.

"Come on," said Max. "Let's join the others. We can talk more about this later."

By now the villagers had clotted together at the foot of the bridge, from where they

would, on the signal from Bill Travis —
"Steady. *Go!*" — wind up their ducks and
set them loose on the water. Inevitably,
there were tragedies: ducks that failed
mechanically, or that were capsized by the
first wave, or driven into the muddy bank.
It was often not so much a matter of which
made it to the finish line as which outlasted
the competition.

It was against the rules to retrieve the
ducks or aid them in any way once they had
set off, although some villagers seemed to
feel that yelling their heads off and waving
their arms about would make their ducks
paddle faster — the din as the finish line
approached for the survivors was deafening.

This day, however, there emerged a clear
winner. Rosamund's duck, wearing tiny
doll's glasses tied on by a narrow purple
ribbon, survived a collision with another
duck, one that happened to be sponsored
by her brother, Peregrine. The collision
actually impelled her duck forward, and it
easily putted its way past the competition
and over the finish line.

Peregrine did not look at all happy with
the result.

Peregrine hated losing.

CHAPTER 16
MAX AND THE BISHOP

Days later, Max was summoned on short notice to the bishop's presence. He adjusted his calendar, putting off obligations where he could, and made the short drive via the dual carriageway to Monkslip Cathedral, home and headquarters of the Right Reverend Nigel St. Stephen.

Cooling his heels in the outer office under the watchful, appraising eyes of the bishop's secretary, Max browsed the magazines on the coffee table with every appearance of absorbed fascination ("No Taizé, Please: We're British" and "Beyond the Fairy Cake Sale: Online Fundraising"), wondering all the while if the bishop might pull the plug at last on his investigative activities. He had been supportive of Max's extracurricular doings in the past, but that was not to say the man's patience was limitless.

At last, Max was admitted into the bishop's high-tech office in the low-tech medieval room with its paneled walls and stunning views over the cathedral close. The bishop was wired for the New Age, and every piece of furniture in the space was functional, with lots of stainless steel and glass and clean modern lines.

With a small inner sigh, Max saw the bishop had a copy of a newspaper open in front of him. This would not be alarming in normal circumstances, but the bishop's office tended to run clear of anything that might resemble clutter; the bishop was an early adopter of the ideal of the paperless office. Also, the *Monkslip-super-Mare Globe and Bugle,* in the minds of most of its readers, was in and of itself nothing but an untidy hodgepodge of fiction dressed as fact, random at least in terms of having a philosophical or even a political through line.

Now the bishop tapped one index finger against the offending headline of the newspaper.

Appalled, Max saw a photo of himself he had not known existed. It pictured him emerging from the Horseshoe side by side with DCI Cotton. The pair had met there just two days before to discuss the case over a pub lunch — it was then that Max had given Cotton the fuller details of Rosamund's deception over the hair clip, pleading her case for leniency. The photographer had caught Max waving his arms animatedly as DCI Cotton looked on, apparently fascinated, and the caption beneath the photo read "Father Max Tudor explains the finer points of detection to the police officer in charge of investigating the shocking Totleigh Hall murder." Great. How Cotton would love that. It made him look like a credulous dolt and Max like Sherlock Holmes. This photo of Max the Great Detective and his disciple ran side by side with a smaller photo of Lord Baaden-Boomethistle, "whose headless corpse was discovered in the woods of Totleigh Hall by the sleuthing priest." The paper had chosen to run a headshot of the lord, a choice Max could only hope had not been made in deliberate bad taste.

The editor also had included, for no apparent good reason, a photo of Bree, Lady Baaden-Boomethistle, taken on her wedding day outside a registry office in London. Her skirt had been caught by the wind, allowing for a sort of Marilyn Monroe moment, which the editor undoubtedly had been unable to resist. She was smiling and her husband, head firmly attached, was beaming. It looked to Max as if it had been a happy occasion.

"Have a seat, Father Gumshoe," said the bishop, not bothering to hide his annoyance. "I hope I haven't interrupted your investigation too much by calling this meeting?"

Max sat as instructed, arms resting on the wide arms of the chair, adopting a relaxed attitude he did not really feel. He ignored the bishop's question, which was clearly meant only to showcase his irritation.

"We have a lot to talk about," the bishop began.

Isn't that the truth, thought Max. He tilted his head to one side expectantly. Much better, he had discovered, to let the bishop guide the conversation. That way the real issues — the things Max was not quite ready to discuss — often went, well, undetected.

"I rang the editor of this execrable newspaper to explain our position."

We have a position? Good, good. Max was hopeful. If "we" had a position, that could only mean the bishop was on his side.

"I did not, overall, sense a keen intelligence at work behind the man's surface geniality."

"No," Max allowed. "No, one probably would not expect to find that." A regular reader of the *Globe and Bugle,* since it was the only game in town for following local events, Max could honestly say *intelligence* was not the word that generally came to the forefront of his mind. *Scurrilous* and *rubbish* often did. The paper was only saved from lawsuits for slander, one sensed, by the comedic quality of much of the sly innuendo, the allegations that stretched nearly into the realm of science fiction. Max and Awena often read bits of the paper aloud to each other of a morning, to start the day off with a laugh. Max had missed this morning's paper only because he had already been on the road to Monkslip Cathedral.

"It is difficult to say what angle of the man's 'story,' for lack of a better word, was most alarming."

Alarming. This could not be good. What did he mean by alar—

"There is, of course, the whole question of whether your parish duties are being subverted by these investigations."

"I assure you, Bishop, particularly now that I have a curate — she is working out wonderfully well, by the way — I have —"

"I am certain that is the case. I would have heard if it were otherwise. You have an . . . an *active* group of parishioners who would not hesitate to complain if anything were being neglected." The bishop stole another glance at the newspaper. "Really, it's quite a good, photogenic portrait of you, Max. You do look dashing, if you don't mind my saying so. How fortunate you were wearing your collar, so the press could play up the whole Father Brown angle. Perhaps we could use you on a recruitment poster. 'Max Tudor, Celebrity Sleuth.' And of course they have emphasized your rumored MI5 background in the article. Too good to resist, along with the cheesecake shot of Lady Baaden-Boomethistle. Let's see — ah yes, here it is: 'According to his parishioners, Father Maxen Tudor, smothered by the Official Secrets Act, is not able to discuss his background, but it is believed he was instrumental in breaking up the more venomous of the drug cartels plying their heartless trade in London.'"

"Regrettable," murmured Max. He couldn't tell if the bishop were more exasperated with the media than with Max himself. Perhaps it was a mixture of both.

" 'Heartless trade.' That's rather good. I must remember to use that in my next antidrug speech when I visit the schools. How are Awena and the baby doing, by the way?"

"Oh!" Max, as often happened, was

thrown off by the bishop's change of topic. "Right as rain. Just fine, Bishop. Owen is such a joy, I can't tell you."

"Remember, I have four of my own," said the bishop, pointing to the family portrait on the credenza — four girls, all redheads like their father. "I know. It is only the beginning. Talk about heartless — they steal your heart and go off with it one day without a backward glance."

Max was sure this was true, and while he hoped it would be different with boys, somehow he doubted it.

"The article goes on," the bishop began carefully, "it goes on to say your wife has a reputation as a healer."

"This is true, Bishop. She . . . it's part of her business, you know. Her shop. She sells homeopathic remedies and so forth."

"The implication is that she does more."

Max sighed. "May I see?"

The bishop handed him the paper and sat in silence while Max took it all in. The reporter had, of course, gotten hold of the whole neopagan angle vis-à-vis Awena and played it for all it was worth. He (one Clive Hoptingle, whose talents clearly were being wasted in reportage, given his driving narrative style) implied without actually stating it that Awena went in for esoteric ceremonies, gathering herbs by moonlight, sprinkling "blessed" water on crops — all the while being married to a priest of the Church of England.

What Clive reported was not wrong, exactly. It was a question of focus, of shading, of innuendo and suggestion, allowing the reader to fill in the blanks with every cliché at his or her disposal. Awena, the most gentle and loving of creatures, was being subtly portrayed as something out of *Macbeth,* a model for one of Shakespeare's three witches. Max felt his face flush with anger. This Clive person was a moron. How *dare* he.

Awena *was* a healer; Max had seen the evidence for himself, had experienced it for himself. It was, however, another reason her growing reputation might make the bishop leery. She sold, for one example, an ointment in her shop that worked fine to alleviate skin conditions; its main ingredient was witch hazel or something innocuous. But, as he once had learned when he injured his ankle, it worked with 100 percent efficacy when Awena applied it to his skin. There had been other, even more profound cures of several people in the village that he attributed to her intervention. There was no other explanation. But explaining to anyone like the bishop, who had not experienced this for himself, well . . .

Max recalled the discussions he and Awena had had on the subject of religion, particularly when they were trying to contrive a wedding ceremony that could enfold both his beliefs and hers.

Awena prayed to the benign and protective being in which she believed absolutely, an entity neither male nor female, but which, as she explained it, resided in the center of a flame that burned with a pure and resolute and indissoluble love for all things living.

It was, she said, a question of faith rather than of belief. A being that just *was,* never requiring conscious thought or invocation, but pleased nonetheless to be summoned.

"The universe is so varied," Awena had said. "No wonder we struggle to name and categorize, in an attempt to understand it all. But when we fight wars over definitions of the deity — or deities — that's when the trouble starts. In the name of religion, we kill one another. How mad we are!"

She had explained to him then what a hand-fasting ceremony was, and had asked, "Would you feel such a thing compromised your beliefs in any way?"

"It depends," he had said. "What are the

vows, exactly?"

She had told him. While they could compose their own vows, they basically would promise to be each other's shelter in any storm: "To love and honor and respect each other as individuals, and to seek the light instead of the darkness in all our dealings with each other and with others.

"I would include a promise to be your soul friend — the one person you can rely on to stand by you until the end of your life. The ancient Celts called it 'anamchara.' "

Max, consumed by the strangely indefinable yet undoubtedly feminine essence of Awena — his lover and his best friend — had said, "I actually think that's all quite beautiful. Is it legally binding?"

"To me, it is. But to answer the meaning behind your question, no, it's not. The UK doesn't recognize the ceremony. Yet."

He found he could not capitulate on this, as much as he loved her and everything about her approach to life. She who could make poetry of any occasion, of any corner of a room, of any meal. Everything she undertook received the same reverent attention: flower arranging, decorating, operating her business, choosing the very ornaments and fabric and clothing she would wear. But alongside her reverence ran that rare ability

287

she had to live in the moment, as the jargon went — it was what made her unique in Max's and others' experience.

He would have done whatever she asked, but on this one thing he had held firm. They would marry, and it would be a legally recognized union. And so after much more back-and-forth, they had agreed they would also have a civil ceremony in order that all the *i*'s were dotted and the *t*'s were crossed. With Owen on the way, it was something Max had insisted they do.

He and Awena had likewise reached a compromise on their living arrangements. It made no sense for her to abandon the lovely horizontal sprawl of her cottage for the quirky verticality of the vicarage, a structure that seemed designed to provide hazards for the very young just taking their first tentative steps.

Although, Max had observed, *designed* was the wrong term. Nothing about the vicarage seemed planned. It was sporadic, haphazard, more as if someone with a compulsion to construct and remodel and build on — someone like the Winchester rifle heiress of California Max had read about — had taken over the place a century before. It was full of rooms that seemed to serve no purpose and yet were not large enough to be put to any conceivable good use. And so the vicarage had become Max's office during the day — an elaborate maze-like study, as it were — while family life took root over at Awena's cottage. The routine with Mrs. Hooser and her children did not change, and, in fact, Max could not find it in his heart to upset what amounted to free baby-sitting arrangements for the Hooser children. They did their homework at the vicarage's kitchen table, as they always had done, and Mrs. Hooser made ineffective forays into the vicarage's many rooms in need of cleaning, armed with her duster, as she always had. For the time being, he and Awena moved easily between cottage and vicarage during the day, as before, the difference being that Max had now moved all his personal belongings into the cottage, which they now called home.

There had been so many things to decide back then, and the few months before Owen's birth had not seemed to Max nearly long enough to decide it all. He remembered a conversation they'd had one day when they were still trying to decide what to do about day-care arrangements. She had been wearing a typical Awena outfit of what he thought of as icon colors: blues and pinks and violets and cherry tones brightly embroidered against a gold background. The long dress was gathered at the waist, Kabuki-style, with a wide belt.

They had been standing before the vicarage fireplace and she had pulled out of his arms, tipping her head back to look up at him. "I don't know, Max," she'd said. "I can watch the baby all day. It's no problem. This will be ever such a good baby, I'm sure of it."

"Yes, but you've a business to run."

"So have you, when you think about it. Really, Max, I'll figure out a way. The other women in the village will help me. And I won't like being away — I know myself; I won't want to miss a moment."

And what she said had proven to be true. Unlike in most young families, where there was a permanent hullabaloo, life with Awena and Owen continued on a serene course, a fact he credited to both their tranquil natures, mother and son.

Awena had held some sort of purification ceremony after Owen's birth. Her sisters Unita, Xantha, and Zoe had all attended, making the journey from the west coast of Anglesey, full of good cheer and unasked-for but useful advice, prattling happily away, their faces wreathed in smiles. Every time Max saw them, one or another was holding aloft some tiny garment or toy, exclaiming over it in lilting Welsh. Max had known Awena spoke the language but had not realized how second nature it was to her. She was alight with happiness from the presence of Owen and her sisters. As she told Max, "It is like the gods are shining on us all."

Max's heart had stilled for a moment when she said that. While he agreed, superstitiously he wondered if it weren't tempting fate to say it aloud. Looking into Awena's translucent eyes that day, eyes Owen looked set to inherit, Max had pondered the path that had led him there, to that very moment, to the only woman who had ever entirely owned his heart. Cocteau had said of Edith Piaf that she had "the eyes of a blind person struck by a miracle, the eyes of a clairvoyant." That was as near a perfect description of Awena — her appearance and her essence — as Max could conjure.

And Max felt he could not live without her. Awena, with her dark hair marked by its distinctive streak of white, and her tea-rose complexion.

He was happy. Sublimely happy.

In early February, halfway between the winter solstice — Yule — and the spring equinox — Ostara — the three sisters had returned to celebrate the onset of spring. In Awena's tradition, this was Imbolc. Their traditions, his and hers, all blended together, making a perfect kind of sense.

One evening not long afterward, he heard himself asking Awena if there were any more of that baked tofu left over from the party, and he had laughed aloud at the "new" Max. He felt he had been thoroughly brainwashed. But if this was brainwashing, he was delighted, happy to succumb. Life, he thought, could not get any better than this, right here, right now, as they lived in this cheerful give-and-take, appreciating and honoring each other's traditions, bound together by their love for each other and of Owen.

Whether the bishop would share this happy appreciation was always open to question.

He might adapt. He had done so before. Max recalled the bishop's initial horrified reaction when Max had explained to him the more esoteric traditions of the handfasting ceremony.

"I don't see how you can participate in what is essentially a neopagan ceremony," the bishop had said at last. "It's rather . . . preposterous for a man in your position." He heaved a mighty sigh, and his face visibly softened, for he liked his scofflaw priest. "I'm sorry, Max. I truly am. But I don't see a way. The media . . ."

Oh, Lord, yes. The media. "The media," said Max, "will find a new dancing bear to keep them and the British public entertained, within a week or less. You know that, Bishop, as well as I do."

When Max had later related this conversation, Awena had laughed.

"Perhaps I should wear an embroidered scarlet letter on my dress: *P* for *pagan.*"

He gathered she had heard about the rather unfunny Hester Prynne remarks. And typically, wisely, she had chosen to ignore them.

He realized now that the bishop had asked him a question. Fortunately, he had rushed on, not waiting for an answer.

"Before you say anything, Max, I have already composed a letter to the editor. I will run it by you, but I don't feel that anything as silly and scurrilous as what this reporter has written and this paper has published should go unchallenged."

The wave of relief that swept through Max made the room practically shimmer before his eyes. He had had no idea how the bishop would react, but Max felt he should have known the man would react in exactly the proper way. For one thing, having met Awena, the bishop knew how ridiculous this portrayal of her was; the bishop and his wife had ended up attending the much-debated hand-fasting ceremony, demonstrating once again their open-mindedness. They had, in fact, ended up staying half the night, enjoying the festivities afterward. It had been a fabulous party, even by Nether Monkslip standards.

"Thank you, Bishop," said Max in all sincerity.

"Now, we come to the difficult part."

There was a more difficult part? Then he remembered the "miraculous" face appearing on the wall of St. Edwold's, which, of course, the reporter had included in his report.

"This image on the wall of St. Edwold's. This face. How convinced are you there is nothing to it?"

"You mean nothing miraculous?" Max hesitated. It almost seemed like a trick question, like one of those tests from the early days of the church, when learned men had debated how many angels could dance on the head of a pin. "To be honest, Bishop, I don't know. I was completely thrown for a loop when Nether Monkslip came up in connection with the so-called miraculous

Face at Monkbury Abbey. It's not that I became convinced there was anything to it, you understand. It is that the confirmation of all the long-simmering legends was just . . . weird." He didn't add, "considering the source of many of those legends was a wildly unreliable narrator like Frank Cuthbert," but he thought it.

"But more than that," Max went on, "I can't ignore the fact that I have had that wall whitewashed and scrubbed and painted more times than I can recall, and the image returns, sometimes by the next day. There is no question whatsoever about that. I've had the roof and ceiling and outside walls checked for leaks. Nothing. And that roof, as you know, is practically brand-new anyway. There is no accounting for it, and yet . . ."

"And yet there it is."

"That's right. By any scientific reasoning, it can't be there, and yet it is. You saw it when you visited Nether Monkslip for the hand-fasting. What did you think?"

The bishop didn't say anything, and when he spoke, he avoided answering the question.

"Why did you become a priest, Max?"

"Why did I — That's easy. I wanted my life to count for something, to mean something. To me, if to no one else."

"And there was an element of turning swords into plowshares in your case, wasn't there? Given your MI5 background?"

This was true, Max realized. The murder of his friend and colleague Paul had done for him. He had grown sick of the carnage, of the tit-for-tat violence, of the stupid bloody-mindedness of it all, of the constant lying to everyone about who he was and what he did all day. He'd wanted out. It hadn't stopped his aching wish that the man who had killed Paul would be killed or captured, but it had changed his life completely, and put him on a wholly different path. A path that led to Awena and to Owen. A path toward — dare he say it? — peace and undiluted happiness.

All he had left to remember Paul by now was the shirt he, Max, had been wearing the day Paul died. It had a speck of blood on the collar, presumably Paul's, and it was tucked on the top shelf of his closet now, carefully preserved. For what, Max could not have said, but he could not be parted from it, and he had given Mrs. Hooser a very hard time when she attempted to use it as a dust rag.

Not long ago, Awena had found it in re-arranging the bedroom closets. He'd told her what it was, and she'd asked, "What makes you certain it's Paul's blood?" Max had been too stunned to reply. Any other explanation had never occurred to him. He had so wanted it to be Paul's.

"I could say the same," the bishop was saying now. "I wanted to make a difference in the world, and this was the avenue that appealed to me — there was so much of the planet in dire straits and I wanted to do something about it, not just spend my short time on earth taking care of me and mine, worrying only about what I could accumulate, and how many channels I could get on my satellite dish."

Max waited, sensing there was more.

"But I also believed, Max. Despite the fact I consider myself to be a rational actor, I was and am a believer. Why, I asked myself, did Christianity succeed when hundreds of cults died off? It was the Twitter of its age, the underfunded start-up that changed the world. Did the early Christians believe in miracles? Of course they did. We know they did. And without joining the ranks of the credulous, the easily duped, the easily separated from their hard-earned money by charlatans, I think we have to believe, too."

Max was taken aback. Never had the bishop spoken to him like this, of matters like this. Max felt he was being given for the first time a glimpse into the man's soul.

"That said," continued the bishop, "this situation has to be handled very carefully. I suppose you could just keep painting the image over, pointless as it has become. Or have that portion of the wall removed, perhaps?"

But even as he spoke, the bishop seemed to recognize the futility of this approach. Any miracle worthy of the name would break through any attempts to stifle it.

"But we come to the real issue, Max. Between the murders and the face and the rampant speculation about you and your wife by the media — well, it may come to this: You may have to be reassigned to another parish."

No. Max's reaction was immediate and heartfelt. Nether Monkslip, like Awena, had come to be a part of his soul. The place not only where he resided but where his soul thrived.

NO.

"I am sorry, Max. We don't have to decide anything today. But the spotlight needs to be turned down a notch. The murders started when you arrived in Nether Monkslip. Perhaps they'll end when you leave."

Or they'll trail along behind me, thought Max.

And from the look on the bishop's face, he was thinking the same thing.

CHAPTER 17
STRANGERS ON A TRAIN

Late that night, Max was watching Alfred Hitchcock's *Strangers on a Train* on DVD. The sound was turned low, as Owen dozed in his arms. Max had figured out that Owen loved old films as much as his father; the sounds seemed to calm him until he fell asleep. Chip off the old block.

The film, starring Farley Granger and Robert Walker, revolved around a professional tennis player and a wealthy psychotic, who suggests they solve each other's personal dilemmas by switching murders, thus providing on each other with an alibi. Farley's dilemma involved the fact that his wife was pregnant with another man's child, and he, Farley, was in any case, in love with another woman. Robert Walker had an inconvenient father standing in the way of his inheritance.

Max, caught up in the portrayal of the thoroughly evil Bruno character played by

Walker, felt a little shiver of recognition, a sense of déjà vu. The theme of strangers chatting casually of death — certainly that had come up recently, and was the reason Max had dug out the old recording to watch. But it was more. What *was* it that nagged at him? Something about pregnancy? The rather doubtful pregnancy of Farley's wife. The top of Max's scalp began to tingle. He had been jiggling Owen to help him sleep, but now he froze, trying to summon whatever memory or idea had been called into play. He rewound the film in his mind: Bruno had been talking about a "crisscross," suggesting the means to establish an alibi, since neither man knew the other and so collusion would not be suspected by the authorities.

But what did that have to do with the current case? Max couldn't fathom it, although he felt certain whatever was nibbling at the edges of his mind had to do with the death — and the life — of Lord Baaden-Boomethistle. And it wasn't just the obvious connection that the removal of Lord Baaden-Boomethistle had meant the estate could pass to his son. It was more than that. Something to do with a train, then?

Max, hitting the pause button, thought back over the facts as he knew them, wondering if two people could have colluded in the crime. That was always possible, even though it was the riskiest way to commit a murder: One had to trust absolutely one's partner's ability to keep quiet. Murder created a pact as "sacred" as marriage or kinship. But he had the idea this whatever it was he was alerting on predated Lord Baaden-Boomethistle's death.

He recalled that Lord Baaden-Boomethistle had mentioned a train. Something about a train . . . how convenient the Chunnel had made train travel but that the Chunnel had just opened one hot summer and he was always one to wait until they'd worked the kinks out of big new projects. The Chunnel opening had been around 1994, as Max recalled — he could look it up, but what did it matter? The lord had talked about how he and his first wife had taken a train out of Spain to catch a plane to England, and how they'd been delayed. How hot it had been that summer. How crowded. The sounds (and the smells) of crying children had added to the discomfort. There had been a litany of complaints about the journey: "I am one of those who firmly believe children should be seen and not heard." And Lord Baaden-Boomethistle had gone on to request — foolish hope! —

that the organizers make sure the noise from children at the duck race be kept to a minimum.

It was gone three before Max put Owen in his crib to be guarded by Thea, the living, breathing baby monitor. Max knew he would need Cotton's help to confirm his wild hypothesis, but there was not much Cotton could do at this hour. He might need a search warrant: That depended on how cooperative the people at Totleigh Hall might prove to be. Somehow, Max thought the odds were not good, but it wouldn't hurt to ask.

The phrase "tilting at windmills" went through his mind.

Owen opened his eyes just briefly before returning to sleep. Max could have sworn his son winked at him.

It was Sunday, and Destiny was conducting the church service. It was her big moment, which made what happened next so unforgivable.

Max fell asleep during her sermon.

Owen, in a departure from his usual placidness, had awakened again and again throughout the night, crying sporadically; drifting off, then seeming to time his awakenings for when his father started to doze.

Max had let Awena sleep through it all.

Nodding off in church — his own church — was an unpardonable lapse, despite the good excuse. Besides, it wasn't a particularly long sermon, as sermons went.

Destiny, who had, of course, spotted him in the congregation, was utterly gracious and forgiving afterward, telling him, "God speaks to us in dreams, too, Max. Probably more helpfully and to the point than in any sermon of mine."

Then she spoiled it by adding, "Besides, I thought you were just concentrating. Thank God you didn't snore."

Or even, thought Max, emit gentle snuffles, like one of Awena's dormice.

His little nap had gone mostly unnoticed, apart from a steely-looking woman in a hat sitting across the aisle from him. Beside her sat Miss Pitchford, also sporting a sort of alpine confection with a feather stuck in the brim. The steely woman appeared to be visiting from another parish, and was possibly a friend of Miss Pitchford's; she was not a Nether Monkslipper. From the look she gave him, she would have stabbed him awake with her hat pin had she been close enough. Max could picture her composing the letter she would send to the bishop to report Max's unsuitability for his posting.

"It is with deep sadness and regret that I, as a loyal member of the One True Church, feel compelled to bring to your most Esteemed's attention a shocking event I myself witnessed this Sunday," et cetera, et cetera. There were people like that, as Max knew only too well.

He had drifted off just as Destiny had been quoting from Psalm 59: "Deliver me from mine enemies, O my God: defend me from them that rise up against me." It was an entreaty that blended perfectly with Max's now-fading dream image of a man in sunglasses — a wavering image Max clung to as he swam against the tides of tiredness and again became aware of his surroundings. This disturbing figure in sunglasses was a recurrent visitor to Max's dreamscape, this menacing half man, half creature, a man trying too hard to look cool, wearing glasses that had not been fashionable for years, if they ever had been. Sunglasses with blue lenses and white frames. Silly, juvenile. Glasses the man had worn the day Max had seen him running from the scene of carnage he had created, the explosion in which Paul had been killed. The man had never been apprehended, despite all the resources of MI5 having been brought to bear.

Like a ghost, he'd vanished, and the

dreaming Max thought something in this ghost idea might be important, so he tried to hang on to it, fighting wakefulness. The figure shape-shifted now into a Robert Walker look-alike — the actor Robert Walker. Max now realized he could see through him, like a ghost.

A ghost, like the headless horseman that chased Ichabod Crane in the old American story. Ichabod, he remembered, had been a superstitious man.

Of course. Who wrote that story? He couldn't think . . . Ichabod, such a wonderful old name from the Bible; his mother named him Ichabod, Max remembered. She died from grief, soon after giving birth to him. *Ichabod.*

It began to snow, and in the distance he could see a church on a mountaintop — not St. Edwold's, but a church with an onion dome. Max suddenly became aware that he stood in a forest, and as he stood, a headless man raced by on horseback. The eyes of the horse he rode were rolled back in fear, the whites of its eyes showing. The horse was not Foto Finish, as Max first had thought, but a sturdy Russian draft horse running impossibly fast.

He heard a voice — surely the man could not speak? But a booming, sepulchral voice said, "Remember: It takes a thief." Max stepped away in horror, and as he did so, he nearly tripped over a head where it lay on the ground among piles of fallen leaves. The head was bearded, a long white beard now soaked in blood. Max tried to run, but his feet were planted, stuck to the ground, mired in the muck of mud and blood and rotting leaves. He became aware of the horse, which was watching him — it must have come back — and of the sound of a cricket's chirp. Beside the head — how odd, almost comical, he thought — lay a smashed pumpkin, its carved skull shattered. The face of the headless man grinned up at him, a jack-o'-lantern grin. The face still wore the sunglasses, but it no longer looked like Robert Walker. It looked like Lord Bayer Baaden-Boomethistle.

At which, Max finally jolted awake, stifling a shout of alarm and dropping his hymnal to the stone floor. It made a *thunk!* which caused heads — heads firmly attached to their owners, thank God — to turn in his direction.

He rubbed both hands over his face, desperate with weariness. Between Owen's awakenings and his preoccupation with the murder of Lord Baaden-Boomethistle, all on top of his usual pastoral duties and the delicate political dance he was engaged in with his bishop, he was exhausted. While he knew that this, too, would pass, he started to wonder when it would.

He realized he'd been listening to Destiny's sermon with part of his mind, anyway, and bits of it had seeped into his unconscious, making the usual incomprehensible stew. For she was now talking about Herodias demanding the head of John the Baptist.

Oh my, thought Max. Good Lord. Given recent events, it was perhaps not the happiest choice of topic. But he knew Destiny had been working on her sermon for ages, polishing it and looking toward the day she'd have a chance to use it, and by this point might not even have seen the parallels.

Stranger things were still to come during this service. The organist began to play the opening notes of hymn number 247 and the choir joined in, warbling with gusto, if a mix of abilities. Awena's voice soared above the rest, sounding like an angel to his ears, Owen apparently content now in his carrier at her side. But, even allowing for the fact he himself generally sang off key, Max couldn't help but notice many in the congregation were singing a different song, until the voices began to trail off and stall in confusion. People were turning to one another, pointing to their hymnals, then pointing to the hymn board.

As in most churches, the board hung at the right of the altar. The numbers for the hymns planned for the service were affixed to a black background using movable plastic white type. Also as usual, the type didn't necessarily match; there had been some attrition over the years, with pieces gone missing, and pieces replaced with numerals in a slightly different font. But what was odd was that the last hymn for the service was to have been number 247.

It was now, according to the hymn board, number 345.

Perhaps some of the village children had been messing about with the board, thought Max. It had happened before. Or perhaps one of the many new visitors to the church had gone in for a spot of mild vandalism. He stole a glance at Miss Steely Eyes. Perhaps . . . there were all sorts of strangers lately . . . but no: Such as she would never stoop to such a thing. Clearly there had been some mistake, however it had happened. Max would have to ask the sexton about it.

As the congregation sang on (at least those

in the congregation who knew the words to hymn number 247 without having to follow the printed lyrics), he took a copy of the hymnal from the rack attached to the pew in front of him. He flipped through the pages until he found hymn number 345, which happened to be "Here We Come with Gladness."

That is odd, Max thought. That is very odd indeed.

CHAPTER 18
MAX AND COTTON

Max, on his way to see DCI Cotton, made a slight detour.

As he approached the stables at Totleigh Hall, he heard two voices, one low and importuning, the other low and dismissive. But at the sound of his footsteps, the voices stopped, and when he entered the row of stalls, it appeared he was alone — except, of course, for the horses.

The horse he wanted to see was not hard to find. Each stall was labeled with a big brass plate with the name of its occupant: Gunpowder, Brio, Mamasito Gold. He wondered idly who had the job of keeping the brass to such a high polish. The fellow who wrote *Downton Abbey* would know, he decided.

Foto Finish, a fine-looking dappled gray, stared from one of his enormous eyeballs, taking Max's measure.

"What do you know?" Max whispered to

him. "What did you see with those big eyes, eh?" He had taken a carrot from the kitchen at home, where it had been waiting to be diced for Awena's famous Root Soup — she was making a video of how to prepare the recipe to upload to her Web site, and he hoped she wouldn't notice she was a carrot short. He held the offering out on the flat of his palm. The horse pricked up its ears, eying Max with renewed interest, and gently nibbled the carrot off Max's hand with his enormous teeth. "What did you hear with those big ears, fella?" Max ran a hand down the horse's withers and stroked the base of his ears. Did horses like being scratched behind the ears, like a dog? This one apparently did. His ears twitched with hope for another carrot.

Foto Finish seemed docile enough to Max, who wondered idly if the animal even realized he was at the center of a murder investigation. Had he been traumatized at all, perhaps by the smell of blood? Probably not. The whole event was for him a chance to return early to the stables and nothing more.

Leaving this mute witness behind, Max walked from the stables to the side of the house. He had arranged to meet up with DCI Cotton where he'd been given permission to set up temporary headquarters.

Approaching a sparkling pair of French doors into the manor, Max noticed the soil in one of the large vases on the patio, holding a small decorative evergreen, had been disturbed — a bit of soil lay on the ground next to the vase. Squirrels at work, most likely. But he cleared away an inch or two of topsoil and saw a blue plastic object had been buried there. It was egg-shaped and of a size to be held comfortably in the palm of the hand. In the center of the object was an orange button. By instinct and habit, he used a clean handkerchief to pick it up. Experimentally, he pushed the button, expecting perhaps an alarm, but it emitted a little clicking sound.

Rosamund appeared at his elbow, the sound of her footfall deadened by the lush grass of the lawn. Today she was wearing round eyeglasses with pink frames and a lavender frock.

Max asked her what the object was, to confirm his suspicion.

"It's a training clicker. You use it to train animals. You know, dolphins, dogs."

"Horses?"

"Horses," she agreed. He could almost see the light switch on as her mind grappled with the implications.

"Where would you buy such a thing?"

She shrugged. She was trying for nonchalance. But failing.

"A pet store. Online. Anywhere. 'Wherever pet products are sold,' as they say."

"Have you seen this before?"

"Well, sure. We have horses, don't we? It's used for positive reinforcement: They come to associate the clicker sound with getting a reward, so long as they do whatever positive thing is being asked of them, either by someone on the ground or sitting in the saddle. Bree is very keen on them because she doesn't like the more punitive training methods: She's a real softy, is Bree, when it comes to animals. There are likely several of the things lying about."

But only one buried in a flowerpot, thought Max. It explained so much.

"I say, you don't think . . ." she began.

Max nodded. "I do."

Max showed the clicker to Cotton.

"Here," he said, handing it over, still wrapped in the handkerchief. "There might be prints on it."

"Yes, I know," said Cotton, smiling. "That sort of specialized detective knowledge was mentioned in the brochure that came with my secret decoder ring."

"Sorry."

Cotton, being even more a city man than Max, leaped to the same wrong conclusion. "What is this? One of those personal security-alert things?" Cotton looked closer. There was an image of an animal embossed on the plastic. "Oh, I see. I've seen people out walking their dogs with one of these."

"Right. And they are used for horse training, too."

Max told him his emerging theory.

"Wow," said Cotton. "So, premeditated, and planned for a very long time."

"With a slight question remaining as to who the intended victim was."

"We've established Foto Finish was the man's usual mount, and that was his standard time of day to ride. There isn't a stable hand who didn't know the drill around here."

"So it is probably safe to say Lord Baaden-Boomethistle was the target," said Max. "Besides, everyone else would have been too short of stature for this plan to work."

"For the wire to hit them right at the neck."

"Right." Max paused, thinking. "Has it occurred to you that we're dealing with a real psychopath here?"

"It has indeed. Although it was a 'clean'

kill, there are surer, swifter ways to murder someone. Less cinematic ways. This was . . . a sort of playing with the victim. A game, and a sick one."

Max agreed. "Lord Baaden-Boomethistle had a collection of guns in his office, just to name one possible method that might have been used."

"That would indicate an inside job, though," said Cotton. "The guns are kept locked. The key is in the desk, but the wife swears he locked the desk whenever he left the room for any length of time."

"But it might be a sort of double bluff. The killing was done the way it was in order to implicate an outsider, someone other than the family, someone without day-to-day access to the house. The stables are easier to slip in and out of. Have you looked at known associates, friends and acquaintances?"

"I've had Constable Musteile on it," said Cotton. Off Max's look, Cotton said, "He's all we had. We're that shorthanded. Sergeant Essex has been in Monkslip Foot working a drug deal that ended in murder. She's just back from consulting with our colleagues in Winfrith."

Cotton punched a number into his mobile, explaining what he wanted when Musteile answered. To Max's ears, Cotton was using a talking-to-idiots voice, but on reflection it was the appropriate tone to use with Musteile, a man whose officiousness was kept in check only by his incompetence.

"Where are we with this?" asked Cotton. "I want to know about mistresses if there were any, old girlfriends, friends of friends, the lot. Get our people at Oxford onto the son. The daughter's at Cambridge."

"I've already spoken with someone there. A Sergeant Fear."

"Good. I'll also need to know about every cyber footprint left by the victim. And by the victim's family. Every e-mail ever sent out into the world is stored for at least six months on a server somewhere. Even deleted e-mails can be reconstructed."

Max could hear Musteile's tinny voice through the speakerphone. "Should I alert the local horse watch members?"

"I don't see why you should," Cotton replied. "Besides, they're probably reading about it in the *Globe and Bugle* right about now."

"Interpol should be notified," Musteile said. Cotton smiled over at Max to see if he'd heard that last. He had. "I'll ask to file a Red Notice with them. That's an international arrest warrant. We could have him extradited. Once we know who he is. And where he's gone."

Ye gods and little — "I know what a Red Notice is, Constable Musteile. I —"

But he was gone. Musteile had a habit of snapping off a phone conversation without a good-bye, something he'd seen detectives do in films.

"Goddamn it," said Cotton, ringing him back. "Damn damn triple damn it. What a blooming idiot."

When Musteile answered, Cotton barked, "Listen and don't hang up, or I'll have your guts pulled into guitar strings, I swear I will. I also need you to get a search warrant *if* we need one. Stand by to move on that." Cotton explained what was wanted — it was a request he was relaying at Max's suggestion. "Got that?"

"Yes."

There was a long, drawn-out silence.

"You can ring off now," Cotton told him.

There was a click as Musteile ended the connection.

"Jeez," muttered Cotton, staring at the phone. Max laughed at his expression.

"I mean," said Cotton, "you have to wonder what recruits were rejected for the constabulary in the year Musteile was applying."

"Oh, he's not so . . ." began Max. "Well, all right, he is, but it could be worse."

"Do you really think it could?" asked Cotton.

Max looked about him at the room. "Nice of them to put you up here."

The investigative team had set up a satellite shop in what appeared to be a drawing room. Or, as Cotton said, "a withdrawing room, a ballroom, an indoor tennis court — God knows. The butler who showed me in called it the Chinese Room. I've been puzzling over why. Something to do with that vase over there, I'd guess." He pointed to a small porcelain vase of green and yellow, preserved under a museum-style dome. "Anyway, this place has more rooms with more specific assigned purposes than Buckingham Palace. How many rooms no one ever sets foot in is anyone's guess. And the stables! The stables can house thirty-six horses, so I'm told. I wonder if the horses have a vase, too. Anyway, as you can see, we have a sweeping view of the lawn and gardens in which to ponder how Lord Baaden-Boomethistle met his death. No doubt my team will find it all inspiring as the sunlight dances in the spray from the fountains."

The spot where they stood overlooked a

flagstone terrace leading to a green lawn shaven flat in lines of a mathematical precision. In summer, the urns on the patio would spill over with trailing flowers; the garden beds now exploded in a blaze of fall reds and oranges.

The two men watched the play of the fountains for a bit, then turned to look about them at the marble fireplaces — plural; at the flocked wallpaper — green; at the Aubusson carpet — worn thin in a manner that broadcast rarity rather than poverty; and at a painting ornately framed in gold leaf of Lord Bayer Baaden-Boomethistle dressed for the hunt, clutching a bugle and a riding crop, and managing to look simultaneously magisterial and ridiculous as he surveyed his opulent future. He looked many years younger and lighter on his feet than when last seen alive, although it was difficult to say if the hefty thighs were an illusion created by his roomy riding breeches. Max calculated the painting had to be two dozen years old. The painted dog at his feet, looking up at its master, seemed to be leaning toward the view that his master was ridiculous. It was a testament to the artist's abilities that he had managed to capture an expression something like contempt on the canine face.

Max's gaze swept the room. It was the type of house *Architectural Digest* might feature, showcasing Elton John or one of the Spice Girls splendidly draped over the furnishings at home, dressed in spangles for a night in front of the telly. No expense spared, no piece of wood or shard of porcelain left unembellished, no edge ungilded.

Cotton himself sat rather primly on a luxurious sofa, slowly sinking like the Titanic into the seductive embrace of its numerous pillows. He drew out his tablet computer and balanced it on one knee. He looked like a child of ten or so, lost in the vastness of red brocade and tasseled yellow velvet. Max stood beneath the portrait of Lord Baaden-Boomethistle, unconsciously assuming the man's commanding pose.

"I think this is what is called a morning room," Max told him. "A sitting room used during the day, to catch the sun." Max's understanding of the uses of such rooms was that the lady of the house would be found here of a morning, discussing plans for that evening's dinner party with the housekeeper. He could almost hear the tinkle of her spoon against bone china as she stirred sugar into her coffee, and the trill of her voice as she issued commands. *"No, no,"* she might say. "The Montesque-

Netherbottoms must be seated *well* away from the Flibber-Jesnots. Bad blood there, you know, going back eons to some siege or another. Seat the daughter next to the vicar, where she'll be out of harm's way."

"So there would be an evening room?" Cotton asked.

"Yes, but they probably wouldn't call it that."

"The drawing room, then? I can't keep up with all of this. I really can't. It's exhausting."

"Most people have only a parlor or living room for entertaining, if they're lucky," agreed Max. "For occasions when they want to be grand."

"My grandmother had a parlor straight out of the Old Curiosity Shop. Footstools went there to die, I swear — but not before they'd spent a lifetime tripping up visitors and sending then sprawling. Still, it was a great place for a young boy to pretend — oh, I don't know: to play cops and robbers, I suppose. This is just — you can't feel cozy in here, can you?"

"It's not meant to comfort, but to impress. Now, what do you say we exchange views, so to speak, and see where our thinking has led us? I know you've been interviewing the locals. Any result there?"

Cotton was himself a local man, or local-ish. His mother had been a performer of sorts, who would drop him off in Monkslip-super-Mare for a long stay with her sister while she herself went on tour. More often than not, she would forget to pick him up again. Fortunately, the sister seemed to have been a basically decent sort and had given Cotton what stability he'd had growing up.

"Not really. Most of them seem strangely reluctant to tip the nobs into it. They may not like them much, but I think there's a certain amount of civic pride in having such a great old family in the neighborhood."

"Can anyone speak to their expertise with horses?"

Now Cotton swiped away a few screens on his computer until he arrived at the page he wanted. "Peregrine and his sister, Rosa-mund, both ride," Cotton told him. "Al-though Peregrine is most often to be seen pedaling about on his bicycle. The family all ride well, according to the stable hands. Except for the dowager — she decided a few years ago she couldn't risk a fall. But she used to ride regularly. The rarity is to see them walking about on their own two legs under their own power — any of the Baaden-Boomethistles."

"What exactly did Lord Baaden-

Boomethistle do before he retired?"

"Not much, from what I gather. He had scads of family money. He had one of those aristocratically obscure occupations, like being captain of the Scottish elephant polo team. So when he drifted over the line officially into retirement, it was scarcely discernible from whatever he'd been doing before, if you follow."

"Yes, I do see." Max had met many such in his career. In almost no case could a job title be applied to men such as Lord Baaden-Boomethistle, or at least none that would stick. They just *were,* and they did the odd thing for charity, and they sat on this or that board, offering unwanted advice and opinion. Overall, however, they probably did more good than harm. And some men and women of the aristocracy were exceedingly generous in giving both their time and money to a cause, particularly one close to their hearts.

"The more competent members of my team have talked to a few of the lord's compatriots," said Cotton. "Their displays of grief seem to be less along the lines of having lost a great friend, and more along the lines of having been made aware of their own mortality. Quite often the wealthy seem to think they'll live forever, and they don't care for reminders that death is the great leveler."

"It is indeed. Beyond that, what do we have?"

As always, Cotton thrilled to Max's use of the plural. His unofficial consulting had helped close several of Cotton's cases. Max could be relied on to see the connections, the little clues, that others often missed. Cotton planned to write up some of these cases one day, when he had time.

"My people have searched everywhere, of course," Cotton told him. "Nothing of a suspicious nature has been found."

"Including on his computer?" Max asked. "Anything that jumps out at one from his recent correspondence?"

"Nothing so far to indicate trouble, but we've only done a quick preliminary. His e-mail account revealed subscriptions to men's clubs, a lively interest in the horse trade, and an overdue bill from his bespoke tailor."

"No threats received or made, then. Is the bill suggestive?"

"The fact that it was overdue, you mean? No. It might depend on what you mean by 'overdue,' however. His tailor is one of those posh outfits that think in terms of centuries rather than weeks. Anything overdue would be handed down to the next generation, all of whom would order its new shirts at the same place. But since you mention it, the overdue bill was for something the son, Peregrine, purchased and put on the family account."

"Ah."

"Yes, a review of Peregrine's obligations does reveal a few debts overlooked. He seems to have a weakness for playing the horses, and a talent for placing losing bets. And when did eyeglasses get to be so expensive? Anyway, I'm picking up rumors that he's involved with a rather gay crowd — gay in the modern sense — *Brideshead*-ish. You know. Not that it matters or has any connection to his lack of financial-management skills."

"I never heard that. Where did that rumor start?"

"With his sister, for one. She says she got the gay bulletin from her stepmother, however. Who, after all, 'is the expert in these matters,' whatever that means."

"What's your read on the daughter?" Max asked.

"Rosamund? Disgruntled. Very bright. Puts the rest of them in the shade, really. She has no use for the brother and barely tries to hide it. I gather she'd like to see him hang for this if we could arrange it. I can see her as she might be in years to come. Competent. Complacent. In charge of something or other, probably some charity she's founded herself, and as sure of her right to rule as Queen Elizabeth I was of hers. It's tough darts for Rosamund to be second in line to the 'throne.' She has never been happy having to share anything with her brother, or he with her. But I think I can see her point of view. She's miles smarter than her brother and doesn't see why his being firstborn and male means he grabs everything."

"She has even less use for her stepmother, I'd say."

"That's for certain. By the way, we've got the tests back on the strands caught in that initialed gold clip. As it turns out, Rosamund lied in vain; the roots of the hair were not intact, so we can't rely on DNA to pinpoint it as Bree's hair. It probably is, though, since she acknowledges the clip was hers."

"And what else does she acknowledge?"

"I have, of course, spoken at length with Lady Baaden-Boomethistle," Cotton replied. "Born Bree Anne Porter." Again a swipe at his computer — Bree apparently rated her own separate page. "She has hazarded the opinion that her husband had no enemies. What she actually said was, 'His many enemies are all dead now, I believe.' But she proclaims that she herself is 'simply horizontal with grief.' Or she will be, once she gets a few social obligations out of the way."

"Interesting choice of words," said Max.

"Isn't it just? Given that there are rumors of the persons with whom she has been horizontal. There is an HRH on the list, I hear."

"Surely not," said Max. "I'd have heard of it long before now, I am sure, during elevenses at the Cavalier: Miss Pitchford and Suzanna are up on all that sort of thing. Besides, there are plenty of gallants in the near neighborhood."

"None of them as highborn," said Cotton. "Perhaps your parishioners were trying to spare your sensibilities. You are the vicar, after all, and perhaps they felt it was all too shocking for your pink shell-like ears. Anyway, Bree, on the occasions I spoke with her, seemed to be quite giddy with relief. And then she'd catch herself and realize it isn't the done thing to dance a jig when your husband has got himself murdered in such a remarkable way. Even if you do have an alibi. Which she does, an ironclad one —

shopping in Monkslip-super-Mare, and staying the night with friends. She's all over the CCTV, and it's unmistakably her."

"The rumors I have heard," said Max, mildly miffed at the idea his parishioners might feel the need to protect him from the harsh realities of life — what sort of babe in the woods did they take him for? — "they indicate that Lady Baaden-Boomethistle is not everything that might be wished for in the blue-blood category — at least insofar as her mother-in-law is concerned."

"You heard right," said Cotton. "She seems to have come rather out of nowhere, and although she has the tally-ho, riding-to-hounds thing down pat, it's only because she is the daughter of a groom. She knew the horsey set and moved in those circles, but as the daughter of a hired hand; she did not know them as someone to the manor born. She's picked up the speech and mannerisms, but at heart I think she loves only the horses, not the nobs who ride them. Still, it brought her into close proximity with Lord Baaden-Boomethistle, who, when his first wife died, was at a bit of a loose end. They got along famously, so I'm told, and I don't think her lack of status bothered him in the least. Besides — well, it has to be said. She's drop-dead gorgeous. I don't think she won his heart by making him a casserole."

"But it bothered his mother, her lack of 'breeding.' "

"Correct. It's odd, however. Since the mother is herself engaged in the low-class occupation of writing, you'd think she'd have been more welcoming to her new daughter-in-law."

"Do you really think so?" asked Max. "My impression, and it is only based on slight acquaintance and hearsay, is that the dowager feels her occupation, as much as she enjoys it and is successful at it, *is* rather a low-class enterprise; she is embarrassed by it. And she writes about the aristocracy, remember. So her son's taking up with someone not of noble blood — well, that might have made her more sensitive to her own lowly status, not less. She needed him to have married *up* the ladder, not down — not just to assuage her own ego but because it would be better for sales if he took up with someone of indisputable lineage — someone like his first wife. It must have felt to her that he was degrading the whole family tree."

"You got all that from barely having met her?"

"Sad to say, one snob is rather like another. And the dowager is a raving snob."

"If daughter-in-law Bree had come a cropper, I guess we'd know who to ask about it, then," said Cotton. "So, who do you favor for this?"

Max replied, "The only person I think likely to have done it has too obvious a motive to have done it."

"Well, come on, then."

"It's merely an idea backed up with nothing. So I'd rather not say."

"Fine."

Minutes passed; then Max mused aloud into the cushiony silence. "I wonder . . ."

Cotton sighed quietly, stoically. "You wonder what, Max? I wonder."

"You have yourself spoken with his mother, the dowager?"

"The lady also known as Caroline?" Cotton asked. He crossed one perfectly creased trouser leg over the other, first hitching up the fabric to safeguard the continued perfection of the crease. "Yes, of course — just briefly. What a complete throwback — all bosoms and ostrich feathers. She looks like an elderly Vegas showgirl — not at all how one would expect a member of the upper crust to look."

"I think some of that is her writerly persona. You know, if you write romance, you probably should dress the part."

"She's more likely to be done up for soliciting if she goes about looking like that. Anyway, Sergeant Essex took extensive notes during her conversation with the dowager and is still doing research on her. The good sergeant has asked if I feel it necessary that she read any of Lady Baaden-Boomethistle's books. I gather she feels plowing through even a chapter of *The Duke's Delight* is going well beyond the call of duty. She flat out refuses even to flip through the pages of *The Prince and the Persuader.* What do you think?"

"That it's asking a lot of Sergeant Essex? I'd agree. And what are the chances the books are in any way autobiographical?"

"Funny you should ask. The chances might be quite good. I gather the dowager was no wallflower in her younger days and was known to, as one old swain put it, 'cut a mean rug.' Whatever that means."

"I think it means she was a good dancer."

"But according to Sergeant Essex, he was hinting at *so* much more, without being able to come right out and say it. She gained the impression he was talking about the lady's postdance behavior more than he was talking about her way with the fox-trot. I suppose those memories of her dancing days might have ended up in her books in some distilled and sifted form or other."

"Really," said Max. "That's an interesting possibility."

"Yes, but does it have anything to do with her son's death?"

"At first glance, I don't see how, do you? Still, it may indicate a wild and impulsive heart beating beneath a now rather stuffy, if highly decorated, exterior."

"Stuffy but fluffy, yes," said Cotton. "And there is no sinner more righteous, more holier-than-thou, than a reformed one. It might explain why she is so down on her daughter-in-law — a sort of 'takes one to know one' mentality."

"The pot is being hypocritical toward the kettle, you think. Hmm."

"Blatantly so. She also mentioned there was a bit of tension circling about the boy, Peregrine. Young man, I guess we must say."

"Tension between him and his father?"

"And his stepmother. The dowager was anxious we should know there were problems that concerned her. She wants rather desperately for Bree to be the killer, you see. She kept saying things to indicate Bree wants the family money all to herself. Money, among other things, like that vase over there. By the way, what do we think of

Bill Travis?"

"I would trust him absolutely with my horse. If I had a horse."

"With your sister?"

"Not so much."

Max fell silent for a long while, staring off into the distance. Or perhaps, thought Cotton, he has simply been struck by a good idea for his next sermon. With Max, one could never be sure. It all tended to be rather the same thing.

"What?" said Cotton finally.

"Oh, nothing in particular," replied Max. "I was just thinking that the genius of Agatha Christie was not that she saw the universal traits of mankind, like Shakespeare, but that she saw we are all quite different people, with differing motivations."

"Agatha Christie," Cotton repeated. "Really? You're thinking about Agatha Christie? As in, what would Agatha do?"

Max smiled. "You jest. But she'd have solved this by now. Or rather, Miss Marple would have solved it. By looking at the motivations and asking, What does this person want, and what does that person want? Want more than anything?"

"Yes," said Cotton with a sigh. "And who in the village it all reminded her of. How villagers are just like city folk, only more deadly. Or something."

"We'll get to the bottom of this," said Max, "with or without Miss Marple to guide us." He looked at Cotton, who had grown up more or less in the country but had been drawn to city ways, city clothing.

And a light came into Max's eyes. He felt the glimmer of a connection forming.

"But it has given me an idea," Max said. "Something my curate said, about people thinking in clichés."

"Now, that I could use. An idea. A clue would also be good."

"Tell me more about how Lady Baaden-Boomethistle is taking this," Max asked. "Bree."

Cotton flipped again to the relevant screen and read aloud. " 'I'm totally shaken and beyond myself,' she told me. Then she asked when she could go and saddle her horse. It seems she had some sort of meet or hunt yesterday."

"And you told her that wouldn't be possible. Besides, the hunt doesn't run on Sundays, not around here. Wherever she was headed, it wasn't to hunt."

"Of course I told her she couldn't go," said Cotton. "You wouldn't think I'd have to point that out, would you? To offer guidelines on the expected behavior of bereaved wives? I should have little cards printed up. 'Before the Funeral: Five Tips on Comportment for Merry Widows.' By the way, she shed not a tear until I told her I needed her to stick around in case questions came up. Only then did she look like she might have a meltdown."

Max pushed himself away from the fireplace mantel, signaling his departure.

"Right, I'll go have a word, then. With the widow and with the dowager."

" 'The Lady, or the Tiger'? Honestly, I'm not sure which is which."

CHAPTER 19
MAX AND THE LADY

Max found her in the stables, the place she would most likely be on any given day. The occasion of her husband's being murdered would not deter her. It might, Max recognized, bring her some solace, this ordinary routine of being around the animals she clearly loved.

Indeed as he walked in, stopping a moment to pet the retriever puppy that ran stumbling to greet him, she was rubbing Foto Finish's long aristocratic nose. Max did not know a lot about horses, although he had taught himself to ride years ago as part of an undercover operation. He could say, with Dorothy Gilman, that he and horses "had never enjoyed a warm or comfortable relationship." He had enormous respect for their majesty but no particular desire to let them become a ruling passion.

This particular horse continued to distinguish himself as much by his unusual dappled coat as by his look of utter complacence. He was probably used to being offered only the finest oats and carrots and receiving the highest praise and gentlest caresses from his mistress. He looked, particularly under Bree's fawning attention, as if it had all gone straight to his head.

The woman turned to face Max, and in that moment he caught the full force of her beauty like a wave. She was stunning, with an old-fashioned loveliness he associated with one of the Victorian showgirls who might have captured the heart of a Prince of Wales. Her dark eyes were enormous, sparkling and long-lashed, and despite her hair's being pulled back into a ponytail, he could see that when loosed it would fall in heavy dark curls. Somehow it seemed impossible for any red-blooded male to view her without wishing to see what that hair would look like as it cascaded down her back. She had the same wide hips, large bust, and narrow waist of a Victorian fantasy, as well, her waist so small that it appeared corseted but of course was not: She wore modern blue jeans and a tucked-in plaid blouse, an outfit that really did not suit an hour-glass figure such as hers.

Lips as pink as rose petals now parted in a tentative pearly smile. There were dark smudges under her eyes, perhaps from lack of sleep. Angels must look like this, thought Max. She did not unleash the vixenish firepower she surely could have deployed if she'd wanted, blasting every man in her path and reducing him to ashes, but instead her manner on seeing him was demure, almost shy. It only added to her impact. Even Max, the happiest of married men in all the world, could sense the potency of her sexual power. He felt he almost needed to grab the nearest post to steady himself.

She undid the tie around her hair and shook her head, letting the ribbons of curls unfurl past her shoulders before unself-consciously gathering it all again into the ponytail. When she spoke, it was in a breathless, little-girl voice. Max could see how the lord had been captivated by her effortless (or so it seemed) charm. Hang the casserole.

He introduced himself, saying how sorry he was she had to endure such a tragedy.

"It's terrible," she said. "It makes me quite ill to think about it. Do you mind awfully if we don't . . ." The eyelashes fluttered.

Don't what? wondered Max, somewhat dazed. Run off together? Mentally, he collected himself, gathering the reins.

"Don't talk about it? Of course, I do

understand. But the police have a job to do, and DCI Cotton has asked me to talk with you. Just a few questions. Nothing disturbing, I promise."

Such a ridiculous promise, and he knew it. There was no such thing as a murder investigation with easy, soft questions. Not unless one were lining a trap for the interviewee to fall into. But he began by getting her to talk about the horse — obviously the way to her heart — how old he was and if she'd raised him from a colt (yes). And before long, he had moved the conversation to include her life at the manor, and from there to how she had met Lord Baaden-Boomethistle. Of course he knew the answer to that from talking with Cotton, but he wanted to see if she would contradict any of it. She did not.

"We met at a horse show. It was love at first sight — the usual story."

Her lovely soft mouth was pouty like a child's; she had a habit of gently nibbling her lower lip as she considered what was being asked of her.

" 'Who ever loved, that loved not at first sight?' " quoted Max.

"Chris Marlowe had it right," she said. He was not surprised she recognized the famous quotation — besides, the intelligence shone from her, alongside her beauty, enhancing it. And certainly he was not surprised that Lord Baaden-Boomethistle's fall for her was swift and final. The question was, Was it also fatal? Max was less sure he believed she fell for him, a much older man, in quite the same way, even though his interest catapulted her near the top of the social hierarchy. He was a powerful, rich man, and those very qualities held their own attractions.

"My husband was devastated by the loss of his first wife," said Bree. "It took him a long time to recover from that." She stood with her small feet apart now, hands on hips, filling the space. It should have been a threatening stance, but it was, in keeping with her general aura, beguiling, commanding. "But the attraction was mutual — even though I know people doubted that." She looked at him knowingly, for the first time engaging him, complicit in acknowledging his own doubts. "We forged a real bond."

Max thought back to his conversation with Candice, the younger of the two nannies. She had not indicated a state of united marital harmony with the first Lady B-B such as Bree was describing. Was one of these two beautiful young women lying? Max wondered. Or was it possible that the

Lord Baaden-Boomethistle Candice knew had changed his spots when his wife died? Shock and grief could alter people, he knew. A shocking loss, out of the blue, could make one reassess. Max had learned that at first-hand.

"And the children? I know sometimes children don't really welcome a new step-mother. Especially when they've lost their own mother in a tragic way."

She nodded her head in acknowledgment, but then she shrugged.

"The fact I was near them in age helped, I think. I didn't try to mother them. I was not at all interested in mothering them."

At least that's honest, thought Max. Why pretend what you don't feel? And why try to force yourself in where you're not wanted? There was wisdom in that. The relationship might be one of benign neglect on all sides, thought Max. The fact that they — the stepmother and the boy and the girl — were of a similar age did make nonsense of any idea that she would be a mother to them, an idea she reinforced with her next sentence.

"Their own mother was a perfectly nice woman and I am sure quite irreplaceable."

"You were their friend, perhaps."

"I also didn't want to be friends particularly. I choose my friends more carefully than that, Vicar. Oh, I see I've shocked you. I didn't mean to. It's just that I don't find I have anything in common with her, or him, especially, although I did try. But he'd launch into these idiot defenses of things that don't need defending. Long-winded diatribes against the government and its policies. I'm sure he's right, but I simply don't care. Except when it comes to attempts to ban foxhunting completely, I pay no attention to what goes on at Whitehall."

Seeing Max's continued surprised expression, she softened her tone.

"I'm not a motherly type," she went on insistently. "Which is good — the children were young adults, rebelling against everything, by the time I came along. They would have rejected any nurturing attempts, from anyone. It's kind of who they are."

"So, who took care of them?"

Again a don't-care shrug. "They were away at school most of the time. There were scads of people taking care of them. I'm just saying I wasn't one of them. It isn't done in these rarified families to keep the children home." She did not add "Thank God," but he sensed if she'd been talking to anyone but him, she might have.

Max remembered a much-wanted child

who had been kidnapped — what had come to be called the Monkbury Murder Case. Here it was different: Here the children of the family did not seem to be much wanted by anyone. They had had only the love of their mother, and she was taken from them. Max felt a surge of pity.

Max thought also of the current Lady Baaden-Boomethistle in a loveless marriage with her lord — if loveless it had been. He supposed it was only natural one so young and beautiful might turn her affections elsewhere; Cotton had said there were rumors of an affair. Or affairs, plural. But it made a nonsense of her marriage vows. Why had she entered into the marriage in the first place? For social prestige? For a little bit of money?

Now he sounded like that policewoman in *Fargo.* Maybe the love at first sight she claimed to have felt had simply worn off. It wouldn't be the first time in history that had happened.

Max wasn't sure what he'd been expecting. All the bad press the woman had received had undoubtedly colored his opinion, in spite of his best efforts. He was reminded, oddly, of a woman he had known in his MI5 days, an expert on serial killers. Before meeting her, he had expected to find a person of sharp edges, clad in leather and red lipstick and jangling metal, a woman who subsisted on wine and canapés, someone who drank to forget what she knew. Instead, he'd been introduced to a woman who fit the stereotype of a favorite granny. She had plied him with tea and biscuits and asked with genuine concern about his life in Five — how he was holding up to the pressure. After half an hour in her presence, he'd felt he'd been through a sort of healing therapy session.

He remembered something else Awena had told him once about the gossip swirling around Bree: "Everything negative I know about her, I came to realize, I heard from the daughter at first- or secondhand. From Rosamund. And only from her."

"But you believed it?"

Awena's fantastic pale eyes, always ablaze with life, had caught new fire.

"Yes, sadly. That's the invidious thing about nasty-minded gossip. It's seldom the truth that sticks in your mind, just the ugly details."

"Should I be frightened?" Bree asked him now, turning from grooming the horse, her own large eyes widened in a classic, silent-film-star look of fear. It was like being caught in the rays of a searchlight, and it seemed to be a calculated attempt to enlist him as her protector. "What if I was the intended target?" she elaborated. "I'm always out riding, and I ride Foto Finish a lot. Did anyone think of that?"

"No. I mean, yes, they did. It seems to have been a . . . a finely calibrated crime. With one intended victim only."

"Oh."

"Do you have any thoughts about what happened? Any theories at all? Did *he* have any reason to fear for his life? Had he been anxious or worried about anything lately?"

Her eyes narrowed slightly with either concentration in forming her answer or suspicion of Max's motive in asking the questions. Again, small white teeth nibbled at her lower lip. In truth, Max didn't know why the questions about fear had occurred to him, but past experience had taught him there was often a clue in the way his thoughts were trending — if only he could fathom what it was.

"He was a powerful man. Powerful men make enemies," she said at last. This was a somewhat cleaned-up version of what she had told Cotton. Perhaps she had taken a moment to ponder the wisdom of being so frank with the authorities.

"I see." He paused a moment to see if

she'd say more. "Well, I am, of course, willing to help you with arranging the services for your husband," he told her. "Perhaps his son . . ."

"Would wish to be consulted? I suppose. Maybe."

"They were not close?"

"It was not a strong relationship, no," she replied. "Most parents care about their flesh and blood children simply because they are flesh and blood. Some care only about their legacy — their children as their legacy. A reflection of themselves." She stopped, as if something had just occurred to her. "Peregrine is Lord Baaden-Boomethistle now. I suppose Pater Baaden-Boomethistle would be pleased by that, if he were still around." She paused, adding, "Or perhaps not. His father thought Peregrine wasn't living up to his potential."

"And you?"

"I never thought he had any potential."

Ouch. "Really?

"He's rather a fatuous young man. It remains to be seen if he'll outgrow that, if the added responsibilities of his title will bring him up to the mark. But he's been protected and cosseted and spoon-fed all his life, programmed into becoming the vapid, mindless oaf you see today. I don't believe the rumors he is gay. He has always struck me as rather a gloomy sort of person. A gloomy oaf. Anyway, his gayness is anybody's guess, but overall, I think not. He seems to be neither here nor there, and it is far more likely he is unpopular with members of both sexes."

Ouch, thought Max again. Peregrine thus disposed of, she returned her attention to the horse. He was taken aback by her harshness, by the hard words emerging incongruously from the petal pink, childlike lips. The initially demure manner had slipped. Certainly Peregrine, from what little he knew of him, would not win any awards for intellect, but even so —

"How do you and your stepdaughter get along?"

"I can stand her in small doses." She paused and added, "I daresay she feels the same way about me."

Again she turned away from Foto Finish to look at him. "Actually, she's not around that much. And he — generally he's away, too, of course, but even before that . . . He's a *strange* boy. Given to mooching about on his own. I never know quite what he's up to. His father allowed him to take his meals alone, in his room."

That struck Max as a sad commentary

right there. This kid on his own all day and even during the dinner hour, when most families manage a passing check-in with one another. And then there was the comment that he was given to mooching about. Looked at another way, a lot can be seen and overheard when one mooches about on one's own. A lot of trouble gotten up to, as well.

He did not fail to notice she had switched the conversation away from Rosamund and back to Peregrine. And he wondered why.

"I did hear there was sometimes sparring at mealtimes."

"Oh, I suppose. There was a bit of business at breakfast the other day. No worse than the usual. Peregrine had done something his father disliked. Between us, I think he was about to be sent down from university. In fact, he seemed to have intercepted a message from his tutor to that effect — the tutor and my husband were great friends."

"But there was already something of an atmosphere before Peregrine arrived home?" Max was fishing, but this kind of rancor generally thrived in a preexisting atmosphere.

"Was there? I don't recall particularly that there was." She looked up at him, calmly assessing, a look of mild humor on her face. "You are thinking I am too hard on him," she said. "You don't know him as well as I do, Vicar — some people bring trouble wherever they go. So you mustn't rush to judge me."

They were words of annoyance but spoken in that silky, insinuating voice, so that the listener was not quite sure where he stood.

"You seem, if you don't mind my saying so, a bit hostile toward him."

"You'd be hostile, too, if he'd slandered you to anyone who would listen. He and Rosamund, and that floozy grandmother of theirs. I've always been in a bad position, all of them running their mouths against me. Accusations . . ."

"I wasn't aware —"

"I've had nothing to do with the estate manager," she rushed on hotly. "With Bill Travis. That slandering, horrible woman."

He could see how tiresome her position was. No one enjoyed being disliked, especially when accusers were stacked three against one.

"Yes, the standards are exacting for being a member of this family," she said. "But if you are thinking I killed my husband to get out from under, I was in Monkslip-super-Mare at the time it happened. I have an alibi: shopping, having lunch, followed by more shopping — with witnesses. I ran into some people from the village while I was there. First it was Elka Garth. Then I saw Chanel Dirkson. We chatted a long while. You know how it is with the villagers. You can't just say hello; you have to stay and have a real chin-wag. This was around seven in the evening. Then I stayed the night in Monkslip Parva. With a *girl* friend and her family."

"Yes, DCI Cotton told me you had an alibi."

"You don't believe me?" When he did not reply, she added sulkily, silkily, that pretty pout cushioning her words, "You seem to be very chummy with the DCI."

"We go back a long way. We first met when I was appearing as a character witness in court, for a young lad who'd gone astray with some bad companions. DCI Cotton was there, representing the forces of law and order."

"Did it work?"

"Hmm? The character witnessing, you mean? Yes. The lad was let off with a warning. And when last seen, he lives surrounded by people who care about him. He's been luckier than most, and more important, he has the wit to realize it."

"I see." She did not elaborate on what she saw. She had been brushing Foto Finish's mane; now she began to separate strands of hair, weaving them into a braid along his neck. Max had never seen this done before. Again he wondered at the love and pampering that went into maintaining this particular horse, probably all the horses here. Did they spoil from the attention, like some people, or did it make them into better horses? The trifling thought led him back to the subject of the young lord of the manor, Peregrine.

"You and Lord Baaden-Boomethistle had been married five years, is that right? How did Peregrine react initially to the marriage?"

"How did he react?" She stopped her work, almost as if pausing to consider the subject for the first time. She seemed to settle on truthfulness as an answer, reasoning quite rightly that Max already knew or could soon find out the truth. "He was almost violently opposed to the marriage, especially at first. I suppose we hadn't prepared him for it — my husband was not one to ask permission or input, particularly from his son. We didn't exactly poll everyone for their views, you know. We were in love." Again that insistence, Max noted. "So we had . . . some bad weeks. Finally, Peregrine agreed to see a shrink. He went weekly for well over a year. It seemed to calm him. I think what really made the difference was that he simply grew out of the bratty stage and came to realize his father had a right to a happy life, too, like anyone else."

"Would you tell me the name of the doctor he visited?"

She named a Harley Street specialist of great renown. Max had actually met him at a religious conference once — something about the nation's spiritual crisis and the effect on mental health. There were many people in search of a church or simply something to believe in; many more who had given up on religion entirely. The majority of the latter felt the need to talk about their lack of religion, which Max and the doctor found interesting in itself. Weren't those people just protesting too much?

The doctor had struck Max as being saner than many of his colleagues. He wondered at the ethics of trying to get him to talk about Peregrine, but he realized the chances the man would be willing to breach patient confidentiality were a million to one against. Max would pass along the information to Cotton and let him worry about it.

"And the dowager?" He could guess the two got along like the mongoose and the snake, but he left the question open-ended.

"I think she couldn't get through the day if she didn't first give everything a base coat of romance" was the silky reply. "In my case, though, she seems to have suspended her usual methods. For me, we are treated to the paranoia and dark worldview of the suspense author. She would be better off focusing her suspicions on Peregrine, but of course she can't allow that into her dollhouse-size mind."

She turned to concentrate on beautifying Foto Finish, at moments nuzzling her face against the horse's cheek. Trying to hide her expression? wondered Max. Or simply overcome by her rather cloying affection for the horse? She exuded such an air of play-acting, Max would have bet the former. For she was hiding *some*thing; no one could be as untouched as she appeared to be about her husband's death — whether or not she were responsible for it. Her world had just been turned — if not turned upside down, then reshaped and molded into an entirely new form and future. Again she busied herself stroking the animal's neck. Even Foto Finish seemed to tire of this extravagant display of fondness, and, snorting, he suddenly threw his head back, stepping away from her.

"You aren't suggesting that Peregrine had anything to do with this, are you?"

She looked straight at Max now. He held her gaze, waiting, wondering if she was trying to toss the boy completely into it. Remembering she herself was not much more than a girl didn't help the dislike he felt for her.

"That in fact is one of *his* theories. That I'm tossing him into it. He is full of . . . theories. Peregrine believes the earth was populated by aliens. Seriously. So whatever he's telling you, take it with a grain of salt. Or Kryptonite."

Max knew Peregrine liked to hang out at Awena's Godessspell shop, which drew an eclectic crowd at times. "There's no harm in him, Max," Awena had told him. "He thinks aliens built Stonehenge and are trying to communicate with us using crop circles, but so do a lot of people. He'll outgrow it."

Max found Bree's manner so disconcerting, he decided on a gamble, trying to shake her seemingly unshakable poise.

"I am afraid I have heard the other rumors," he said. "About the estate manager, for one example."

355

A flicker of apprehension crossed her face, like the flash of light through tree branches blown by the wind. He remembered the indistinguishable voices he'd heard as he'd approached the stables earlier. But she collected herself and said with every appearance of coming clean, "My husband and I were happy together for a very long while. Happier than most, I daresay."

"And then?"

She shrugged.

"And then we weren't." She looked as if she might go on and then decided against it. She closed her mouth so tightly, he would not have been surprised to see her pantomime turning a key in a lock. As it was, she looked defiant, but scared.

"This is rather bad timing for you, isn't it?" said Max, not entirely without sympathy. "Apart from losing your husband, the timing of losing him is a bit awkward, I mean."

She relaxed her shoulders and rubbed a hand across the back of her neck in a gesture that spoke of tensions being released.

"I am sorry," she said, surprising him. "I didn't mean to make it sound as if that's my first concern. Of course losing my husband is awful; he was good to me. He gave me a good life. But this all looks rather . . . you know."

"Convenient."

"Yes, too convenient. And it is anything but. The police are bound to look at the whole thing with suspicion. We've all seen those shows on the telly. The spouse is the first suspect."

"Or in this case, the spouse's lover."

"Oh my God, Max. What am I going to do?"

Max, was it now. The appeal to the man, not the priest. But again, he was not without sympathy. If one believed in divine punishment and retribution, here was a doozy of an example. In the midst of a reckless affair, her husband is killed, and she and this man are thrown right into the lineup of suspects — put right at the head of that line. But Max knew there was a certain class of criminal that never considered or cared about appearances. There was a type of personality that believed it was immune and could get away, literally, with murder. He had met many such in his MI5 days, many of them sociopaths.

And Lady Baaden-Boomethistle was in a special category, bestowed by her God-given looks — there was no question. Possessed of a natural, flawless, and effortless beauty, she must be so used to having men open doors for her and rush to do her bidding that she wouldn't give it a second thought. The way one takes health for granted until one's health fails. Thus would Lady Baaden-Boomethistle go through her days, finding the universe organized to her liking, until old age caught up with her at last.

Such thoughtless, innate beauty might make one come to believe one was invincible.

As for getting men to do one's bidding — might that even include murder?

There was a great rectangle of hay just outside Foto Finish's stall, and now, as if suddenly tiring, she moved to sit atop it. She removed her boots and tucked her stocking feet beneath her. It was a casual movement, a strangely intimate one, as though she were in her bedroom, preparing to change for dinner. Max felt this sort of unconscious act on her part was part of her charm. She was not being rude, never that; she was simply following whatever impulse came into her head. It was a gesture that reminded him of someone, and then he realized that just so did Awena sometimes sit, graceful and relaxed and serenely unaware.

He didn't reply, and she continued to gaze at him, although with a certain lessening of favor. With a slight change of gears, and a certain edge to the little-girl tone, she said, "When can we arrange for the . . . how do you say it? Celebration . . . of his life?" Had the pause in her last sentence gone on a bit too long?

For *celebration* was clearly the key word as far as she was concerned.

"I'll be in touch," Max told her. Relenting a bit, for his tone had been abrupt, he added, " 'Jesus, Son of Mary,' number three sixty-three, is a favorite with many."

She looked as if she couldn't care less if they sang ABBA's greatest hits. Then she surprised him by saying, almost shyly, "I always liked 'I Sing a Song of the Saints of God.' Could we have that, do you think?"

He smiled. "Of course. You may choose whatever you like."

Bree watched Max's back as he walked away, out of the stables, headed toward the main house. Really, she thought. *Such* a dishy man; it was just ridiculous. But she had not been brought up in religion and she had no use for religious people. Although she found them wonderfully pliable, particularly the men, she trusted none of them.

And so she found the several small untruths she had told Max bothered her not at all.

A dark figure emerged from one of the stalls at the back of the stables.

"That was perfect." Foto Finish pricked up his ears at the sound of the deep, warm voice.

"Perfect," the voice repeated. "You played him brilliantly."

CHAPTER 20
MAX AND THE DOWAGER

The Dowager Baaden-Boomethistle received Max with a show of pleasure, tempered by a nicely calculated recognition that while he was not to the manor born, he was the village vicar and his office must be accorded respect. She established this fine distinction by addressing him as Father Maxen and pointing him into a low seat before her own place on the sofa. Max ignored the gesture and sat in the chair nearest her.

"Please call me Father Max," he said. "Or Vicar, if you prefer. I am most deeply sorry for your loss, Lady Baaden-Boomethistle."

"It is dreadful. Simply dreadful. To lose an only son. And in such a common way."

"You mean . . . for him to have been killed in such a way."

"Murdered!" she said.

Max reflected that there was in fact a long tradition of those in the upper classes getting themselves murdered. While he had never seen statistics to back up the premise, certainly the nobs put themselves in the way of offending people, and perhaps more often than did those in the lower classes. After all, they had wider scope and opportunity to give offense.

She had taken a handkerchief from inside the long sleeve of her low-cut black dress and was now dabbing at her eyes. The handkerchief came away spotted with black goo, the makeup she liberally applied to her false lashes. He also noticed that one corner of a false lash had come loose, giving her a startled, cockeyed appearance. He reminded himself that while snob she might be, she was a mother mourning her son.

"I am so sorry," he repeated.

She nodded, taking this as her due. She also was busy taking Max's measure: tall and striking, she thought, her romantic writer's brain automatically flipping through the pages of her internal dictionary. A dashing, heroic figure, utterly, *melt*ingly masculine, hard-bodied and with the slightest and *most* attractive hint of the rogue playing at his edges. And those gloriously penetrating gray eyes! If, she thought, I were twenty years younger. Even ten years younger! And not in mourning. And if he were not married. *Well*. Not that the married part had always been an impediment, but now she had her position to consider. That business with Lord Stag-Hazen did follow her around so, his rather ill-bred wife kicking up such a tiresome fuss, and she —

"I did wonder if you might be willing to talk with me about the, well, the atmosphere in the house in the days leading up to your son's demise," Max Tudor was saying.

She trembled ever so slightly and then threw back her bejeweled and feathered shoulders, braced to withstand any onslaught of questions, however unseemly.

"We must get to the bottom of this," she said, and Max could only agree. "Someone tried to attack me the other day as I was taking my constitutional in the woods. Only my screams frightened them away. And I think someone tried to break into my bedroom from the tree branch outside my window. I *told* the gardener that branch should be cut down."

Max took a moment to consider how much fact was mixed with fantasy here, but meanwhile, she had hared off in a new narrative direction.

"You must understand, Father, how out of my element I am here. I've led a rather sheltered life — oh, I'll admit it! So I don't know how I can help with such a sordid matter. I can but try!"

She cast him a look of bewildered innocence, a look exquisitely misjudged for her shrewd, rather worldly audience. Max decided to let pass this deft burnishing of past peccadilloes. After a suitably respectful pause to take in his plush surroundings — really, it was as if he'd stumbled onto a set for *Downton Abbey* — he said, "You have no ideas of your own, then. About what might be behind this?"

"Well . . . since you ask. My daughter-in-law is not all she might be. Oh, I'll say no more about it! Nothing could pry more out of me. I shall not stoop to it! But, then again, I suppose I must not conceal what I know. My son's killer must be caught! She and the groom . . . the estate manager . . . I have seen them together, you know."

Max decided to feign ignorance. "Really?"

"There could be no mistake." She said this with an operatic gesture, throwing back her head and placing the back of one hand against her temple as she gazed at the ceiling. "They were in the pagoda. Caught them in flagrante, I did. I was that shocked." She seemed to recall the sheltered life she had claimed to lead, and opening her eyes wide, fingers splayed against her chin, she assumed a look of innocence outraged this time. She and Bree must have the same acting coach, reflected Max.

The pagoda . . . that little folly or summerhouse in the woods. So his guess as to its alternate uses had been right.

He struggled to come up with something that would drag her attention down to the level of normal conversation. Finally, he came out with a question: "When did you last see your son that day?"

"In the morning, was it? Really, I'm not sure. When I am writing my little books, it is like I'm in a trance. It's a form of magic, you know. I could be anywhere, in any time period. There was, as I recall, conflict at the breakfast table earlier that week between Bree and Peregrine. I have a little confession to make. . . ."

"Oh, yes?"

She leaned in closer to him. "I borrowed some of the conflict of that morning for a scene I was writing. Really, the passions and the struggles between that little trollop and everyone else — the hostility and bad blood! I rather thought it might make an intriguing title for the book. *The Trollop and the Duke.* Or perhaps, *Prince* would be better."

Why hold back? Max wondered. Why not go for it with *Emperor*?

"She came from nowhere, you know. Bree. Even her name — so common. She sounds like a canapé."

For the second time that day, Max was taken aback by the viciousness and backbiting in this little group. Seeing the truth would not be easy: There were so many shades of dark running through this family tapestry.

Particularly since the dowager's past, by all reports, would not hold up well to scrutiny, and she would do what she could to hinder the investigation in that regard. As Cotton had speculated, perhaps her own past was the reason she felt she understood Bree and her motivations so well. Or was it simple jealousy?

"How did they meet, Bree and your son?" Max asked, certain she would have her own spin on what he knew of the situation. "I know he was a widower. . . ."

"You are quite correct," she drawled, her voice dripping with venom. "His wife — lovely woman; a Pratt-Knodlebaum, you know — was barely in her grave or so it seemed. My son went to a horse show or auction or something like that and Bree made a dead set at him."

"She was flirtatious. I see."

"No! No. Of *course* not." Max was treated

to a pitying look: For such a handsome man, he was certainly a babe in the woods when it came to women. "The easiest way into a man's heart is to act as if the man doesn't exist," she said, speaking slowly, as if to give Max time to absorb the esoteric knowledge she was imparting. "That he's beneath the woman's notice. It's catnip to their egos. Particularly if the woman is from the lower orders, like Bree. Everyone knows that."

Max bowed to her superior knowledge of tactics deployed in the war between the sexes (this was the woman who had brought *Priscilla's Passion* to a waiting world, after all), hoping not to appear to fall in line with her views on the social classes. "Lower orders" indeed. What a dinosaur the woman was.

"Why, oh why, did he have to go and marry her? He was greatly sought after when his wife died. He would have had his pick of great ladies." She rolled her *r*'s on the words *greatly* and *great* in her rich contralto voice, as if to emphasize not only their greatness but her own highborn, strained speech pattern. "There was Alexandra 'Tinky' Leggett-Fitzcalder, just for one — dazzling on the dance floor and in the field and forest."

"I beg your pardon?"

"I mean," the dowager said slowly, enunciating for his benefit, a manner she had perfected in issuing instructions to the housekeeper, "she was at home with all the highborn of the land, and with the hare and the hound. She could skin a rabbit in the wink of an eye, or gut a stag, but then bring a man to his knees with her plunging décolletage by eight that very same evening."

The ultimate multitasker, then. Max gained the clear impression the Dowager Baaden-Boomethistle had wandered off inside one of her own books, from which she would continue to quote the most appalling drivel if he could not pull her back out in time.

"But Lord Baaden-Boomethistle passed all this by for the sake of Bree," he said quickly. "I see."

"She also had many suitors, did Bree," the dowager admitted, but grudgingly. "That only added to her appeal for my son. Women like Bree have their ways and their wiles."

Women like Bree. "And I suppose she was a good cook." Max could not resist playing with the dowager just a bit.

"Really, I've no idea." She looked at Max as if he'd taken leave of his senses. "I've never seen her do so much as boil an egg. We have servants for all that." She sniffed, adding, "I can only guess at what she *was* good at, and I prefer not to be reminded of it, if it's all the same to you, Vicar."

"Yes, I do hear Bree's an expert horse-woman." Max beamed at her, the picture of innocence.

The dowager sighed deeply into her own rather impressive décolletage. Really, the man was hopeless. How on earth anyone this naïve had managed to father a child? . . . Still, what could she expect? He was a priest, after all. Her fingers itched to dial up her wellborn friends and relay this conversation. They all seemed to agree that Bree was a gold digger who should be clapped into irons immediately. And now this credulous priest was somehow assisting the police with their investigation. She would just have to get on the horn to Whitehall. *And* to the bishop of Monkslip. This outrage *could* not stand. Had her son been killed in a duel between equals, she felt she could bear it — just. But for him to be murdered by the low-born Bree — and he had been, she just knew it! She knew it! — well . . . It was an insult to the proper order of things, that's what it was. And now it looked as if Bree was going to be allowed to get away with it, the truth overlooked and swept under the rug by an incompetent constabulary.

Away with murder.

Away with murder, *and* with access to the family millions.

Max assumed much of this venom came from worry about her dowager rights, with this little "trollop" Bree coming in from the gutter, as the duchess thought of it, and taking everything. People who feel their basic security is being threatened will lash out in all sorts of ways, Max reflected, which went a long way toward explaining the savagery of some divorce proceedings. Even though she was protected by law and tradition, who would want an unseemly tussle over who owned that silver tea service, and who owned that painting? And, more important, who lived where. Bree no doubt could make things very uncomfortable for the dowager if she chose.

Bree, for her part, might fear a smear campaign, along with being "outed" for having an affair. That mattered less with Lord Baaden-Boomethistle out of the way, of course. But gossip and innuendo could make life a bit uncomfortable for her in the village, with the dowager claiming to be an eyewitness to carryings-on in the summerhouse. But, *had* she seen anything? It was always possible she was testing the waters, seeing how Bree would react. Or causing mischief for the sake of mischief. That tendency of hers toward fantasy might blur the edges of reality. He would ask Cotton to look into any other witnesses to this behavior on Bree's part. It was possible she had let herself open to a spot of blackmail.

"I must bid you farewell now," said the dowager. She eased gently back into her pillows, as if her back troubled her. Max was reminded of Cotton as he'd left him just now, wrapped in cotton wool like a rare artifact. In such a manner did the Queen dismiss her courtiers. It was courteous, but it let the listener know who was in charge. Her courtiers would be sent scurrying to open doors if she were leaving the room, and to offer arms to escort her to her final destination in Buckingham Palace or in whatever palace she managed to find herself. Max stopped to wonder at the life of evident privilege, and to try to will himself into such a place and setting, and he found he could not do so. His natural habitat was the little vicarage study, where he wrote his sermons and dandled Owen on his knee, not this gilded cage.

Max made the usual sounds of regret at

being parted from her and rose to leave.

"I hope I have not imposed on your grief," he told her. "Please remember that I am here to help. You need only call. And of course there will be arrangements to make."

"Arrangements?"

He could clearly see her flipping through her mental file, looking under *A* for *Arrangements*. Flower arrangements, seating arrangements — ah, of course, here it is! Of course, yes: funeral arrangements.

"You mean arrangements for his . . . erm . . ."

"Yes, I'm afraid so," said Max. "Please don't trouble yourself about it now. Plenty of time. Perhaps your daughter-in-law would —"

But this mention of Bree seemed to galvanize the dowager. Gone was the mask of genteel and noble suffering, to be replaced almost comically by a Kabuki-style warrior mask — her painted red lips drawn back and her heavily made-up eyes narrowed into a menacing guise of anger. Gone, too, was the look of simpering helplessness. The Dowager Baaden-Boomethistle looked fully capable of taking care of herself. And of dealing with anyone who might try to stand in her way.

"No," she said flatly, crossly. "Not her. I

will *not* have her involved." It was almost as if it had just occurred to her that arrangements *would* have to be made, and of course her daughter-in-law would be consulted first about them.

"I'll see her in hell first," said the dowager.

CHAPTER 21
DESTINY REMEMBERS II

Max had asked Destiny earlier to stop by the manor house whenever she could fit it into her schedule, to see if she could offer any help.

There was never a shortage of need for pastoral care in the village, and Destiny was already much in demand. Max somehow thought a woman's sense and sensibilities might be useful in this case. A referee between the two ladies up at Totleigh Hall, he realized after speaking with them both, might be even more needed. He thought Destiny possessed the right diplomatic skills, possibly enough to get everyone through the funeral service in one piece. He felt sometimes she was wasted here and would have better served the world in the Hague.

It was late in the evening when she visited the hall, and early the next day she headed straight for Max and Awena's cottage. She found Max alone at the breakfast table, lingering over his second cup of coffee and the newspaper. He apologized again for his unplanned nap during her sermon.

"Really, don't worry about it. I say, that was odd about the music, though, wasn't it?"

"The hymn board? Yes."

"Eugenia was in a complete tizzy. She says she saw a woman changing it. Changing the hymn numbers before the service."

Not a teenager messing about, then. "Did she say who it was?"

"She thinks Chanel Dirkson. Can you imagine? She's starkers, Max — Eugenia is, I mean. Or she needs her eyes examined. I wouldn't pay much attention whatever her answer. Why would a grown woman do such a silly thing?

"Anyway, why I'm here: I went to the manor house, as you asked, to see where I could be of help. At all cost we need to avoid having the lady and the dowager engaged in unseemly squabbles over the lord's remains — I've seen that happen in the best of families. And this is not the best of families, I'm sure you'll agree. Anyway, it was a pea souper out there — fog so thick, you couldn't see your hand in front of your face. I was on a shortcut through the woods, which is particularly spooky, I don't mind saying. Especially once you know what happened to Lord Baaden-Boomethistle in those woods. But it was when the fog cleared momentarily that I had my first good look at him."

She realized, she said, that she must have been walking the same path through the woods that Max had taken the night of the murder. And that was when she saw him.

"Him who?"

She had not known his name — he went by one of those posh nicknames at Oxford, like "Cosmo" or "Smurffy" — or that he was from a manor house near Nether Monkslip. But she recognized him on sight, in that split second the fog had cleared, despite the odd haircut he had adopted. She thought maybe he was trying to dumb himself down for the police investigation, but why he would do that defeated her.

"It does seem far-fetched. You are talking about Peregrine, of course. You passed Peregrine in the woods outside the manor house. And you recognized him from your recent Oxford days."

"I do mean him. He just passed me by, pretending not to have seen me in the fog. But he had not wanted to be seen and definitely did not want me to waylay him.

He turned his head and sort of scuttled off."

"Was he wearing glasses?"

"Hmm? No, I don't think so. Are you saying he couldn't see me without his glasses?"

Max did not reply.

"And you knew who he was?" he asked. *So?* he wanted to add, but this was Destiny. There would be a point to this, however long it took to get there.

"Just wait for it," she said. "There's more to tell you, Max. Loads more."

"I knew the son only by reputation at Oxford, but it was quite a reputation he had." She put down the piece of wholegrain toast she had appropriated from the rack on the breakfast table. Max pushed a little bowl of currant jam toward her. "This sounds like the most dreadful gossip, doesn't it?" she added.

It did, but Max was not about to stop the flow of these revelations. Gossip and unsubstantiated rumor were terrible if indulged in for entertainment or cruelty. They had been the saving grace in more than one investigation, however.

"He was not at Oxford what he appears to be now: a sort of überdork. He was famous for partying in a town known for drinking clubs and out-of-control gatherings. He was also famous for affairs and breaking hearts, generally — a bit of a ladies' man. More than a bit. He was not famous for intellectual achievement, not surprisingly. Where would he find the time?"

"Surely you recognized him when you saw him here in the village? Recognized that name?"

She shook her head.

"I only saw him as he flew by on his bicycle, generally muffled in a scarf. There were photos of him in *Cherwell* and other student papers — generally holding a glass aloft — so I know what he normally looks like. In the woods, I came face-to-face, within a few feet of him. I didn't *know* him — here or at the university. He arrived at Oxford pretty much as I was leaving. And I only heard rumors, you understand — his arrival was like a rock thrown into a pond. I was on the farthest shore of that *Brideshead* sort of thing, but even where I was, I felt the ripples. He wasn't a member of St. Barney's, obviously; he was at Christ Church, carrying on with his little foxhunting friends.

"He wasn't like you, Max," she added, thinking, You could have had your pick of anyone you wanted, but you never took advantage of the fact. Which only made you that much more desirable to every female of every age and persuasion for miles around. "Peregrine was known to be predatory. Famous for it. Again, I know only his reputation, but that's what it was. Among the women, especially. Not that many of them seemed to take the warning. He's the type to give the Bullingdon Club a bad name."

Since the Buller, a famous drinking club, already had a bad name, Max reflected this was probably saying something. While at Oxford, he'd once investigated the murder of a member of such a club. The trouble had been that everyone's memory of events on the night in question had been so hazy.

"But can you be sure it was Peregrine?"

"Who else could it have been in that particular place in the woods, so near the manor house?"

"The estate manager, for one."

She shook her head. "I know what he looks like. I've visited his mother — she lives nearby." Max had not been aware of this. Destiny, Max reflected, was full of surprises. "She must have a hundred photos of her handsome son in her sitting room. Besides, I said, 'Hello, Peregrine' — his name has been on everyone's lips around the village lately. And he didn't stay to correct me. He just scuttled on by."

"I see."

"But there's more."

"More about Peregrine?"

"More about his stepmother."

Max stopped in the middle of spreading preserves on his toast, his knife, dripping with currant jam, poised in midair. "Do go on."

"I wonder if there's any more of that wonderful coffee?"

Max went to make another pot. The conversation stilled for a moment as he fed fair-trade coffee beans through a hand grinder.

It transpired that after spotting Peregrine, Destiny heard again the voice of one of the women she'd overheard in the steam room.

"The thing is," she told Max, "after talking with the dowager — and what an interesting fossil she is; I kept thinking of Mae West — and after recognizing this son as someone I sort of knew by reputation at Oxford, I heard a *voice* I recognized. All of this happening at once made it a bit difficult to process, you see."

She told him that after passing Peregrine and walking on toward the village and her cottage, she heard a voice: a woman talking. And she followed the voice as she heard it coming through the fog, dumbstruck to realize it was the same disembodied voice she'd heard once before. The voice led her to the templelike summerhouse in the woods.

"It was all *just like* before, in fact, because of the fog. The identical sort of hazy setting triggered the memory of the voice in the 'fog' of the steam room. There could be no mistake. Problem is, I couldn't see inside the summerhouse through the windows — I didn't dare get that close. They'd have heard me and there'd be no good explanation for my being there."

"Tell me again what you heard in the steam room," Max said. "Word for word."

Destiny made a moue of effort, trying to remember. "I'm not sure I can." She summarized the overheard conversation as best she could, adding, "The odd part was when she said she knew someone who could obit someone. Who says that? I figured it was some slang term I didn't recognize. But it didn't sound like a positive outcome for someone."

"Might she have said 'omit'?"

"Yes, of course, that makes more sense, doesn't it? There was also that odd phrasing I told you about, that 'not yet.' "

"The voice you heard in the summerhouse

381

last night — it was Lady Baaden-Boomethistle speaking, perhaps?"

She shook her head. "I don't know. Never got the chance to meet the woman — the butler told me she wasn't at home when I came to call. That may or may not have been true, although I think he would have said she wasn't receiving visitors if he'd been trying to cover for her. It wasn't the dowager — I'd just left her, and she'd really have had to hoof it to get that deeply into the woods that quickly."

"That can be remedied," said Max thoughtfully. "Hearing Lady B-B's voice, I mean. It is a voice she has polished to a high gloss, rubbing away all traces of her background, and yet it *is* most distinctive. Whom was she talking to?"

"That's what's so frustrating. She was on a rant, really not allowing whoever it was to speak. My sense is that this time, the person she was speaking to was male, though. It might have been Peregrine — perhaps that had been where he was headed in such a hurry, to meet her. She was agitated, her voice sort of urgent — hectoring is the best I can describe it. I'll just scoot over there to the hall before I start my hospital visits today and make sure. See if I can catch her in."

"Don't you dare do that. Don't even think of it. I'll arrange to have a policewoman with you when you go, or we'll figure out a way you won't be seen."

"But I —"

"Promise me. Whoever is behind this killing is quite, quite mad. Ruthless. Even given the horrors we are becoming accustomed to seeing and hearing on the news every day, this stands out."

Off her look, he added, "It's not what you'd expect in Nether Monkslip. I know."

CHAPTER 22
GASLIGHT

Max rang Cotton after Destiny had left and related the gist of her story. Cotton was in court all that day, testifying in another case, so Max invited him to stop by later that afternoon to talk over a pot of tea laced with whiskey.

He arrived at five. Awena was away taping her cookery show for the BBC at a studio in Monkslip-super-Mare. Max, Owen, and Thea had stayed behind at the vicarage with a fire blazing against a settling autumn chill.

"Destiny and I both read theology at St. Barnabas House," Max told Cotton. "She was an undergraduate at the time I was a graduate student of the college."

"And you trust her — her judgment, her testimony?"

"Implicitly, although much of what she knows or thinks she knows may be clouded by time. You know how unreliable eyewitness testimony can be, even given an honest and well-intended witness. She heard that conversation in the steam room many months ago now. And then she overheard two people talking in the forest. She went off the path in the fog and didn't realize quite where she was. Only this time, one of the voices Destiny overheard was, she thinks, male. Although he wasn't really talking, just listening and agreeing with the woman — perhaps pretending to agree. A grunt of assent or protest here and there."

"Young male? Middle-aged?"

"She couldn't say."

"Was it Peregrine?"

"Again, not sure. He veered off the path after nearly running into her and might have been heading for the summerhouse. She rather assumed it was he, and I probably would have assumed the same. Otherwise, the woods were teeming with people that night, which seems unlikely."

"Well, what did she say?" Cotton asked. "The woman who might be Lady B-B, I mean."

Max cast his own mind back to the exact words as relayed by Destiny. " 'When it's over, we can do as we please. Not much longer now. We'll sell up — the National Trust would kill to get its hands on this place — and we'll go where no one knows us.' " Again he replayed the conversation with Destiny in his mind.

"Bora-Bora, I believe, was mentioned," Destiny had told Max. "Do you know it?"

"I was there once on a case," Max had replied absently. "Smuggling. Anything else?"

"No. Just then I snapped a twig underfoot and they heard it, because they shut up right away. I nearly fainted, it was that loud, or so it seemed to me. I had to duck behind a tree, holding my breath. God knows what I'd have done — what they'd have done — if they hadn't decided it was a wild animal in the woods scuffling about. But it spooked them and they ended the conversation."

Max again summarized all of this for Cotton, who sat studying the play of light on the whiskey bottle that sat between them on the low table.

"She didn't really say anything all that helpful," Cotton remarked. " 'When it's over' — well, yes, that might mean the murder and the investigation of the murder. But it would have been jolly helpful if she'd said, 'When they're through investigating me for killing my husband, which, by the way, I actually did do, and I'm not at all sorry, not one little bit. Here, let me put that in writing while I'm thinking about it.'

"But the need to go where no one knows them," Cotton continued, "somewhere far away, like Bora-Bora . . . Doesn't Bora-Bora have an extradition treaty with us?"

"Lady Baaden-Boomethistle and whoever it was she was talking with might have more luck heading to some of the larger stretches of Africa if the idea is to disappear. But I think she meant it as a for instance. They'd take the money and run as fast and as far as the money would take them. They'd do a disappearing act, like Lord Lucan."

"Are we saying we like Lady Baaden-Boomethistle for this murder? Or the son? Or both of them in it together?"

"Certainly. But there are other suspects. The victim was not universally loved. Even the people who cared something about him — and I include his mother, the dowager — seemed to feel he was making choices that threatened them."

"There are various live-out staff, of course," said Cotton. "One needs a mob of day help to run a place like theirs. They are out of this picture as suspects, though."

"How do you know that?"

"We asked them if they had anything to do with the murder and they said no. Seriously, Max, they've all been cleared by my team for the time in question."

"Which is?"

"Precisely seven. Ish. Nothing has changed there. You know the medical examiner will never be held to anything without twenty minutes wiggle room either way. Even if he'd been an eyewitness to the murder, it seems to me he'd try to stretch the time frame."

"But no one really needed to be there on the dot," insisted Max. "They only needed to set the trap, which could have been done maybe a half hour before."

"Agreed. Still, you couldn't just leave a snare like that hanging out there for long. It would be spotted; people would ask questions; it might harm someone you didn't intend to harm. Our guess is it was put in place only minutes before, and taken down right away. The lord was very particular about his routine. An evening ride, a quick shower and change, dinner at eight."

"I see. That means whoever did this had to stand about, hiding and waiting."

"Yes."

"And, of course, there is a houseful of people who knew the routine well — who might have chatted idly about it, and to anyone for miles around."

"What do you see as the next step?" Cotton asked.

"Right at the moment, I'm thinking in terms of 'dynamic inactivity.' "

"What?"

"What Harvey Schlossberg, a well-known hostage negotiator, used to call 'dynamic inactivity.' In other words, if all else fails, you wait and do nothing. That in itself may flush out your suspect. The bad guys get as tired and restless and antsy and bored as we do."

"Ah. Very Zen-like. Well, grasshopper, I'm not sure that won't lead to all the clues just drying up, in this case."

Max hid a smile by taking a sip of his tea. If anyone lived an existence like an illustration from *Zen Life,* it was Cotton.

"The clues, such as they are, have already dried up," said Max. "I do think the solution in this case is more psychological than forensic."

"Meaning?"

"The suspect may let something slip if left alone — left to his or her own devices. The waiting makes most people anxious, and can make them act irrationally — make them give the game away."

"I'm afraid I must come down on the side of actually doing something, Max. My super will raise objections if I'm found in downward-facing child pose when I'm supposed to be investigating in my usual dynamic and results-oriented way."

"It's called simply 'child pose,' " corrected Max. Because of Awena, he could command an entirely new vocabulary. "You're mixing it with downward-facing dog pose."

"If you say so. How about if I bring the 'child' in to help with our inquiries? Peregrine? From what Destiny has said, he's gone to some trouble to change his appearance, his manner. The most likely reason is that he's up to his neck in this. Oh, sorry — what an unfortunate choice of words."

Max said merely, "It's an idea."

Cotton gathered that while it was an idea, it was a wrong one. Max was too diplomatic to come right out and dismiss any plan or theory. Also, he was too wise not to know the wildest ideas were sometimes the ideas closest to the truth.

"Well, what've *you* got?" Cotton asked.

"I have an idea who's behind it."

"So do I. But now I hear I'm wrong."

"My concern is we'll never be able to make a case that will stick." He shifted in his chair. "Have you got any further with the search warrant?"

"Yes. He went along with it, dying of curiosity but meek as a lamb. 'Anything to be of help.' It may take a while for us to find what we want. There's always a backlog, you know. *If* there is something to find."

But Max had moved on, pursuing a different thought. "The question of motive is puzzling me still," he said. He reached over and topped up Cotton's drink, then his own. "This crime took a lot of motivation to be done the way it was done, even given that the killer is unbalanced. There was no going back once it was set in motion."

"Good old greed? Lust runs a close second, in my experience. Mindless hatred spinning out of control — not for a crime like this, I don't think. This was not spontaneous."

"But hatred may well have played a part. I suppose everything you say is correct. And it might be a combination of motives. It generally is."

"Lady B-B has got to be behind this," said Cotton. "She paid a hit man — something like that. But our usual informants in that department have nothing to contribute this time."

Max was shaking his head. "She strikes me as someone who will do whatever is necessary to remain in control, and to protect herself above all. So if she's involved, she thought this through and she wouldn't have casually recruited from the local criminal population. She is not a risk taker in that way — in her mind, it is for other people to take risks on her behalf.

"The thing is, Lady B-B was doing fine and was very well off just staying with her husband — so long as she could keep him in the dark. Scandal would not be part of her plan; divorce would be out of the question. She was comfortable. Why upset the applecart? She didn't need to run off with Peregrine or with anyone. She just needed to let things be.

"If she and Peregrine, especially, were in a relationship, it was bound to bring scandal down on both of them. However, his fear would be that he would be disinherited by his father, whose anger over this would be epic, I'd imagine. That fear existed only so long as Lord Baaden-Boomethistle lived. The risk has been eliminated. The boy can relax. And so can she. He inherits, and she lives happily ever after *with him* — if she chooses. After a certain amount of time, the scandal would pass. I think she'd be comfortable with that. I'm not sure he would be. Thus the need to make him think an island escape was in his future."

"So how do we catch the killer?" Cotton, leaning in, said. "A confrontation, some deftly choreographed, drawn-out interrogation at the station?"

Max shook his head. "Too risky — too likely to make him clam up, call in counsel, claim he's being persecuted by jackbooted thugs. And all you'd get out of her is that she has an alibi and you're harassing her. And at this point, you would be."

"So let's do a spot of gaslighting."

"What do you mean?"

"You know. Smoke the murderer out. Make him — or her — believe what can't be true is true. Frighten the living daylights out of them."

"Yes, okay," said Max, metaphorically taking off his clerical collar. "But exactly how?"

"It shouldn't be hard. The situation at Casa Totleigh is deteriorating. Everyone is ready to tip the next one straight into it, if you ask me."

Somewhere behind Max's gray eyes, a thought flitted past, too fast for him to capture, leaving behind a strange queasiness and uncertainty. What was it? What was the trigger? Something Cotton had just said? Some word, or some angle of his head as he said it, some light in his eyes? It was there, Max knew, and it was real. And the only way the thought might return would be to let it run wild and then, hopefully, return to him.

There he goes again, thought Cotton. That quizzical, rather fierce look Max got as he made some connection that had eluded all the best minds on his team. Including, thought Cotton, my own.

Trying desperately to hold several strands of thought in his mind simultaneously, Max asked Cotton to repeat what he had just said.

Max listened, and said at last, "Interesting choice of word."

"What word?" Cotton stood from his chair and restlessly began pacing the room, ending up before the little crèche scene from Monkbury Abbey.

"Interesting," Max repeated. Cotton spun his lean body around now to look at Max. The DCI knew Max's *ah-ha* tone too well.

"I need to clear my head a bit," said Max, also rising from his chair. He left the room and returned with two glasses and a pitcher of water. He placed these on the low table before the fireplace, within reach of Cotton, and poured out water from the pitcher. Owen stirred briefly and Thea opened one eye to see what was up. Cotton watched as they both fell back asleep. He felt as if he had walked into the middle of a children's tale and stood now in an enchanted little cottage where children and dogs dozed through the most terrible conversations about murder and mayhem.

Max stood staring at the fire, his head bent and his arms straight out as he clasped his glass on the mantel before him. It was, Cotton noted, nearly an attitude of prayer.

Max turned around and said, "Okay."

"Okay what?"

"I've thought of a way to bring the cat to its milk. It will sound absurd, and even the legality of what I propose is doubtful. But when you consider the gullible nature of at least one of our suspects . . ."

"You mean you've thought of a way to gaslight the mother," Cotton said happily.

"Language!" But Max was smiling. "Something like that."

Max thought back to the sermon he'd been working on before all this had happened. "Thy will be done" had looked somehow easier to accept at the time. As for "Do the ends ever justify the means?" he had not known how soon he would come to appreciate the irony.

But God acted through man, and it was up to man to take action. At least so Max reasoned now. Sitting and waiting would not be possible and might let the suspects get away. There was nothing to keep them here, after all. They had nothing on anyone, no concrete evidence. Just one witness to some overheard garbled conversations.

He explained his idea to Cotton and told him what — and who — was needed to put the plan into action.

Cotton tried his mobile. The connection failing, as was often the way in remote Nether Monkslip, he picked up the enormous Bakelite phone on Max's desk. He got through to the headquarters in Monkslip-super-Mare and asked to speak with Sergeant Essex. Max pictured her at her desk, even this late in the day: tough, wiry, and bright-eyed as a terrier, her short hair standing out about her head. She would likely be reading through the case files for the tenth time: *Some*thing would be in there. Something she'd missed.

When Cotton had finished describing to her what was needed (Max could hear her excited questions and yelps of agreement from across the room), he put down the receiver to meet Max's questioning gaze.

"She's thrilled," he informed Max. "It gets her away from Musteile for the day."

"I thought she would be. She told me once she grew up around horses."

"Full of surprises, she is."

"One more thing," said Max. "Be sure to keep up surveillance on the summerhouse

— the temple or whatever it is."

"I've had Musteile on it."

"Try putting someone competent on it. It's important."

CHAPTER 23
RED HERRINGS

Two days later, DCI Cotton returned to the vicarage. Both Awena and Owen were there with Max.

"It went off well, did it?" Max asked him over coffee and biscuits.

"Like clockwork." Cotton gently withdrew a finger from Owen's sticky grasp. Max thought the fastidious Cotton would find all the baby effluvia upsetting, but he clearly had made an exception in Owen's case. "But with an added bonus. You were right about Musteile. Once we put someone competent in place to watch the summerhouse, we got results. Maybe not the results we expected, but results."

"Can nothing be done about him?"

"He's being reprimanded, but it won't stick. He's 'Someone's' nephew — that's 'Someone' with a capital S. It will take dynamite to get rid of him. His family doesn't want him at home causing havoc, you see."

"Yes. Much better to let him muck up a murder investigation. Anyway, Destiny was right about the son?"

"Peregrine, thinly disguised as a loser? Yes. We've learned he's taken a turn or two on the stage at the Burton Taylor Studio in Oxford. It helps that the family spends most of its time in Spain — no one quite remembers what he used to look like growing up. So he shows up in the village looking gauche and undesirable — daft as a brush. He's always to be seen traipsing about, doing nothing much. If anyone remembers him from before, they probably assume some sort of slow decline into dweebdom."

"And the purpose of this was to throw suspicion off the affair he was having with his stepmother."

"Right," said Cotton. "To make him look like the unlikeliest of candidates for the lady's affections. For any lady's affections."

Owen was making a reach for Max, so he paused to pull him out of Awena's arms and settle him on his lap. As he spoke, he gently ruffled Owen's hair, soft as lambs wool. "When the dowager claimed she was attacked, I paid little attention," Max said. "It was exactly the sort of self-dramatizing story I felt she would make up. But now I believe there was truth in it, even if she later decided to downplay the danger. I think she *did* know something; I think she saw something going on between Lady Baaden-Boomethistle and the son of the house."

"And she had a decision to make," Cotton said, agreeing. "In the end, she felt she had to lie to cover for her grandson, despite having seen him in a passionate clutch with Bree. Why lie? Because she wants her grandson to inherit: He must not be disinherited for any reason. So she creates this fiction of Bree's infidelity with another man — the truth that Bree is embroiled with her own stepson is too ugly a truth to come out, so the dowager tries to push us in a different direction, toward the estate manager, for one."

"The dowager's claim that someone tried to climb through her bedroom window from outside. Any evidence of that — or was it all a red herring?"

"As a matter of fact," said Cotton, "we did find a broken branch outside her window. The lab boys and girls thought it may have broken off accidentally when someone stood on it — the wind didn't take down that branch, in other words."

"So there really was an attempt to warn her off? To frighten her into silence? Perhaps by someone masquerading as one of the ghosts said to haunt the old house?"

"It looks like it — something like that. But if someone climbed that tree, it was clearly an athlete at work. Someone who was fit from, say, horseback riding. Or football. There may be some forensic evidence left — there appear to be some scrapes of shoe leather on the bark. They're looking into it."

"But," said Max, "that will only prove someone was up to mischief — trying to scare her off. It may not even have been necessary — her own self-interest may have been enough to keep her quiet."

"I agree," said Cotton. "Anyway, the dowager was right to be worried. The butler did report that at breakfast she sort of lost it and said, 'I saw you!' That made Bree and Peregrine think she suspected or knew they were having affair. She could have been just wildly thrashing about, hoping for a reaction, but in any event, after that they felt they could not entirely rely on her discretion."

"But," said Max, "they weren't to know that it was better from her point of view that word of the affair not seep out. The scandal would have been enormous, and costly. I think she was toggling in her mind

401

between the lesser of two evils, and unable to decide. I think she expected fair treatment from her grandson if she played along. But Bree was another matter."

"We are still left with the question of whether this need for secrecy constituted a motive for murder," said Cotton. "Would the son kill his own father? Was that just one easy step away from sleeping with his stepmother?"

Max shrugged. "He had a lot to lose. Anyway, her husband's death was so convenient for Bree that whoever did it, she was not going to toss them in it — at least not right away."

"But she would create as much distance from them as she could." Cotton paused, thinking. "Because we were so sure to suspect her involvement, guilty or not, she wouldn't want to draw attention to the weak link — the one who might break under pressure. And I think she views all men as the weak link, don't you?"

Max nodded.

"All the rumors about Bill Travis . . . you think there's nothing to it?" Cotton asked.

"I only know that Bree herself is the one who brought it up, only to hotly deny the rumor in the next breath," said Max. "Then she seemed to admit to it — almost. No one could be allowed to suspect the truth of her involvement with the son of the house. And if Bree had to drag innocent people into a murder investigation, I don't think she lost any sleep over it."

"It seems the purest luck for Travis that he had an ironclad alibi," said Cotton. "He was at some horse show or other in Devon. There's even video footage of him in the crowd — I've just been watching it."

"Right. Anyway, Bree's dismissive way of talking about Peregrine, calling him an oaf and so on — this was all a blind. An elaborate bluff. Insinuating he was gay — that was meant to ensure we never saw him as one of her romantic conquests, but of course he was.

"She protested too much, portraying him as some sort of aristocratic buffoon, emphasizing his unattractiveness — to either sex, making a joke of it, and of him. Still, what did it mean? Stepmothers and stepchildren can be natural enemies, as Destiny's memories of some people in her old village reminded me. One is seen as a threat to the other. That part was understandable. But Bree's denial of any involvement with other men, like the groom or the estate manager — now, oddly, that rang true. She was indignant — for at a guess, she was aiming much higher. For someone wealthy and, this time, closer to her in age."

Awena spoke for the first time, lifting her gaze from Owen, now asleep in Max's arms. Apparently he was dreaming, his small fists waving almost comically in the air. Awena might not have been listening, but if Max knew anything about Awena, it was that she was always listening, and seldom dropped a stitch in the conversation.

"I don't follow," she said. "Was Peregrine involved with the murder or not?"

"I haven't filled Awena in on everything you told me when you rang," said Max to Cotton. "I thought I'd let you do the honors."

"Right," said Cotton, settling back in his chair. "First you must consider that when both parties are risking a fortune by having a completely inappropriate affair, suspicion must be thrown elsewhere. So Peregrine, with his experience as an amateur actor, came up with his rather silly plan to make himself look like an unlikely prospect for romance. He comes down from university acting like a spoiled child, probably to emphasize the difference in age between him and Bree, and looking like a rube. The disguise worked, until he had the bad luck to cross Destiny's path the other night. He was not wearing the glasses he'd adopted, which made him easier for her to recognize, and he had dropped back into his normal walk and demeanor. Apart from the haircut, he was the dashing ladies' man Destiny recognized from photographs of him at university."

"He may have felt in his arrogance that a rustic audience is easily duped," said Max, turning to Awena. "Certainly he felt that way about his sister. Anyway, Peregrine also went to some trouble to get me to believe he had a girlfriend elsewhere. Someone he was dying to visit in Italy. But he doesn't and didn't. He's in love with Bree, but of course he can't admit it — is too ashamed to admit it. Plus, would his father have thrown him out if he knew? Undoubtedly."

"His father did keep him on tight purse strings," said Cotton. "Peregrine pretended to blame Bree for this. All part of the plan to indicate there was bad blood between him and Bree, when the opposite was true. And by the way, Bree was also kept on an allowance. Not a small allowance by my standards or yours or even the Sultan of Brunei's, but probably by hers."

Max nodded. "And there's your motive. So, Awena, everything she said about Peregrine was bluff — that he had no potential in her eyes. She was trying to toss red herrings in my path and succeeding for a while. She saw lots of potential in Peregrine — he was her means to an end.

"She liked to emphasize the difference in their ages, and certainly she was the more mature of the two — her upbringing was not cosseted as his was — but she was only five years his senior. Even so, it's like the difference between human years and animal years. He couldn't possibly keep up."

Cotton said, "According to the boy, who broke quite nicely once we'd frightened him out of his skin — thank you for the idea, Max — their affair started not long after her marriage to his father. He was a teenager and she was just out of her teens and finding herself tied for life to a very old man."

"Something she might have noticed before she married him," Awena remarked.

"Oh, she did," said Max. "I believe she certainly did. It was her bargain with the devil, and she went into it with eyes wide open, or so she thought. She wanted to escape the past, and her looks were her ticket out. But she was marrying into one very unhappy family. And Lord B-B could be bit of a brute."

"Tolstoy was right, although he couldn't have reckoned on this lot," said Cotton.

When, Max wondered, did Cotton find time to read the classics? The remark made Max remember his disturbing dream of the severed head with the long Tolstoyan beard.

Max said, "I suppose having an affair is a lot like being a spy. All the skulking about, all the lying and passing coded messages, and varying your route in case you're followed."

"Maybe that is part of the appeal for some people. For a certain type of person. They enjoy the secrecy, the danger of being caught."

"And for others, the secrecy does them in," said Max. "The guilt overwhelms them. I do not get an overriding sense that was a drawback for Bree, do you?"

"Not at all. Lady Baaden-Boomethistle is a very cool customer. And the son is not exactly wallowing in guilt at betraying his father."

"I will grant you remorse is not in Bree's repertoire," said Max. "But Peregrine might be caught up in a web of several emotions. I am not sure we can write him off entirely, even though he nearly was tempted into patricide. He was the means Lady Baaden-Boomethistle first tried to use to get what she wanted."

"Which was what, precisely?" Awena asked.

"Apart from the money? Freedom — much the same thing in her mind, I would imagine. The freedom to do exactly as she pleased, when she pleased, and the money to do it with. To buy horses and ride horses and travel the world, following the sun."

"And this she couldn't do with him alive?"

"Not with him controlling the finances for both her and the boy. And according to her prenup, if she left Lord B-B, she'd leave with not much more than the clothing on her back. She was not well advised by lawyers, perhaps. In fact, she seems to have signed the papers without giving it a thought. She was young and maybe not as smart in the ways of the world as she became later. That would breed anger, too — that her youth and inexperience with lawyers had been taken advantage of.

"So she may have started by leading Peregrine on, perhaps out of boredom and a taste for revenge as much as anything, not really sure he would do anything so mad as to kill for her, but trying nonetheless to turn him into the unthinking instrument that would extricate her from this marriage. It was fun. It was, if nothing else, a challenge."

"But she failed."

"She might have succeeded over time — my money is absolutely on her in that regard — but then she came to know she was backing the wrong horse, to continue the racing metaphor. And that's when she decided to try elsewhere. She needed someone without the emotional complications of a son's guilt. Someone more mature and steady, whose love for her was primal, beyond question. Certainly that is what she had in Chanel."

"Chanel?" said Awena.

"Yes, didn't we say?" said Max smoothly.

"No, Max, of course you didn't say!"

CHAPTER 24
CONNECTIONS

"Once Cotton got someone capable of staking out the summerhouse over there on the property, whom did they see?" Max asked. "The son, yes — we expected that. But the surprise was Chanel, meeting up with Bree to discuss what happened next. Taking time out from her busy day of advising others how to live, writing books stuffed with good advice, to engage in a spectacularly ill-advised scheme.

"The two women organized the times for their meetings by using the hymn board. I did wonder why Bree had taken a sudden interest in the church, when none was evident before."

"The hymn numbers. Three forty-five. Of course!" Awena said.

"Once I saw the usefulness of that board to people wanting to set up a private meeting, it made surveillance of the summerhouse a bit easier — I made the assumption

410

that any secret meetings around Totleigh would take place there, and now we knew when to keep an eye out. Generally, the board is changed late Saturday afternoon for the Sunday services, so it doesn't matter what numbers appear there during the week, when services aren't accompanied by music. Generally, the old numbers from the week before stay in place. If they were messed about, no one would notice, and it didn't matter anyway. Kids playing, people would think. The pair avoided anything as risky as sending a phone or text message or letter, which could too easily be discovered or seen by prying eyes. Eugenia was spot-on when she said she saw Chanel Dirkson changing the numbers."

"It was clever of them," Cotton put in. "Anything digital would be too easily tracked in the mobile records."

"The old-fashioned methods are so often best for anyone wanting to escape detection," agreed Max. "That is why bin Laden successfully communicated via courier and got away with it for so long."

He felt he'd been looking at the truth the whole time and missing it. It is said that when your eyesight degenerates, it can be like that. You can look straight at someone's face but see only the trees behind them. It all made him think of Monkbury Abbey and miracle cures, and missing the forest for the trees. How could he have been so blind?

"It's like something out of a spy novel," said Cotton.

"The ultrasecrecy was essential. Imagine the lord's reaction if he'd suspected — and I think he did suspect something was going on. He just didn't know the exact nature of what was being planned. That may have been why he called me to the manor house that night to talk. From his manner, I knew something was troubling him.

"Anyway, it was Chanel, with her deep voice, and Bree, with her similar voice, whom Destiny overheard that evening — these names! It all sounds more and more like one of the dowager's plots, doesn't it?"

"Tame by comparison," said Awena. "So Chanel . . ."

"Was another of Bree's conquests, in a way. Another person under the spell of Bree's charm and beauty. She was being 'groomed,' so to speak, to do what Bree wanted. Manipulated and lied to, pressured to act on Bree's behalf, yes. A team united — at least Chanel thought they were. Partners in crime? Oh yes." Pair they were, something Max felt he should have realized. That conversation Destiny had overheard, conducted miles from here, in a place of privacy. That location suggested — could only mean — a close bond between two *women.* It had nothing to do with Peregrine or any other male. And their conversation proved this was more than two women friends idly chatting.

"Partners in crime," repeated Awena. "So Bree is the killer?"

Max and Cotton exchanged glances and sighed. "Bree is certainly responsible — I would say directly and indirectly — for her husband's death. Did she goad Chanel? Insinuate? Inveigle? Make promises and paint a beautiful picture of their glorious future together? I think she did, and I think she's guilty as sin as a sort of instigator."

"A starter," mused Awena. "A provocateur."

"But Chanel isn't talking anymore," said Cotton. "She's clammed up. The prints we found on that clicker Max uncovered are hers, interestingly enough. It's not airtight evidence, but every bit helps. If Bree put that thing in the planter, by the way, it seems she was smart enough to wear gloves doing it."

"Chanel isn't talking *yet,* you mean. That day may come — unless Bree does a magnificent job of making sure she doesn't feel forgotten, rotting in her cell. If Bree is really smart, she'll hire the best solicitors and barristers to handle Chanel's case."

"But you do think she talked Chanel into this?"

"Not exactly *talked,*" said Max. "She's too canny for that. She'd choose her words wisely, and never say anything that could be brought home to her door. I think she only had to drop little hints of how much she longed for freedom. Mention how the pair of them could be together, and how nice it would be if they were. They could go and live on a tropical island, perhaps, if only she were free . . . with all that money. . . . How desperately unhappy she was, but it was all impossible. You know the sort of thing. It is likely that the full extent of Bree's involvement might never be known, but I would not be at all surprised if she used the oldest trick in the book, claiming that Lord B-B was unfaithful or abused her in some way. I noticed there were faint smudges under her eyes when I spoke with her, like healing bruises. I think now they were bruises, and I think they were self-inflicted. Either that or it was cleverly applied makeup. Even Chanel may not realize how much she's been manipulated."

"She acted as though the whole thing were

414

her own idea, and claims that it was. She's staying with that story, Max."

"What made her talk?" Awena asked.

Again, Cotton and Max exchanged glances.

"Chanel fell into the trap we'd laid for Peregrine," said Cotton. "We arranged for a headless horseman to ride through the woods, just after the sun went behind the trees, and the setting was properly spooky and cast with shadows. And we made sure Peregrine and Bree were there to see it — I'd asked them to meet me to look at some evidence near the murder site."

Max said, "Cotton tells me that Bree, as we rather expected, kept her cool — the benefit of being suspicious by nature is that you're harder to fool. I almost wonder if she knew the famous story of Ichabod Crane and the Headless Horseman of Sleepy Hollow — one of her horses is named Gunpowder, the same name as the horse Ichabod rode. A brass plate with that name is on one of the stalls in her stables. Anyway, in the story, there is a strong suggestion the whole thing is a hoax: a pumpkin is involved, as I recall." His mind caught on the pumpkin in his dream, smashed in pieces. "Peregrine quickly came apart and confessed to the affair, but denied he had anything to do with murder. She tried to shush him, but he was past listening to her. This was all much more than he had bargained for. I'm sure he will forever have nightmares about the headless corpse of his father."

"And then Chanel, who had been waiting for Bree in the summerhouse, arrived on the scene," interjected Cotton. "She heard Peregrine yelling blue murder — remember, he's not much more than a boy — and she came running, just in time to see the 'ghost' race by. Then *she* came undone. Once we'd reduced everyone but Bree to a quivering mass, the truth came out quickly enough. There was not a lot of point in Chanel's claiming she didn't know what we were talking about, not once we told her her conversations in the summerhouse had been overheard. We implied we knew more than we did, but no matter. She confessed she'd done it. She was gibbering to the point I had to interrupt the flow to caution her."

"Wait a minute," said Awena. "Everybody just wait a minute. Headless horseman?"

"Horsewoman, actually. The very diminutive Sergeant Essex, atop Foto Finish. With a cape covering her head, the horse thundering down the forest path in the flickering moonlight, it was an amazingly lifelike apparition. Essex carried an old-fashioned lantern as she rode, which I think was rather a nice touch — her idea. Quite frightening, actually — even I was shaken, though I knew who it was and what was going on."

"Is all this legal?" inquired Awena.

"More or less," said Cotton lightly. He toggled one hand equivocally. "It got the confession we wanted from Peregrine, as to his involvement with Bree. And a denial of involvement in the murder she had urged him to commit — a denial that was utterly convincing. The added bonus came from Chanel, as to the commission of the murder itself. She simply threw herself under the wheels to keep Bree out of it, once she saw the way the whole thing was trending: The blubbering Peregrine was, by this point, accusing Bree openly, quoting chapter and verse. From a legal standpoint, it's hearsay, of course, even though I believe him."

"But Bree admits nothing," said Awena.

"I am not holding my breath that she will ever own up to the extent of her involvement. It is very likely she cannot be held culpable, as things stand. And she knows it." Cotton shuddered slightly. "She's like a spider, that one."

"But how was it done?" Awena asked, clearly appalled. "The beheading . . . the wire."

"How exactly did Chanel pull off the murder? The horse had been trained from a colt to obey the sound of a clicker. All of this was quite a normal part of his training. Then at some point, over and over, he began to be taught that to get a reward, he had to lower his head at the sound. And keep his head down and keep running until the clicker sounded again."

"I heard what I thought was the sound of crickets that night," said Max. "As I walked through the woods with Thea."

"Crickets don't live in forests," said Awena. "They live in fields and meadows."

"I know. It took me a while to realize what a country boy would have known right away."

"We have got," said Cotton, "to get more local farm people to join the force. Musteile doesn't count."

"So Chanel — ironically, the self-help guru — became besotted with Bree almost from the moment she moved to the village?" asked Awena. "A case of love at first sight?"

"Something like that," said Max, remembering Bree's comment that Chris Marlowe had it right.

"It may not have been first sight — we're looking into that," said Cotton. "They are both from Wiltshire originally. But first sight or old friendship, they forged a bond either way. I gather Bree is rather good at forging bonds."

"Or at making other people believe they have a bond with her," suggested Max.

"She killed at Bree's unspoken bidding," said Cotton. "That took some doing."

"Shades of Salome," Max pointed out, "the topic of Destiny's recent sermon. Rather, Herodias and her dutiful dancing daughter, whom we have come to call Salome. What a totally appalling mother, I have always thought. Pushing your daughter to dance before your husband — probably an erotic sort of hoochie coochie, snaring him into getting your enemy John the Baptist killed for you."

Awena and Cotton looked at each other and laughed. "Hoochie coochie?" said Awena. "Honestly, Max. Who says that anymore?"

"What?" said Max. He was mildly irritated — not that they were laughing at him, the old fuddy-duddy, but that their laughter had distracted him from an idea he'd been chasing. Something struggled to emerge from the depths of his mind, something slippery and dark, a murky connection that slithered maddeningly out of reach just as he reached to retrieve it. He thought it was connected with the dream he'd had in church, the dream that had given him the idea for shaking the truth out of Peregrine. He'd awakened, mortified to realize he'd surfaced in the middle of Destiny's sermon. What was it that eluded him now, though? The ghost? The pumpkin?

"I do, apparently," he told them. "Hoochie coochie is a time-honored and useful phrase." Again, Cotton and Awena exchanged glances. "Anyway, a woman who didn't do the actual killing but had it done for her. A woman well aware of her power to command. In any event, the purpose was to free Bree from a loveless, abusive marriage. Something Chanel felt she knew all about, having survived a loveless and abusive marriage of her own."

"Bree," put in Cotton, "was stringing along both Peregrine and Chanel. Chanel was particularly useful to her because she knows everything about horses. Because, as she tells us, she grew up on a farm — a horse farm."

"I guess that is why Brat Farrar came to mind," said Awena. "The story with the rogue horse." Owen was stirring now but listening intently. He liked the sounds of adults talking, and would listen, all eyes and ears, completely still, drinking everything in. Like his father, thought Awena.

"Not completely," said Max. Half of his mind was still on the rogue idea that had popped into his head and immediately vanished. Deliberately, he released the thought now, letting go of it like a kite on a string, knowing that was the only way it might return. "Only later did I realize the other reason the Brat Farrar story stuck in my head. The story has to do with an imposter, a man who passes himself off as a rightful heir. In this case, there was no imposter, but the creation of a rightful heir where there had been none before."

CHAPTER 25
BORN AND BRED

"I don't follow, Max," said Awena. "How do you create an heir? Apart from the usual way, that is."

"By adopting one," Max replied. "Or by stealing one. In this case, a foundling was adopted to ensure the family line did not die out entirely, at least in the eyes of the world. Only the adoption was kept secret, from everyone. It was, it turns out, a deadly secret." Max was coming to think this was a fairly common occurrence among the families at a certain stratum of high society. Was anyone up there who he thought he was? Modern DNA would surely put a stop to this sort of deception, but then only if a deception were suspected.

That Peregrine was adopted was probably known only by the man he called father — and his father, when angry, had threatened to disinherit Peregrine, telling him he was no son of his. Did Bree know? Max wondered. Did her husband tell her Peregrine was not his heir? Was not of his flesh and blood? Max thought it likely.

Because that was the end of her need for Peregrine. Max imagined the moment her husband had confided Peregrine's true status to her would coincide precisely with the day she started to ease out of her relationship with Peregrine. For she would be out on her ear if their affair were uncovered, and Peregrine would be out, too, with no inheritance for them to live on. For her to continue her relationship with him was simply too risky — foolhardy and with no payoff in the end.

Max also thought, and wanted to believe, that Peregrine would have balked at any suggestion he help Bree murder her husband. Peregrine was no angel, but Max thought he would draw the line at doing anything so completely amoral as to kill the only father he had ever known.

So Bree had had to look elsewhere for help in killing her husband.

The case in the end really had little to do with horses, Max reflected, except that a horse had been used as the means to an end. There was something clinical and detached about the method used — like killing secondhand. A knife or gun would have

423

been a more direct and intimate method.

And perhaps it had been decided that was the problem with using a more conventional method: An opponent could dodge a bullet, or overcome a woman wielding a knife.

Finding the clicker had been pure chance, even though squirrels liked to dig wherever soil had been recently disturbed. Perhaps it had been Bree who had buried it in the vase on the patio, figuring it would not be found, or, if found, could not be traced to her. Having left it in a temporarily safe hiding place, she probably decided it was better not to return too soon to dig it out.

So many red herrings. The case had to do with love or lust, call it what you will — Chanel's wish to free the desired one of an unhappy marriage, in the mistaken belief it would win her heart. There was also some element of greed, of course. A beloved with a huge inheritance would be an improvement on a beloved broken financially by a prenup.

"The Brat Farrar story nearly led me astray," said Max aloud. "There is a rogue horse in that book, as you say, but what we were dealing with here was just the opposite of a rogue. Not a "killer" horse but a perfectly trained, even docile, one.

"There was also an heir in that story making false claims to an inheritance, but the heir in this case wasn't attempting to impersonate anyone. He honestly did not know he'd been substituted into his position almost from birth.

"One further parallel is that, like Brat Farrar, Bree is a true horse lover. She is also charming and utterly dishonest."

"Back up, back up," said Awena. "Peregrine is not the heir to Totleigh Hall?"

"No," said Cotton. "He is not his father's son. He agreed to let us test his DNA — he seemed to think it had something to do with the crime scene. And since he knew he had nothing to do with the setup for his father's grisly death, he was more than happy to comply."

"Really," said Awena, arching one perfect dark eyebrow.

"It was your husband's idea," Cotton told her.

"Really," she said again.

"Still, it didn't clear Peregrine as a suspect," said Cotton, "because he may have had no clue he was not the heir. It is likely Bree didn't know this, either, going into the relationship — that he was not eligible to inherit in the first place. Otherwise, it is very doubtful she'd have wasted time on him."

"So where exactly did Peregrine come

from?" asked Awena.

"He was kidnapped shortly after his birth from another blue-blooded family. Via some orphanage where he was left, and then through the offices of an adoption agency — probably a rather dodgy one — he came to be taken into the B-B family. This likely was done, the illegal 'adoption,' at the instigation of Lord B-B's first wife. Desperate for a child, she talked her husband into this scheme to pretend Peregrine was their own. When Cotton made a joke about the people up at the casa, it reminded me of Peregrine's origins — that he was born in Málaga, where the family had long had a home. The story about his remaining in hospital for some imaginary illness was a ruse to fudge his age, to cover the fact he was too big to be a newborn.

"I came to realize Lord Baaden-Boomethistle and his wife were in Málaga at the exact same time a baby was kidnapped in an internationally famous case that took place near Monkbury Abbey. It was in that summer of 1994. He had a distinctive birthmark at the top of his back, this baby — in case he was ever found, officials could readily identify him, because that mark was so unusual. It was a port-wine stain in the shape of a heart. Photos of the mark were distributed far and wide through police channels. Both nannies confirm Peregrine had a birthmark, by the way. Elspeth Muir alluded to Cain, and she may have had the "mark of Cain" in mind. But they never connected Peregrine with that missing child, and they never saw the police photos.

"I was already thinking in terms of a switch: The film about the switch of murders on the train. Then I realized — perhaps there was another sort of switch altogether? A switch of babies? Then I thought, That can't be right; they brought their baby out of Spain together and the dates of pregnancy don't match up. I asked Cotton to pull the birth certificate.

"Peregrine's mother — the woman who raised him — tried to claim it was a preemie birth to waffle the dates, but who ever heard of a nine-pound preemie?"

"And you know this how?" Awena asked. *"Ouch."* Owen had grabbed a fistful of her hair and was pulling on it like a rope. Awena gently disentangled him.

"Partly because the woman who was the nanny at the time, Elspeth Muir, has taken the advice of her minister. And his advice was to tell the truth and shame the devil, mirroring her own inclinations. She knew

Peregrine was adopted; they tried to buy her silence and she wasn't having any."

"My head is reeling," said Awena. "So Rosamund? How does she fit into this? She's not adopted also, is she?"

"No. Rosamund is the true heir, not her brother. As so often happens, once a couple adopts a child, they conceive a child soon after. I have to emphasize though that this child, now called Peregrine, was stolen in the first place, then substituted for the child Lady Baaden-Boomethistle could not successfully carry to term. All of it strictly irregular and highly illegal, not to mention immoral. There was a worldwide manhunt for that child. What we don't know is whether the Baaden-Boomethistles were aware of his true origins. They may have thought the baby they adopted was a foundling, left by a local woman who was, for whatever reason, unable to care for him."

"So sad . . ." said Awena.

"I kept remembering that the butler overheard an argument between Peregrine and Lord Baaden-Boomethistle. 'You're no son of mine. You're unnatural, that's what you are. No son of mine could do what you did.' Lord Baaden-Boomethistle was angry and not to be taken literally — or so it was assumed. But no: He was being precise and literal, and not just blowing off steam. Peregrine was no son of his."

Cotton said, "As part of the investigation, Max had us check all the birth records for Málaga for around the time of Peregrine's birth. Peregrine had said he was born there, and on paper he was. But another child born there to Lady Baaden-Boomethistle did not survive, and that is in the records."

"Along with what is, on close inspection, an altered certificate of birth for Peregrine," Max added.

Awena looked down at the beloved face of her own child. "That poor woman," she said, then corrected herself: "Poor *women*. The one who lost her baby to kidnappers, believing it had died, *and* Lady B-B."

"Yes," said Cotton. "Having lost the longed-for son and heir, I don't think she and her husband took time to think it through. They acted. She may have believed it was her only chance to have a child."

"And so there was a scramble to find a 'replacement' child," Max continued. "Lord B-B put his agents on the case. Just then, a baby boy of a few weeks of age turned up in the local orphanage. It was said to have been abandoned. We were able to track down this transaction — I won't call it an adoption. The baby came from out of nowhere, but its birth date matches exactly that of the child who was kidnapped from near Monkbury Abbey so long ago. The same date, even to the same hour."

"This seems like no more than a wild coincidence," insisted Awena. "Except — except for . . ."

"Precisely." Max nodded. "There's no getting around that birthmark. The kidnapped baby was very tiny, practically a newborn when it was taken. They claimed Peregrine was large for his age, to forestall questions — his size had to make sense for his supposed date of birth. But who would question it, really? They were of a class of people who could buy what they wanted, and they were operating in a country where poverty allowed them what they — what Lady Baaden-Boomethistle — most wanted: a child."

"And the kidnapped baby? No one ever knew?"

"The authorities assumed he had been killed. That is the case in most kidnappings, sadly. His own brother had arranged cold-bloodedly for the kidnapping — out of pure jealousy, I still believe, among other motives. He — the fifteenth earl of Lislelivet — didn't ask or care to know what became of the child. He just needed the child to be legally declared dead. Which it was."

Max paused, then added, "If Peregrine had taken part in killing his father, it would have been for nothing. Because Lord Baaden-Boomethistle was not really his father. And Peregrine was not the heir to the estate. His sister was."

"I see. Goodness, what a story. Well, I must say —" Awena began. Seeing her husband's face, she stopped. "What is it, Max?"

Something had clicked in his mind. Max could almost have sworn he heard the satisfying little sound a jigsaw puzzle piece makes when it is snapped into place.

"All the talk of babies and mothers," he said slowly. "I have been such a fool."

"Hmm?"

Max turned to Cotton. "We've overlooked something. Who do you have in Wiltshire who can look through the birth records there? I mean quickly."

"It's all computerized, Max. Anybody can do it quickly."

Max told him what to look for.

"And — this will please Musteile no end — get on the line to Interpol. We'll need one of their Russian speakers."

"You think? Really?"

"I do," said Max. "We talked of love or

431

lust, assuming that is what drove Chanel to do this. But what if only the stronger of the two emotions was in play here?

"What if love is what drove her?"

CHAPTER 26
AWENA

A week later, peace had been restored to the village of Nether Monkslip.

Or so it seemed.

The vicarage had a garden front and back; a gated path led from its front door to Vicarage Road. Max, working at his desk, waved to Awena as she passed the casement window, headed for the High, having left Owen in Max's care. She planned to stop at the ironmonger's for some paint: The dark vicarage kitchen needed cheering with some yellow cupboards.

"We may as well do it ourselves," she had said. "It's not worth asking the diocese to pay for it. And it will make ever so much difference to your day when the afternoon sun creeps past the window. Feng shui is based on what the mind perceives without our knowing it. It is such powerful stuff."

Max loved it that Awena worried about this sort of thing. Someone had to. Furthermore, she was always right. He returned to the e-mail he had been composing. The Parish Council was meeting to discuss whether to host a spiritual retreat or a weekend outing to London, to include a visit to the theater. As usual, the issue had divided into two bitter camps.

Of all the things to fight about. Max was always surprised that they seemed to find something ever more trivial to take sides over.

The door flew open at that moment, flung back on its hinges by Mrs. Hooser. She announced, "That detective is here to see you."

Mrs. Hooser had interrupted Max as he was, greatly daring, making a case for the spiritual retreat, so he welcomed the interruption.

DCI Cotton strode in and took his customary place by the fire.

"I'll be right with you," Max said. He ran his eyes over the e-mail one final time, said a brief prayer, and hit SEND.

"I just wanted to say good-bye before I head back to the office," Cotton told him. "We've cleared out of Totleigh Hall, all done but the mopping up."

Max stood up from his desk. "I was thinking again this morning of the motives behind this case," he said. "Of the fact that when it comes to love . . . desire . . . all the things that drive the human heart — those things should never include money. And yet they so often do."

Somehow the topic of love had also made him think of Eugenia, who had vanished from his thoughts until the night before when Awena had said, just before drifting off to sleep, "I think Eugenia has developed a crush on you, Max. You'll need to step carefully there." His first reaction had been to laugh — the situation was too ludicrous to take seriously. Wasn't it? But he realized he'd been hoping it would resolve itself. Perhaps he'd have to brave a more direct route.

Awena had added, "I'm afraid she sees me as a bit of a rival. Don't worry, I'm sure it will pass, and I'm also sure she's not dangerous. But we need to be aware — gentle with her feelings, both of us. I don't think many people in her life have been tender with her."

Max, remembering the poisonous look he'd seen Eugenia aim at Awena — at all of them, really, at their tightly knit little family group, at their happiness — felt a slight frisson of alarm. He thought he should have spotted the signs of her infatuation earlier

— and wondered that he had not. But surely it required an inflated, even monstrous, ego to imagine a woman losing her grip over him.

Eugenia happened to pass by his window just then, almost as if he'd conjured her up. She carried a flat gathering basket overflowing with flowers and was obviously on her way to the church to tend to the altar. As he watched, she surreptitiously eyed his study window, trying to see if he was there. Max quickly stepped back out of view.

He hesitated but then decided Cotton should be made aware. If there were any chance Awena was in danger . . . "I'd like a word," he said. "It's about Eugenia Smith-Ganderfort. I seem to have attracted a bit of attention from that direction. It's ridiculous, but I think she has developed some sort of . . . well, some sort of a crush."

Cotton followed his sight line to Eugenia's broad retreating back. She moved with an odd, unhurried grace, much like Awena. Almost as if she had been studying Awena . . . copying her. . . .

Owen started to make his waking noises, and Max went to lift him from his cradle.

"A crush on you, you mean," said Cotton. Max nodded, not meeting his eyes, the picture of abashed and confused misery.

Cotton laughed. "It's a fairly common occurrence," he said. "A lonely widow, a handsome and respected man such as yourself . . ."

"Who said she was a widow?"

"She came forward as a witness and we ran a background on her, as we do with any overeager witness. It turned out she'd seen nothing but was hoping to get information out of us. That frequently happens with murder. People want to be a part of it — they find it exciting. Sometimes they find it exciting because they're the murderer. That's why we ran the background. Whichever of my people she spoke with found her a bit odd."

"I hadn't realized she was a widow," said Max. "Most people assume she was divorced. I did."

"It was years ago. Some sort of accident. Automotive, I believe. Shall I look it up for you?" He made as if to reach for his ever-present briefcase holding his ever-present computer.

"Funny, is all. She never spoke of him. Perhaps she just wanted to forget."

"Anyway, if you think it worth pursuing, I could ask Sergeant Essex to have a word . . . about the crush, I mean. But these cases usually resolve themselves. You are probably just a hobby to Eugenia for now, like a new knitting pattern. She'll move on to other interests soon enough."

"I'm quite sure you're right. It's just that I completely ignored the undercurrents, which were quite obvious in retrospect, and that wasn't smart. She was always banging on about the altar flowers, trying to engage me, I suppose. You know the sort of thing. It all seemed so ridiculous. And then there's Awena to consider. You don't think she —"

Mrs. Hooser, even knowing he had a guest, burst into the room again. She had her young son, Tommy, in hand.

"Right," she announced. "I'm leaving now for the shops. Will you be needing anything for the next hour or so, Vicar? Awena popped back in just now to ask if I could pick up some twine," she added inconsequently. "Something about tying back the sweet peas. It's a lucky thing I were still here."

"Right. Thank you, Mrs. Hooser."

"While we were talking, a man come to the back door. He asked if she were Mrs. Max, the healer. I thought that were strange. That he come to the back door and all."

Awena's reputation had spread, making this not such an unusual occurrence. He had not been aware anyone called her Mrs.

Max, and wondered what Awena thought of that.

"I think he were blind," Mrs. Hooser went on. "Hard of seeing, like. He asked Awena if she could show him where the church were. So he could go and pray, like."

"That's nice." Max settled Owen back in the cradle, tucking him in with the blanket Lily had made just for him, moons and stars on a background of deep blue.

"You know how Awena is. She can never say no to no one in need. He come here asking for help, so she offered to walk with him to St. Edwold's. Even though I know she were so busy today. Isn't that just like her?"

Max, wondering if Mrs. Hooser were ever going to leave, started to say "That's nice" again, but then some instinct made him look up from Owen's face.

"What did this man look like?"

Cotton, who had been browsing the book-shelves that lined the study, suddenly took notice at the tone in Max's voice.

"Oh, tallish. Medium tall," I guess.

"Yes? And?"

It was little Tommy who spoke up with the salient detail.

"He wore funny glasses. Sunglasses."

Max felt the blood start to drain from his

439

heart. Very slowly and carefully, so as not to frighten Tommy, he asked, "What made the glasses funny, Tommy?"

"They were blue and white," he reported. "Blue inside and white outside."

Blue sunglasses with white frames. No one wore naff sunglasses like that, thought Max. Absolutely no one, except . . .

"Are you sure, Tommy?"

They were interrupted by the sound of a gunshot, a single loud report that roiled through the air and made the old mullioned windows rattle in their frames.

"What the —" said Cotton.

"It's coming from the church," said Max. Oddly calm now, deadly calm — for who would bring harm into the sanctuary of St. Edwold's? Who would dare? — he scooped Owen from his cradle, wrapped in his blue-sky blanket, and followed Cotton, who was already at the door. His expression reflected Max's own — still, unruffled, as if gunfire in a small village church were an everyday occurrence. If either stopped to think at all, they hoped some mechanical failure was behind the sound — the temperamental boiler indulging in some new outburst, perhaps. Both men wore a mask of calm, trying not to alarm Tommy. His mother, who had let out a bloodcurdling shriek, was doing a good-enough job of that.

But the boiler? That made no sense, Max realized on the instant. Twenty thousand pounds sterling had just gone toward replacing the old boiler. And what was that man doing in his village?

What was *Paul's killer* doing in his village?

Holding Owen tightly against his chest, Max hastened after Cotton.

The church vestry was locked from the inside and precious moments were lost as the two men raced around the side of the church to the front door. Owen, sensing something was very much up, played the uncanny trick he had of becoming preternaturally still, waiting to see what would happen next.

By now, a small knot of villagers, attracted by the ruckus, had gathered to gape in amazement as DCI Cotton and their vicar, babe in arms, ran through the churchyard, threading their way past gravestones and monuments.

Cotton reached the entrance first, bursting through the heavy wooden door and throwing it back on creaking medieval hinges, Max still right on his heels.

Once inside, the first thing Max saw as his eyes adjusted to the dark interior was Eugenia at the altar, looking for all the world as if she were celebrating the Eucharist. She held the wine flagon in one hand, staring at the vessel as if she weren't quite certain how it had gotten there.

Is she mad? Is she quite, quite mad?

Suddenly, she reared back and let fly with the flagon. Her target was the man in sunglasses, who sat next to Awena.

To his horror, Max saw he held a gun to her head.

The heavy flagon hit its mark — the man didn't see it coming. It didn't knock him out, but the liquid it contained connected with the earphones he wore around his neck, startling him and making an audible hissing sound. Either the sound or the small shock rendered by liquid shorting electronics gave Max and Cotton the split second they needed. Max put Owen, now bawling at full throttle, into the collection basket as Cotton flung himself at the man. Max flew right after him.

But it was Eugenia who reached the man in the nick of time. Sailing off the chancel steps in superhero fashion, she aimed herself at the hand holding the gun, dislodging it safely; it clattered on the stone floor. Picking up the empty flagon, she reared back and gave the man an almighty blow to the side of his head, knocking him sense-less.

Max retrieved the gun, and ran to the back of the church to retrieve the baby.

It was then the walls of the church shook to their foundations with a resounding *boom*. Max turned to see the stained glass of the St. Edwold's window shatter out of its frame — just as coils of smoke and flying debris obliterated his sight.

Chapter 27
Aftermath

"We got all the details later from Eugenia." DCI Cotton and Sergeant Essex sat in the Monkslip-super-Mare police station as he recounted the events she'd missed in not-so-peaceful Nether Monkslip. "Eugenia who, by the way, is recovering nicely, thank you very much, and basking in her role of least likely heroine you are ever going to meet in this world. She'll be selling her story to the *Mirror* any day now — you just watch."

"She should set her sights higher." Essex had been fuming for days at having missed the action, at assuming that it was safe to leave Max Tudor alone for five minutes.

Cotton nodded. "Anyway, Awena and the man wearing those strange glasses had come into the church, where Eugenia, she told us, was fiddling about with the altar flower arrangements and the altar cloth, and doing something or other with the flagon of unconsecrated wine. The man's name, as we know now, was Konstantin Konstantinov. The man who killed Max's MI5 colleague, Paul.

"Eugenia luckily had ducked behind the altar to retrieve her scissors just as this man and Awena came in, and once she heard the way the conversation was going, she stayed ducked down. This was common behavior for Eugenia, if you ask me — it was how she gathered information for her friend, Miss Pitchford, aka the Tokyo Rose of Nether Monkslip. Anyway, unnoticed, Eugenia overheard the entire conversation. Despite her adoration for Max, which skewed her common sense in many ways, I think we can take what she told us as gospel.

"What she overheard was Konstantin asking Awena to say healing prayers over him. So far so good. Awena, completely used to this type of request and finding nothing odd about it, asked him to remove his glasses. He was wearing earphones — I guess he'd been listening to music or a podcast on his mobile, and the glasses got entangled in the earphones, so there was a bit of a fuss to disentangle him. Then she sat with him in the pew, talking with him, praying for him, holding his hand. Completely unafraid of helping this strange man who had come to

445

her. You've met her — you know how she is. Compassion personified."

Essex nodded. "Go on."

"So there she was, holding the hand of a killer as deadly as a neutron star, as unstable as antimatter. And Awena looked carefully into the eyes of this creature and told him she had an ointment that would ease the dryness but that some things were beyond her ability to cure. When she told him the truth — that she could not cure him; only the gods could do that if they chose — he flew into a screaming, incoherent rage.

"He told her he had been praying to the face on the wall, and it had not healed him, either. 'For seven days I've come here, like some peasant fool, and nothing's changed.' He called her a fraud. 'You are all frauds. You're all phonies. Priests and shamans, witches and charlatans, all of you.' He grew more and more agitated, frustrated that his prayers had not been instantly answered — he'd lost faith in her power, which he had counted on as his last resort, and he quickly flipped over to a place where he wanted to destroy all that was holy. He pulled out a gun and fired a shot into the ceiling. According to Eugenia, the situation just spiraled out of Awena's control. One minute, he sat quietly listening to her, and the next, it seemed, he had her in a chokehold.

"Next he held the gun to her head: 'Your husband will pay. While I still have light to see by, I'll make him pay.' "

"Holy mother," whispered Sergeant Essex. "Pay for what?"

"God knows. He was ranting, out of his mind. Eugenia, now practically collapsed with fear, realized he was a madman. And knew that she had to do something, find some weapon to hand, before he spotted her. Or killed Awena. Or both.

"Then there was a sound. A scuffling sound near the face, coming from beneath it somewhere. It was little Tommy. Deliberately, we think, drawing attention to himself and away from Awena."

"Tommy? Mrs. Hooser's son? What on earth was he doing there? Is that child never in school?"

"Not if he can avoid it, apparently. He'd escaped from his mother and ran just ahead of us to the church. Anyway, this is when Konstantin really lost it; he turned toward where Tommy had been and shot four bullets in a frame around the face in the wall. The next shot was through the forehead of the face. A lucky shot, given his eyesight — a perfect bull's-eye, obliterating it. Tommy took the opportunity to run like hell out the door. Fortunately, he's so small, the pews hid his progress.

"Of course, Eugenia would not know that six shots fired meant the handgun held one more bullet. Her knowledge of guns came from six-shooters she'd seen on the telly. Awena, the last person to know or care about guns, had no idea, either. She kept her cool, saying nothing to provoke him, and Eugenia stayed hidden. Then Eugenia thought she heard Awena say softly, 'Please let me go. I have to get back. . . . Owen . . . Owen.' It was, says Eugenia now, like a prayer."

"And that's when you and Max burst in," said Essex. Like a child hearing a favorite story, she loved the retelling and was anxious that Cotton leave nothing out.

"That's right. Just as Eugenia was collecting herself, Max and I burst in. And because she is honing this story for the *Mirror,* here is the version she insists on telling: 'I was suddenly overcome with a raging thirst. And all I could think of was the wine flagon on the altar. There was no reason for this thirst. What on earth is wrong with me? I wondered. It was hardly time for a drink. Although, when you think of it, when was there ever a better time?'

"I think Eugenia may enjoy a tipple or two

in a private moment," Cotton told Essex. "Anyway, 'in a flash,' it all was made clear to her. Grabbing the flagon, she threw it straight at the man's head. Bull's eye. It didn't knock him out, but because he couldn't see it coming — remember his eyesight — it completely startled him. Even better, the liquid connected with the elements in the earphones around his neck. The resulting shock was minuscule, just unexpected enough to jolt him. It was the split second Max and I needed. Max put Owen into the collection basket; I flung myself at the guy, Max flying through the air right after me.

"But Eugenia reached him first."

"Right. It was just chaotic." Cotton shook his head. "Pure chaos."

"And then came the explosion. Max had the gun and was already turning back toward Owen; taking him from the basket, he shielded him from the blast. You, meanwhile, had wrestled the suspect to the ground — both you and he and Eugenia were behind one of the pews. Protected."

"That's right."

"And only Awena still sat near the bomb," said Essex. "The guy had planted it in that makeshift altar beneath the face — an IED hidden among all the flowers and petitions

449

and photos people had left. Perhaps he was hoping it would go off while people were praying there."

Cotton breathed a sigh. "Right. But thank God," he added, "he didn't use shrapnel. We'd have had a far worse outcome if he had."

"Wait a minute. Not that it really matters — we've got him for this — but how can we know this was the same guy who killed Max's friend Paul? We have Max as an eyewitness, sure, but it was ages ago, and he barely had a glimpse of the suspect. I think it was the glasses he remembered more than anything."

"There was a security camera near the scene of Paul's murder. Grainy footage, but good enough. Enhanced, as we can do more and better these days, it will help ID him. It shows him attaching a magnetic bomb onto the car — the car Max would have himself been killed in had Paul not taken his place.

"But there was more — evidence we at first knew nothing about. Max had a grim souvenir of that day of Paul's death. Preserved on the top shelf of his closet was the shirt he, Max, had been wearing the day of Paul's murder, and on it was a spot of blood. Max handed it over to the prosecutors. He had assumed all along it was Paul's blood on the collar, but it turns out it is not — it is the killer's.

"The DNA on that collar is a perfect match for the blood of Konstantin Konstantinov. He managed to injure himself that day; he didn't run fast enough after planting the explosive.

"Analysts need only a speck of blood to tie him to the scene. And thanks to Max, we have it."

CHAPTER 28
FROM RUSSIA WITH LOVE

One day many weeks later, as the case wound its way through the court system, Essex and Cotton met again, this time over bangers and mash (her) and a vegetarian Cornish pasty (him) in the police canteen.

"When they searched Konstantin's flat, they hit pay dirt," Cotton told her. "Sulfuric acid, nitric acid, phenol, wiring, lab equipment, you name it. A one-way ticket to the U.S., flying under a false ID, of course. He also had some experimental stuff — MI6 is not talking about it, not to the likes of us yokels. But according to Max, who still has his channels, it's the sort of thing that is not routinely screened by security. Pity is Konstantin didn't blow himself up long before, but we have him now. He had to have had accomplices, given his eyesight, and that's where they're putting the pressure on him, to find out. He'll talk."

"There is the strangest rumor going

around," began Essex hesitatingly. "They say he's already made a written confession to the whole thing. Helpfully, he's naming names of some of his worst colleagues."

"Good. Glad to hear it."

"But . . . Remember he came to Nether Monkslip on a sort of pilgrimage, seeking a cure. For his eyes?"

"Right."

"The face drew him there, and stories of Awena's powers, and legends of Nether Monkslip as a place of healing. The stories of miracle cures, especially for people losing their vision — the ties with Monkbury Abbey and the nuns and so on. He hung around the pub at the Horseshoe, where he was staying, soaking up the gossip. Of course he heard of Max, and probably recognized him from the news photos. Came to hear all about him, Awena, the baby."

"Yes," said Cotton tersely. He was terse because he was having the most unprofessional thoughts about the case, in rare moments wishing he'd used a little more force on the guy. Just a little more. He'd had him in a chokehold, and . . . He had talked about this to Max, who did not surprise him by saying, "Paul's wife has a right to see justice done, in court. As for me, I am satisfied to think of him spending his life in jail, detained at Her Majesty's pleasure. Besides, think of what he knows, what he might tell us one day."

Cotton returned his attention to what Essex was saying.

"They say his sight has come back."

"What?"

"Konstantin. Our guy. Our *bad* guy. His sight has been restored. And that's why he's confessed."

"He had some operation? What?"

"No, he was *cured.* A miracle. He says he woke up one morning and his sight was restored. Presumably by the face on the wall."

"Impossible."

"So the prison doctors say. That's why he wore those glasses in the first place, to protect what was left of his eyesight. His world was going dark, and so he flailed about looking for a cure."

"Impossible," Cotton repeated.

"Me, I think he may have been cured by Awena," Essex continued, ignoring him. "I wish my gran had been around for this; she lost her vision the last few years of her life. Remember Awena sat by him and tried to comfort him, urging him to open himself to what was possible but to be ready to accept what wasn't possible. Eugenia said she held his hand. There was nothing about this guy that wasn't scary — the owner of the Horseshoe said he was grubby, dirty and disheveled, and he'd soon been ready to toss him out — but nothing scared Awena. We will never know for sure, will we? What cured him? But something did. Make that Something with a big *S*."

Cotton, who up until now had had little use for the supernatural, still found himself shaken to his core. But he would not let it show. Essex was apparently more easily swayed by reasons beyond this world.

"Konstantin will end his days in prison," said Cotton. "So now he'll have a clear view of those concrete walls. On a good day, he might see birds flying free overhead and wish he could join them."

He became lost in thought, separating the peas from his pasty with a fork and lining them up into a grid of four across on his plate. He surfaced to hear Essex say, ". . . Chanel doing?"

"Hmm? Well, she'll do a lot better if she wises up and throws Bree into it, but so far she won't. If Chanel were Bree's lover, a conclusion we simply leaped to, there might be hope that she'd see the light. But since Chanel is her mother — a mother protecting her child, as she sees it — that whole mother bear thing . . . well. She may turn, but it's a much, much longer shot. In a sort of role reversal from the John the Baptist story, it was the mother doing the daughter's bidding.

"Max was right, of course. Bree's maiden name was Porter. Of course, we knew that, but since Chanel was nowhere near to being a suspect, we never made the connection. Never thought to look at Bree's birth record while we were busy looking up Peregrine's. But there it was, clear as day. How many Bree Porters born in Wiltshire to unwed teenagers named Chanel can there be in the world? Of course, Chanel later married briefly and became Chanel Dirkson. Even so. She lied about that, by the way: she told several villagers that she'd never been married. I suppose that in pretending that Dirkson was her maiden name, she was trying to bury the fact of her relationship to Lady Baaden-Boomethistle, née Bree Porter. Which suggests she was planning something bad when she moved here. Had probably moved here at a summons from Bree. Otherwise, why lie about something so innocuous?

"Looking back further, with the help of Interpol — Musteile remains beside himself

over that and will *not* shut up about it —
we found Chanel's birth record in Russia."

"I still don't get —" began Essex.

"How Max made the connection? That
conversation Destiny overheard — part of
the problem she was having was that they
were speaking partly in Russian, Chanel's
native tongue. Chanel was born in Russia
but came to the UK as a young girl when
her mother married a Frenchman, later settling in Wiltshire. It was in Wiltshire that
Chanel gave birth, as a young unwed
mother, to Bree. I wondered at the names,
the way they were sort of Frenchified — I
mean really, Chanel and Bree? — but Porter
in this case is not of English origin, but
French.

"Anyway, the mother taught the daughter
what she remembered of the Russian language and they sometimes slipped into old
habits as they talked. What Destiny heard as
'not yet,' for example, being used in a way
that was slightly out of true in English, was
nyet, or no.

"I'd imagine a lot of the garbled language
Destiny overheard and couldn't understand
that day had a Russian phrase or two thrown
in — this was a sort of private language, a
pigeon Russian, if you like, that the pair had
adopted. Another example: Destiny heard

one of the women say the word *obit,* used in a strange, ungrammatical way. What the woman actually was saying was *ubit.* The English *obit* was close enough in meaning that it made sense, but not quite. The Russian word *ubit* means 'to kill' in English. The woman, probably Chanel, knew someone who could *kill* for them.

"And what Destiny heard as 'duh' was probably *da,* or yes."

For heaven's sake, thought Essex. "And Max figured this out how?"

"I asked him the very same question."

Cotton thought back to an earlier conversation with Max: "I know some Russian," Max had told him. "And there was this dream that lingered in my mind. . . ." He told Cotton some of the Russian symbolism in his dream — the draft horse, the head with the Tolstoy beard, concluding, "Really, it was obvious, once I thought it through. What cinched it was when Bree told me she saw Chanel in Monkslip-super-Mare, providing her with an alibi for the time of the murder and shoring up her own alibi. Why would she do that — alibi Chanel? I would believe the blameless Elka if she said she saw Bree, but Bree could *not* have seen Chanel. As we now know, Chanel was busy killing Lord B-B at seven."

Cotton had mumbled something that sounded like "for Chrissake" but said merely, "I thought it was Italian you spoke fluently, Max."

Max had shrugged modestly. "That, too."

He'd gone on to explain, "I really don't see how I missed it all so badly. Because Bree's impact was so sexual, I assumed wrongly that she exerted power only in that way. I was wrong. Chanel loved Bree, too, as did many people who should have known better, but of course she loved her in a different way. I think Chanel, a woman of somewhat ordinary beauty, may have been astounded to have created such a perfect beauty, to have brought such physical loveliness into the world. That created a powerful bond, too. A love, of sorts. Perhaps more like a fierce adoration. Whatever. Known for her common sense, Chanel threw all common sense aside when it came to her daughter." Max had paused and said, "It was a classic case of 'Physician, heal thyself.' "

Essex was saying now, "And so long as Chanel believes Bree was being abused by her husband . . . the same way Chanel was abused by her husband, as she claims — this Dirkson fellow . . ." Essex let the thought drift. Was there a mother alive who wouldn't have tried to intervene? But a saner mother would have found a saner method. Aloud she said, "Right. In killing Lord B-B, Chanel was saving the beautiful daughter she adored. Avenging the wrongs done to her." She shook her head. "She'll never talk."

"I can only hope you're wrong. People have a way of talking in prison, though. Too much time on their hands, you know. I'm thinking of putting a policewoman in there to cozy up to her, get her talking." He looked at her. "How do you feel about working undercover?"

"Are you serious?" Essex, who probably weighed a little over seven stone sopping wet and wearing riot gear, didn't hesitate, for she was fearless. "Yes, of course! I'll get her talking. When can I go in?"

"Think about it awhile." Even though her street smarts would protect her, Cotton feared he might have spoken too quickly. It would be like sending her into a badger baiting, with her the badger. "Anyway," he said, to change the subject, "as for all the folks at Totleigh Hall, they've recovered nicely. People with resources like that always do. Bree is enthroned as the new dowager, and all hint of scandal will be washed away by passing years and amassing money and dignity.

"As for Peregrine, he has petitioned to be recognized as an earl in his own right — the rightful earl of Lislelivet. For now, he's still hanging about the village, tootling around on his bicycle, smooth and dapper with a new haircut and clothing, his usual public-school sheen restored.

"By the way, apparently Peregrine was not the only one attempting a disguise. Chanel's child-of-nature, organic getup was her attempt to blend in with the folk of Nether Monkslip. Her real style runs more to heels and false eyelashes. Although right now, of course, she's wearing prison garb.

"Anyway, Peregrine's come down from university or been sent down, whatever version you choose to believe. His sister inherited in his place, you know, and, fortunately for him, she is being magnanimous and wise — at least for the moment.

"The same goes for his grandmother — if it were up to Bree, she would have to fight for her food and shelter, but Rosamund stands as protectress to all, defending against the worst impulses of the old regime. She seems to have taken quite a fancy to the estate manager, by the way. Bill Travis. That certainly will shake things up if she marries him, which I think would be most unwise. However, no one consulted me."

"These old families," said Essex. "Like with heirloom tomatoes, you can get some strange and wonderful varieties."

"You sound like Awena. That's exactly like something she'd say."

"What about Father Max?" asked Essex slowly, dreading the answer. "How is he?" A sure sign of her distress was the spiky confusion of her multicolored hair, which seemed to stand on end in sympathetic disarray.

"Not good," replied Cotton. "He's taken some time off to make sure Awena's completely well and back to normal, but I don't think there's enough time in the world . . ."

"I know. It's unthinkable." She paused, watching Cotton as he sorted small cubes of carrot into a tic-tac-toe design with the peas. "Do you know, I wouldn't be surprised if Max became a bishop himself one day."

"I think that's the last thing Max would want. An archdeacon, perhaps — there is no way they won't try to promote him upstairs. They probably think he's wasted in Nether Monkslip."

A pause. Cotton moved the salt and pepper shakers on the table into perfect alignment on the checkered oilcloth. He did this sort of thing, Essex knew from long acquaintance, only when he was worried.

"The explosion?" she asked him. "Did

they ever figure out . . ."

Cotton looked up from the table and nodded. "The guy had an IED attached to his belt. But he'd removed it and — I told you — left it hidden in that sort of makeshift altar by the face. The idea may have been to blow himself up along with Awena and whoever else was around. But here is the tricky part: The IED was set to a timer, and that timer was attached to an alarm on his mobile.

"He seems to have forgotten the time change — that is what we think happened. His own wristwatch had not 'fallen back' at two A.M. Sunday to become one A.M. But the mobile clock reset itself automatically, of course. He never noticed the discrepancy, and when the explosion failed to go off, he just assumed the bomb was a dud and tossed it."

"Fool" was Essex's brief summary.

"Most of these guys are. It makes them no less dangerous, but they're all fools. So perhaps changing his mind, losing his courage, thinking the thing worthless — whatever — he had unstrapped it from himself and thrown it away. And when it went off . . ."

Cotton could clearly remember, would remember until the day he died, the sensation of his body being blown back by the force of the explosion, of twisting in the air, and finally coming to a thudding landing in the nave. He'd been knocked senseless for a moment, and when he came to, he was staring straight into a ripped-apart copy of the Book of Common Prayer. The pew had saved him. Him and Eugenia and the wretched Konstantin. Awena, unshielded and nearer the explosion, had caught the worst of it. She'd been knocked completely out, suffering a serious concussion.

But the doctors said she was fine now. Rather, she would soon be fine. Whether she would ever regain that unflappable grace and composure was anyone's guess. Being on the receiving end of rampant and mindless cruelty had a way of changing one's belief in one's fellow man.

"By the way. It's a very odd thing . . ." Essex began.

"What?"

"Nothing really. I hesitate to bring it up. But that face on the wall? Or the 'Face,' as some would have it?" Essex made quotation marks in the air with her fingers. "I went by St. Edwold's the other day to talk with the sexton. There's been a crush of visitors to the site. 'Pilgrims,' as he calls them. He's asking us to help with security."

"Yes? He'll be lucky. We're short-staffed as it is."

"Yes. Well. It seems to be sort of knitting itself back together."

"What does?"

"The face. Where Konstantin put a bullet through the center. The damage is shrinking, like a wound or scar healing."

"Don't be ridiculous," said Cotton. The whole conversation was starting to irritate him. "The sexton or somebody has been busy with a plaster knife."

She moved the salt shaker a fraction out of true. "Do you really think so?"

EPILOGUE

Max had looked at the wailing bundle thrashing in his arms that day in St. Edwold's and wondered what on earth he would do.

He spent the ensuing months in a constant shuttle between the hospital and home and the vicarage or — when Awena was released at last — working in Owen's nursery, next to their bedroom and sleeping on a cot outside the door, so he and the baby wouldn't disturb her. He could hear her cry out in her sleep, something she'd never done before. That was probably the worst sign, that Awena's impenetrable serenity had been shattered.

But she was alive, and for a long time that was all that mattered.

One way or another, every waking moment was spent praying for Awena. Bargaining with God, at times pleading, at times angry.

For Awena was his alpha and omega. And life without her could not be endured.

The most bizarre thing was the impulse he kept having while she was in the hospital to pick up the phone to talk with her, to share some trivial event from his day. To tell her of Eugenia's newfound celebrity, or to update her on Owen's astonishing progress.

To sit alone without her in the evening was agony. The nights never seemed to end, and only remembering he had to keep his health for Owen's sake helped him catch what hours of sleep he could. More days than not, he greeted the dawn as Nether Monkslip slipped into winter. Her sisters arrived in rotation to help him out — a godsend, all of them. They fed him until he thought he'd burst, plying him with calming teas and root-vegetable soups, which they claimed held the secret to his own recovery. Seeing how completely Awena and Owen were safe in their hands, he began to sleep at last.

He began praying to the face on the wall, sitting in a nearby pew for hours on end, asking for a miracle. Sometimes young Tommy would join him, silently, harnessing all his powers of stillness, extraordinary for a boy not yet five.

Max realized his pleading went against all

he'd been taught by his religion, the teaching that he must accept whatever happens, whatever God has sent. One day in the gloaming light, he thought he saw the eyes of the face flash open. It startled but did not frighten him, and he sat for a long while, staring until his own eyes watered, forcing himself not to blink. It was as if this were his new standard, that the laws of physics should be upended in this way, for his benefit. This was his new normal. But he blinked at last and he saw the eyes were closed, as they had always been. As they were.

A visual distortion, merely.

A hallucination brought on by worry, by lack of sleep.

Someone had left behind in the pew a fine leather-bound copy of the psalms. It fell open in his hands to Psalm 85: "Righteousness shall go before him, and peace shall make a pathway for his feet."

Peace eluded him.

He had often thought he would give anything to see the man who had killed Paul punished. He had got his wish, but what he had nearly lost was Awena.

I can accept anything, he thought, but not that. Never that.

Awena recovered completely; in fact, she

healed so quickly that her doctor called it a "miracle." When he said that to Max, when he used that word, Max had had to bite back the hysterical laughter that threatened to escape him. For how to explain to the man that of course, of *course* it was a miracle?

Wasn't it a given that Awena, the healer, would herself be healed?

Thank God. He should have known.

Yet in the end, he found he could not accept any of what had happened: how near he had come to losing her. Only Awena could have achieved that quietude and stillness — Awena, who had somehow mastered the art of taking the world as it was, of people as they were. Of accepting everything and not trying to change anything. And despite all the evidence for ill and evil in the world, still seeing the beauty everywhere.

She also long ago had mastered the art of forgiveness, and Max struggled and prayed and found he could not.

It was some weeks later when he picked up the phone and rang his bishop.

And then he rang his old boss at MI5.

ABOUT THE AUTHOR

G. M. Malliet won the Agatha Award for best first novel for *Death of a Cozy Writer,* which initially won the Malice Domestic Grant, was nominated for both a Macavity and an Anthony Award, and was chosen as one of the Best Books of 2008 by Kirkus Reviews. Malliet's first three books in the Max Tudor series — *Wicked Autumn, Fatal Winter,* and *Pagan Spring* — were all nominated for the Agatha Award as well. She lives in the Washington, D.C., area.